PROPOSAL OF MARRIAGE

"I assure you, sir, you need not do anything about me at all," Linnea said.

Rothwick frowned. "And I assure you, Miss Ashley, that as I am responsible for your predicament, I need very much to do something about you. How many families, do you suppose, will send their daughters to a school which has amongst its faculty a man's cast-off mistress?"

Linnea's hands clenched. "But I am not your mistress."

Rothwick sighed. "It matters not. It is what they will assume, will you, nil you."

Linnea stood up abruptly, feeling the heat of anger and frustration. "So you!" she said furiously. "You who have effectively ruined my reputation and any means to earn my bread—what do you suggest? What do I do with myself, your high and mighty lordship? You have left nothing for me. Nothing." She bit her lip, shaking with the effort to suppress her sobs.

She heard his high and mighty lordship draw a deep breath. "You could always marry me, you know," he said.

By Kathleen Elliott

The Marriage Scheme
A Special License

A SPECIAL LICENSE

KATHLEEN ELLIOTT

HarperPaperbacks
A Division of HarperCollinsPublishers

This is a work of fiction. The characters, incidents, and dialogues are products of the author's imagination and are not to be construed as real. Any resemblance to actual events or persons, living or dead, is entirely coincidental.

HarperPaperbacks *A Division of* HarperCollins*Publishers*
10 East 53rd Street, New York, N.Y. 10022

Copyright © 1995 by Karen Eriksen Harbaugh
All rights reserved. No part of this book may be used or reproduced in any manner whatsoever without written permission of the publisher, except in the case of brief quotations embodied in critical articles and reviews. For information address HarperCollins*Publishers*, 10 East 53rd Street, New York, N.Y. 10022.

Cover illustration by Bob Berran

First printing: April 1995

Printed in the United States of America

HarperPaperbacks, HarperMonogram, and colophon are trademarks of HarperCollins*Publishers*

❖ 10 9 8 7 6 5 4 3 2 1

A SPECIAL LICENSE

1

William Staynes, *seventh Earl of Rothwick,* sat at the breakfast table, immersed in his newspaper. He had almost finished a short article on a Whitechapel ax murder when a feminine voice pierced the breakfast parlor.

"He will surely let me in when he understands the urgency of my case!" The door opened, and Lady Wrenton stepped in, followed closely by a profusely apologetic footman. The footman encountered my lord's uninterested eye, subsided abashed, and slipped quickly out the door.

Except for a momentary movement of Lord Rothwick's eyebrows, however, my lady's entrance did not seem to pierce his concentration on the newspaper. She sniffed. It had always been so. He had been an annoying baby brother; now that he was grown, with a title and vast estates, he was no less annoying. Less impetuous, perhaps, but that was hardly saying anything at all.

Lady Wrenton twisted a lock of her hair nervously. She did not feel very hopeful in appealing to her brother when there was any sort of trouble, except, of course, when it dealt with his duty as her trustee. It was not in William's nature to put himself out for anyone. She thought there was a lesson in it somewhere—it had always seemed to her that one so indulged as a child ought naturally to be indulgent toward others.

This was not true about her brother, however. He could almost be called a care-for-nobody, except he was unrelenting in his determination to make her stay within her allowance. And he had a disagreeable habit of jumping to the most unpleasant conclusions—at least not the conclusions one *wanted* him to come to. She sighed. Perhaps she could persuade him by appealing to his sense of duty, although her problem had little to do with the trust.

Her ladyship plumped herself down upon a chair, gazing at the newspaper that separated her from her brother. For all that it was only a newspaper, it almost acquired a personality of its own in the hands of the earl. It was as if it set itself up as a guard between Rothwick and the rest of the world. Lady Wrenton sighed, knowing his attention would not go past the newspaper until he chose. She surveyed the laden table instead. "Sausages!" She made a face. "I am surprised you have such a vulgar thing at your table." She herself never had more than her cup of chocolate or tea and toast in the morning.

"I am grieved you have found me out," replied the newspaper calmly. "I trust you will not spread it about, Lydia. I am sure I would not be able to show my face for more than a fortnight should you do so." That face, revealed during the turning of a page, was the picture of unconcern. "I am glad you sought to warn me so quickly, my dear. A serious case indeed." A cup of coffee disappeared behind the paper, then reappeared, empty.

Her ladyship looked taken aback. "Serious? Sausages, serious?"

"Of course. Anything which reflects a vulgar light upon me is a serious matter. You relieve my mind, Lydia. I had thought at first you had come to me about that tiresome boy of yours. I see I was mistaken. My eyes have been opened. Your sisterly affection for me was more than I knew. How fortunate it is to have someone who looks out for my interests—fond older sister that you are," he added wickedly.

A fork pierced the offending sausage. Lydia could see its shadow briefly behind the advertisement "Dr. Thompson's Superlative Baldness Cure" before it merged with Lord Rothwick's.

"Hardly old!" She patted her thick black hair. "Why, we might even be mistaken for twins."

A corner of the newspaper tweaked down for a minute, exposing her brother's ironic eye. "Perhaps I am mistaken, but I thought you had the advantage of me in years—ten, is it not?"

Lady Wrenton shifted uncomfortably. How they had got off the subject she wanted to pursue, she did not know. "Well, as a matter of fact, I did come here about Paul. And he is not tiresome! I do not know why you should call him that, for he is the most darling boy a mother could want for a son." She hesitated. "It is only . . . he is so susceptible to those who would lead him astray."

The eyebrows moved again, but not with total skepticism. Though Paul was the younger of Lydia's two children, he was twenty years of age and could not be called a boy much longer. Indeed, thought Rothwick, briefly reviewing some of his nephew's forays into the muslin company, Paul was entering into more manly pursuits than before. One could suppose that meant he was susceptible to being led astray. His lordship's expression gave away none of what he was thinking, however.

"Astray." Rothwick put down his paper, touched his lips with his napkin, and gazed at his sister with resigned boredom. "What has he done now?"

She sat back on her chair, raising a hand to her eyes with a small sigh. "It is a—a . . . it is that vulgar creature he is escorting lately."

"Yes?" His voice was uninterested.

"You must stop him before she brings ruin upon him! She is nothing but a common strumpet!"

"If she is, as you say, his light o' love, there is no reason to do so."

Her ladyship's lip trembled. "William, I do not see how you can be so unfeeling. He is your heir, after all. You cannot let him sink so low as to marry her."

Rothwick laughed. "I hardly think he will do that. He has been out on the Town long enough to avoid any such tangles. The only thing he needs to learn is not to let such rubbish reach your ears." He picked up the coffeepot, gauging by its weight whether it had any coffee left. It did not. He glanced at his sister, then again at the empty pot. Life has its irritations, he thought, sighing. "I will allow some exaggeration arising from mother love, Lydia, but you do have a penchant for tragedy making when it comes to Paul. You are making something out of nothing, I assure you."

"He is only twenty, and—and persuadable, Will! And he himself told me he was going to marry her." Lady Wrenton was overcome. She pulled out a lacy square and dabbed her eyes. "I do not know how I could bear it if he should go through with it!"

Rothwick seemed to pay a little more attention to this but said, "Nonsense."

"He *did* say it! And she had the effrontery to nod to me when they passed in his carriage," cried Lady Wrenton, incensed. "Her name is Cassey Pickens. She is supposed to be a widow—grass widow, more likely! When I saw her, she was dressed in half mourning—which was, no doubt, what took my poor boy in. Nothing, however, could have hidden her vulgarity from me!"

Lord Rothwick sat back, and his sigh was exquisitely full of ennui. Lydia's chair felt suddenly uncomfortable, and she was annoyed at him for making her wish she hadn't come. But he said: "How tedious. It looks as though I shall have to intervene."

"Oh, William!" cried Lydia, running around the table to him. "I knew you would come to my rescue—dear brother!"

He held off her embrace. "Yes, yes. Just don't interrupt me at my breakfast again. You know how I dislike it. I might have sausage again if you do."

His sister wrinkled her nose. "Well, I won't then. Only get that horrid creature away from Paul, and I will, well, I promise I will keep better account of what I owe my dressmaker!"

Lydia was clearly willing to sacrifice a great deal for her beloved son. She had never before been able to keep her bills in any order. A hopeful light glimmered in Rothwick's eye, then faded. He sighed again. "You may rest easy, sister. I doubt I shall hold you to it."

It was true Lord Rothwick did not put himself out for others. He had never had to do much in the way of pleasing people, and like most mortals he avoided change, for he felt satisfied with his life as it was. This was not, of course, to say that he was not a fair and generous man when he chose to be. His many mistresses could attest to that. Though indulged in childhood, he had not escaped without a sense of responsibility—instilled in him, perhaps, by his old nurse, who was always alternately scolding and petting him.

Certainly his parents had had nothing to do with it. He was the result of a last attempt by the sixth earl of Rothwick and his lady wife to beget an heir, and his mother had been almost forty when he was born. It had weakened her, and though she had lived another fifteen years, she never did recover enough to keep up with the active, vital boy he had been. His father did not live very much longer than his mother, but that did not make much difference to the young man; the sixth earl had always seemed a distant figure who appeared only at quarter day to give him his allowance and admonishments toward proper behavior.

Of the two things his father gave him, William was properly grateful for the first and ignored the second. How else was it to be, after all? He was a handsome youth when he finished Cambridge, with black hair and eyes as grey as slate. Fast on the heels of his diploma came invitations to social functions, both select and not select at all. At the former he flirted happily with maidens and the hopes of ambitious mothers but never succumbed to the matrimonial mousetrap, no matter how prettily baited. At the latter he flirted with the hopes of ambitious courtesans and succumbed happily to the lascivious lures of his light o' loves, especially if prettily baited.

This last occupation, alas, was soon to end. Or rather, the obvious flaunting of his activities was soon to end. He was to marry a sophisticated miss named Sophia Amberley; he had to do his duty and bring forth an heir, after all. He felt Miss Amberley would do quite well.

He brought forth her image in his mind's eye. Ah, yes. She was a honey blonde, with periwinkle-blue eyes and full, pouting lips. She was a ravishing sort, because he never consorted with any but diamonds of the first water. She was clever and not so much in love with him as with his title, he was sure. That was all he required. He would go on with his usual activities, and after she bore him an heir, she could do as she wished—discreetly, of course. His activities would not make the marriage an unequal one for Sophia, for he was a reasonably intelligent, realistic man and knew well that the cover of marriage often gave special license to women to act more freely than was customary for a spinster. He shrugged at the thought. His life, for all intents and purposes, would remain pleasantly unchanged.

He was not married yet, however. They were betrothed but two days—nothing had been announced officially yet—and he would enjoy himself to the fullest first. He was fully cognizant of the realities of marriage; he had to give up some of his time to devote to Sophia, put in an appearance at her side once in a while to satisfy convention. Duty was duty, after all. And Sophia's looks and voluptuous figure were such that fulfilling at least part of that duty would not be distasteful at all. . . .

He shook his head, setting aside Sophia's undoubted charms to an easily accessible corner of his mind. Paul. He must attend to that troublesome brat's damned brumble-bath. Rothwick would not bother rescuing the boy except that he remembered the scrapes he himself had fallen into at that age and wished he had had someone to drag him out of them then. Though my lord would never say so, he had a certain fondness for his sister and did not like to see her worried. He sighed, resigned. It was one thing to have a few mistresses, but a man did not marry any of them. Well, if he saw Paul in the course of the next couple of days, he would warn him off.

Rothwick found him sooner than he thought he would. An invitation to meet at White's by a crony of his took him out on a warm spring day to Bond Street. He would not have noticed the tall man a few yards in front of him had it not been for the man's companion. He appreciatively eyed the lithe, full-bosomed figure clothed in lavender half mourning, but he jerked almost too hard on the reins when he saw Paul's profile bending above her solicitously.

It *was* Paul—he could not mistake that yellow-striped waistcoat. Rothwick had attempted to dampen Paul's enthusiasm for it only a week past by saying it was too dandified. The young woman was not anyone he recognized. She must be that bit o' muslin Lydia was so upset about. He would certainly find out. He handed the reins to his tiger and stepped from his curricle.

The situation between the two was no better at close range. Rothwick noted with disgust an absorbed look in Paul's eyes; that harpy had her claws in deeper than he would have thought. She was not, obviously, very intelligent. If she had any notion of propriety, she would not allow herself to be seen in Bond Street, even upon his nephew's arm. She was probably clever enough to discern that Paul had not yet any notion of it, either. It must be Cassey Pickens. He came directly behind Paul, tapping him on a slightly padded shoulder.

Paul turned. "Uncle Will!" he cried. "Glad we bumped into each other. Not that we bumped, precisely, but you know what I mean." He turned to the woman at his side. "Uncle, this is—"

"Yes, I know very well who this is," growled the earl. He gave a cursory bow, then scanned the woman's face with more intent. Hers was a piquant face: full of liveliness, humor, and just a touch of sadness about the eyes to make her thin, heart-shaped countenance interesting. A few dusky curls escaped her bonnet; they looked soft, like down from a chick. It was a face that could draw a man to look and look again, for her eyes attracted and her soft, pink, innocent lips invited kisses.

Innocent? Rothwick shook himself mentally. Nonsense. This must be Cassey Pickens, and thus she'd be far from innocent. "Ma'am, your servant." He turned to Paul and with a jerk of his head indicated to his nephew that they go.

The woman turned a startled gaze upon him. "But, sir, we are in the middle of Bond Street! You cannot leave me here alone!"

"I am sure," Lord Rothwick said tightly, "that you will not be alone long." He noticed her face flamed red with apparent understanding. There were no ladies' shops on Old Bond Street; there could be no reason for her to be there.

"I say, Uncle!" protested Paul, but he was cut off by the young woman.

Eyes flashing, she cried, "The sort of company I would encounter here would put me at some peril, as I am sure you are aware!"

Bold as brass, thought Rothwick, reluctantly admiring her angrily flashing eyes. But he relented, though he would not stoop to converse with her further. The earl motioned to his tiger and instructed him to escort Paul's companion to her destination. She accepted with a haughty grace, which almost caused Rothwick to smile, but he suppressed it.

He seized Paul's arm in a viselike grip and propelled him firmly away from his fair companion.

"I say, old boy! No need to be rough! Just got this from Weston's, you know." He managed to pull himself away and smoothed down his sleeve with an injured air. "And not quite the thing, abandoning a lady. Just escorting Miss—"

"Quiet!" thundered Rothwick. He had needed only one look at the "lady" to confirm his fears. He would bet his inheritance the woman was the harpy his sister had told him of. It was easy to see how Paul would be caught by one such as she. Her figure improved at close range, and though her half-mourning dress seemed on the surface modest enough and even dowdy, it fit her too close in the bosom for absolute modesty. He had surveyed her half mourning in reluctant admiration. She was obviously posing as a widow to lure young men with the double attraction of her looks and supposedly pitiful situation. The earl was experienced enough to fence with women of that caliber, but Paul was not fair game for women of that sort.

Paul gazed at him warily. "Not in a scrape now, I promise you. Just escorting a lady on an errand: no harm in that."

"Your mother told me about her, Paul; there is no need to hedge the matter with me," said Rothwick. "Good God, boy! Don't you know it has reached your mother's ears? I thought you knew better than to take a woman of that stamp so seriously."

Paul stiffened. "Never thought you were that high in the instep, Uncle! Seems a perfectly respectable girl to me. Just orphaned, daughter of a vicar—no portion, of course, but that's no matter—related to Lady Boothe!"

Rothwick almost gasped at Miss Pickens's audacity. He had heard that old orphaned-daughter-of-a-vicar story before, but to claim relatives amongst the ton! That was gall indeed. He sneered. "And of course, Lady Boothe being one of the best-dressed ladies in society, she sees fit to dress one of her own likewise."

"I—I, well, she's someone's companion right now, and they don't treat her right, I can tell you that!"

"They never do," replied Rothwick. "Good God, Paul, I thought you were more up to snuff than that. Can you not see when you've been taken in? That story's as old as Eve! Why, my father heard that one when he first came out on the town."

"It's true!" protested Paul.

"They are always true." His uncle sighed wearily. The earl looked down the street. He could see his tiger driving atop his curricle, threading his way back through the afternoon crowd. "But if I have anything to say about it, you are not going to marry a woman like that."

A quick puzzled look crossed Paul's face but was erased with his next words: "By *that,* I suppose you mean Miss Pickens. I can marry whom I wish!"

Lord Rothwick smiled grimly and stepped up into his curricle. "That you can, but it will be a bit difficult to support two on your allowance. Pray remember: you do not gain the whole of your inheritance until you reach five-and-twenty."

His nephew grew pale, then reddened in anger. "As if that would matter with anyone! I shall do well enough!"

Rothwick laughed and gathered the reins. "You tell her! I'll wager she hedges off!" he threw over his shoulder.

Lord Rothwick was more worried than he cared to show when he told Lydia of the incident. It was just as well, for she was anxious enough for two. "And he refused to cut the connection?" she cried.

"Yes, but he is at the height of infatuation. We shall see if it lasts," he replied.

"'We shall see'! Why, it may be too late. It must be nipped in the bud!"

"I have said, my dear sister, that his infatuation is already full-blown."

Lydia jumped up from her chair and paced agitatedly around the room. She stopped, clasping her hands. "William! You must pay her off!"

He grimaced. "That is hardly any guarantee she will leave him. What is to stop her from taking the money and marrying him all the same?"

My lady sank back onto her chair. "We must think of something! I know if he is pushed to it, my dear boy might, just might, run off with her."

Rothwick gave a short laugh. "Well, she is comely enough. Perhaps I shall run off with her myself."

Lydia turned, gazing at him round-eyed and hopeful. "Oh, Will! That is a wonderful idea!"

It is not to be thought that Lady Wrenton would countenance her brother marrying a courtesan any more than she would her son. She well knew, however, the charm her brother could turn on the most disagreeable of women that rendered them meek as doves; could he not do this with the despicable Cassey Pickens? Of course he would not marry her, but she was sure that woman would not mind being carried off by someone as rich and handsome as her brother. And William, after all, was no innocent boy. He could easily fob off the woman when he was done with her.

Her brother was wont to protest, of course. "I might remind you, Lydia, that I am newly betrothed. Hardly the time to be selecting a mistress, don't you think?" he said ironically.

"Oh, pooh. You are scarcely going to announce it to the world, after all. If it should come to Sophia's ears, why, she knows the ways of the world and what is expected of your wife. It is hardly a love match, after all." Lydia could not resist sticking this last pin into his cool veneer. It irritated her that he had barely acknowledged her candidates for matrimony and had selected Sophia Amberley, whom she had always thought an ice-hearted chit. To be fair, it hurt Lydia, too. For all her lightness and frivolity, she loved her brother and would have liked to see him in love as well as married. But with Sophia! She could not conceive how it could happen, for all the girl's beauty. Certainly he had not changed his ways at all since his betrothal.

The pin, if it pierced, made no mark. Rothwick waved a careless hand. "You are right, of course. Nevertheless, one must be careful of appearances. . . ."

Lydia smiled smugly. "You, of all people, should know how to keep up appearances. Why, it is rumored you have had a string of mistresses, yet I have never seen you with one."

He said nothing but gazed at her sadly and raised his eyebrows in mocking reproof.

"Well, I did—" Lydia stopped and gave an irritated moué. She would not be diverted from the purpose of their tête-à tête. "So you will lure this—this creature away from Paul?"

"I have not said it, have I?"

"You are disobliging!" she returned crossly.

"No, sensible, I think." Rothwick sighed. "We shall see."

"Ha! I wager that you are afraid you cannot!" Lady Wrenton leaned back on her chair. She was not going to ruin her challenge by seeming too eager.

"I said, 'We shall see,'" he replied. But then the earl smiled slightly and said: "How much do you want to wager, dear sister?"

2

Linnea pulled her cloak closer around her. She wished she had something other than the lavender half-mourning gown she wore, but it was the least shabby one she had. The cloak was not as warm as her pelisse, but it was a dark grey, and she did not want to attract any notice. She was glad of the gas lamps put in but a year before in Pall Mall, but the streets between Cousin Boothe's house and Lady Strahan's in Pall Mall were not so well lighted. She looked about her, peering into shadowed corners, and walked as quickly as her tired feet would let her.

"I will not have to be Cousin Boothe's unpaid servant for long," she said to herself. "The employment registry will send me a message soon. I will then be out of Cousin Boothe's house and into a respectable home where I can be a governess."

Linnea allowed herself a little smile. Her words were

her litany against fear. She felt frightened more often these days, for Lady Boothe had suffered reverses at the gaming table lately and could not afford a servant to accompany Linnea on the errands she had to run. It was very late; she had told her cousin that it was past eleven o'clock and Lady Strahan's ball would be half over by the time she arrived there. But her cousin had slapped her, accusing her of being ungrateful; it did little good to argue with her. Linnea had left, hoping she would not meet anyone on the way to Lady Strahan's house. She was prepared, however.

Twice a man had accosted her while she was delivering messages in the evening. The first time the man was inebriated, and she managed to wrench herself away. The second time she brought a small knitting-pin, which proved very useful. She also had a large rock in her reticule.

The walk always seemed long at night. Linnea knew it was because she was anxious, for Pall Mall was but a few streets away from Lord and Lady Boothe's house. *You are tired as well,* a stubborn part of her insisted. *Yes, but it is only right that you earn your keep,* she argued back to herself. But for all that she had been the sole caretaker for her father and the vicarage when he became ill, she had never worked as hard in her life as she did now at Lady Boothe's. She wished again that her brother Jack had not died at Ciudad Rodrigo, that her father had not given up on life at the news, that she did not have to make her own way in the world. She shook her head. Useless to think of it! The employment registry should call for her any day now; two weeks had passed already. . . .

"Eh, what's this?" cried a man's voice, hoarse with drink. "A little grey ladybird, do you think, Charlie?"

Linnea's heart hammered, and she walked faster. She slipped the knitting-pin from her sleeve.

"Aye, but I think she won't be flying to your arms, eh, Arnie?" The second man sounded equally foxed. Linnea started to run. "Wager a yellow boy I'll catch her before you do!"

"Done!" said Arnie.

Linnea picked up her skirts and ran as fast as she could. She could hear the men's footsteps coming closer. Wildly she glanced around, but she could escape nowhere. A hand pulled at her skirt, and then another grasped her arm.

"Let me go!" she cried.

"Now, now, my dear, I won. Let me have a look at you." A grinning face peered into hers. "Well, Charlie, look at this! We've got ourselves a pretty little pigeon for our supper. Let's see if she tastes as good as she looks—" The face came closer.

"Stay away!" hissed Linnea. She whipped out the knitting-pin.

"Ow! What the devil!"

"Get away from me, you horrid man!" Linnea turned to Charlie. "And you, too! How dare you accost a respectable woman!"

"Respectable—ha!" jeered Charlie. He glanced at Arnie. "Seems you're too foxed to do much, eh, old man? Let me try." He made a grab at Linnea.

She jumped away and waved her knitting-pin. "I'll hurt you!" she said through gritted teeth.

Charlie grinned and lunged for her.

Linnea stepped aside, but not quickly enough to avoid him. He took hold of her arm and pulled her toward him. The knitting-pin struck again, and for good measure she kicked whatever parts of him she could reach. Charlie fell, clutching himself. A large scratch on his chin bled freely.

Arnie came at her. "Leave me alone!" Linnea cried, and swung her rock-laden reticule with all her might. The string broke, and the reticule escaped her grasp. She lost her balance and fell. Pain shot through her right ankle. She closed her eyes. Lord help me, she prayed.

She heard horses, a yell, the sound of someone falling; and then a different voice said: "A female David, and two drunken Goliaths! How novel."

The voice sounded familiar, but the man's beaver hat obscured his face. "Please go away," she said. She looked around her. Charlie was sitting on the ground, holding his jaw, and staring with dismay at her rescuer. Arnie lay unconscious on the ground. A snore emanating from his open mouth reassured her that he was not hurt badly. She rose slowly. "I must go." She clenched her teeth at the pain in her ankle and started limping away.

"But you are hurt! Come, let me help you."

Linnea could hear his steps behind her. She tried to walk faster but stumbled and cried out with the pain. She felt a strong hand supporting her elbow.

"Come," the man commanded, and led her to his waiting carriage.

She felt sick with the terror just past. Her body ached with fatigue, her ankle hurt, and she knew when she came back to Cousin Boothe's house she would have more work to do. It was so very easy to do as her rescuer bade her. She could not know whether he was truly any better than Charlie or Arnie—but he *did* come to her rescue. Just for a little while, she thought. It would be heaven to sit in a carriage.

At the door of the carriage, she brushed briefly at her skirt, then looked up at him. "I thank you, sir, for helping me. . . ." She faltered, then stopped. The man was Paul's rude uncle, Lord Rothwick. She drew back at the look of surprise on his face, then said: "But I think I can do well enough by myself."

"My dear ma'am, I was only jesting when I called you a female David," he said irritably. "There are other Goliaths who may not know they are supposed to be defeated. I suggest you do as I say, and I will take you away from here."

"No, I cannot! That is . . ." She hesitated. "That is, I should not go with you. It is quite unseemly."

"As it is quite unseemly for you to wander out in the evening without escort, I hardly thought it would matter to you," he replied with a hint of irony.

She hung her head. "I know, but my—my cousin wanted a message delivered, and there was no one else in the house to do it, so she sent me."

"Your cousin?"

"Lady Boothe, sir."

It seemed he grew suddenly still. "I know where she lives," he said finally. "It is but fifteen minutes from here by coach, while you would take nearly an hour to hobble there on foot."

Linnea looked at the open carriage door. The lamp within put a glow upon the soft cushions and upholstered interior. She could not help glancing at the dark streets, and the comparison made her want to weep. The temptation of just a few minutes' comfort was too great. She stepped up into the carriage.

"Unusual, is it not, for someone to send a female relative unescorted into the night?" Lord Rothwick said after he gave direction to his groom.

Linnea's head lifted quickly, and she looked squarely at him. "Not for Lady Boothe!" she said acidly. She paused, then looked away. "I should not have said that; it was uncharitable in me. I am tired, sir. Do excuse me." She *was* tired, tired to the bone. She would not have almost let slip her opinion of her cousin's hypocrisy otherwise. All must be respectable and proper for Lady Boothe's own daughters; their chaperonage could not be spared for a poor relative, and a distant one, at that.

"Of course," said Rothwick, and patted her hand in what she felt was a most comforting manner. "You have had a most terrible assault on your person; I do not blame you for your frame of mind. I would not count it as a discourtesy if you rested your eyes for a few minutes, at least until we arrive at your, ah, destination."

"Yes, I think I will, sir, if you do not mind," replied Linnea. Certainly her first impression of him the other day had been grossly incorrect. How kind he was! Perhaps he had only been angry at something Paul Wrenton had done and had not meant to be rude. Linnea closed her eyes. The squabs were soft beneath her, and the body of the well-sprung carriage swayed rhythmically. Even her ankle seemed to hurt less. Her eyes drooped, and she dozed.

Well, well, thought Rothwick. Opportunity knocks. Although, if he had known at the outset that the woman was Paul's so-called inamorata, he would have left her to her fate. No doubt it was all some squabble about money or jewels.

He grimaced to himself, feeling the knuckles he had bruised on one man's jaw. Untrue. He could no more have let her be assaulted than if she were his own sister. In truth, no woman should be assaulted, regardless of what she was. Besides, he had not known who she was until he had seen her face.

However, he could teach her a lesson. What an actress she was, to have claimed kinship with Lord and Lady Boothe, and with such an unconscious air! But she had slipped, and slipped badly. He had heard long ago that Lady Boothe was a woman of rigid propriety; he would bet his estates that she would never let a young female relative out of her sight or from the close proximity of one of her dragons. Much less would Lady Boothe let a female of her household walk alone at a time of night when only men and prostitutes dared appear. He felt himself confirmed that this woman was no innocent maiden at all, but as sly a bit of muslin as he had ever come across.

Rothwick pursed his lips slightly, as if a sour taste had entered his mouth. He did not like liars. His past mistresses had been honest, making no claim to be anything other than they were. He would not bother making her his—but most certainly he would teach her a lesson. She would learn to stay away from members of his family.

The earl turned up the carriage lamp and surveyed her in the dimness. She neither moved nor spoke during their ride, and though she was not deeply asleep, he thought she dozed. The lights made shadows under her closed eyes; she looked very tired. Rothwick shrugged. The light was muted, and if she was tired, it was no doubt from dissipation. Women grew old quickly in the oldest of professions, for all their knowledge of paints and lotions.

The carriage slowed, and Rothwick could see that the Boothes' town house was near. He quickly made a decision. Leaning out of the door, he murmured a few words to Grimes. The groom's brows rose, but the man said nothing. The carriage continued down the street. Rothwick gazed at the woman, thinking about what he would do. Should he expose her charade at the nearest stopping place, or should he continue to his hunting box? He reviewed the various inns on the periphery of London and thought better of it. An inn was too public a place—if she set up a screech, it would cause no end of scandal, and he wanted to keep his—well, he would admit it—abduction of Miss Pickens quite private. It would have to be his hunting box. Once more he leaned out the door and gave his groom the new direction, then smiled to himself and settled back down on the carriage seat.

When she finally opened her eyes, she sighed, looking around her for a few seconds. Her eyes rested on the earl and lost their sleepy vagueness, looking embarrassed instead. "I am truly sorry, sir—I think I actually slept for a while. Your carriage is remarkably well sprung." She laughed tentatively. "It must have been terribly dull for you. Was it long?"

"No," replied the earl. "It was but a moment." He did not want her to know they had been traveling for more than half an hour. It would be most inconvenient if she made a fuss before they were out of London; indeed, he had hoped she would actually sleep. They were already at the outskirts of town, however, so it was not likely she would be able to make much headway in escaping if she did find out. He smiled briefly at her. "I do wish you would not call me 'sir' every time you address me. It is quite tiresome, you know."

She blushed but said with a touch of spirit, "I can hardly address you otherwise, since I do not know your name."

He raised his brows. "I am remiss; you must forgive me. I am William, Lord Rothwick, at your service." He inclined his head slightly.

She returned his bow with quaint dignity, he noted with reluctant admiration. "I am honored, my lord. And I am—"

"I know who you are, Miss Pickens. You have become quite well known to me." He laughed shortly.

"Pickens?" she said. "I am afraid you are mistaken; I am not Miss Pickens, I am—"

"Come, come, my dear—shall I call you Cassey? No matter. There is no need to pretend you are other than you are. I know what you were up to with my nephew, Paul. He may still be wet behind the ears, but I am not. I have had experience with your sort, and I needed only to look at Paul's expression when he escorted you that day to see he was almost secured in your trap."

"Of—of my sort?" She looked confused. "What can you mean? And who is this Cassey? It is not I, I assure you, my lord. My name is Linnea—"

"Really, Miss Pickens," Rothwick drawled. "I concede you are a good actress, but did you really think you could fool me with that story about Lady Boothe? It does your case no good to change your name, either." He leaned back in a leisurely manner. "It was a good story—one I have heard before, however—though the invention of a relationship between you and Lady Boothe was a bold stroke, I must say! But I happen to know Her Ladyship is extremely strict in her observance of the proprieties, and would never let a young woman of her household leave without escort. So, my dear, why don't we dispense with this unnecessary pretense and engage in some pound dealing, shall we?" He smiled genially.

Her face was the picture of stunned astonishment,

and she seemed bereft of words. Really, he thought with a touch of irritation, she was an excellent actress, but he would prefer she be open with him now.

"But—but, I assure you, sir, I am not who you think I am," she managed to croak. She cleared her throat and said more calmly, "Please, you need only let me down at Lady Boothe's and she can identify me."

He laughed. "And have you make a run for it?" She opened her mouth to reply, but he held up a hand. "Or, no. You seem to be an imaginative young woman. . . . Let's see. You will be so bold as to approach Lady Boothe and demand her presence. She will not recognize you, and you will then protest that she is against you and seeks only to cast you out from her house."

The young woman opened her mouth again, only to shut it. A hopeless look came over her face. "But, my lord, she must acknowledge me!" she whispered. "I am her kin, after all." She seemed almost to be talking to herself. He could see she was on the edge of giving up her act.

"Come now. You know she wouldn't," he said soothingly.

She looked at him as if bewildered. "But wait—wait! Am I to assume from this conversation you are not taking me to Lady Boothe's?"

"No, I am not."

She half rose from her seat. "Then where—" She stared at him in horror. "You must be mad! You cannot just—just abduct someone and carry her off!"

"Your presence here proves that I can."

"No. I cannot go with you, it's impossible!"

"What, another assignation with a . . . er . . . paramour? Or is it Paul?"

Her gaze was one of incomprehension. "Paul? What has Paul to do with all this?"

"So you are on a first-name acquaintance with him, are you?

"Why, yes, I have known him for a good while."

"Your mask slips further and further, Miss Pickens. There is no one in Lady Boothe's household who is closely acquainted with Paul."

She pressed herself into the seat, away from him. "You jump from one thing to another! You must be mad or—or full of drink! I cannot see why you chose to abduct me and then talk of people I don't know, and acting as if I should!"

"People you don't know," mocked Rothwick. "You just said you knew my nephew!" His distaste grew. She was playing the innocent maiden role, an act that often lent some spice to other men's pursuit of women, but it was one he detested.

"Ah, sir! Why do you do this to me?" she exclaimed. She looked about her wildly. "You *must* be mad—or I! I cannot go with you!" She jumped up and seized the carriage handle, tearing open the door.

She moved so swiftly that she was halfway out of the moving carriage before he seized her about the waist and pulled her back in again. From out the swinging carriage door, Rothwick could see the quick flashes of reflected moonlight on the road's rocks and pebbles. She could have been killed. He turned his head and looked at her. She had fallen against him, and he still had one arm around her waist and a hand clamped around her wrist. She breathed in small gasps, and he could feel how thin her wrist was in his hand and how little flesh covered her ribs that were pressed against him. Her eyes looked up into his, and in the turned-up carriage lights he could see a spark of defiance beneath the fear and fatigue in her eyes.

The horrible suspicion that had risen in Rothwick's mind when the woman had gone for the door now turned into certain consternation. Women of the demi-monde may act the unwilling maiden to tantalize, but they soon gave way to seduction at the end. They did not try to escape into what might have been death or at least severe injury.

"Who are you?" he whispered tersely. He let go of her waist and let her down gently on the seat opposite him.

She pushed herself into the corner away from him, her hands clutching the cushions. "I am Linnea Ashley. I live with Lady Boothe, my—my cousin. She lacked a footman to send a message to Lady Strahan, and she sent me instead."

"Oh, my God." Rothwick sank his head into his hands and wearily ran his fingers through his hair, pulling a little. He glanced up at Miss Ashley. "You can stop trying to wedge yourself into the woodwork. I don't ravish women, much less ladies of quality." She relaxed a little but kept a wary eye on him. "Please," he amended.

She lifted her chin mutinously. "You might change your mind," she said. "Indeed, I do not know what you will do next."

"Surely you don't take me for a madman—yes, well, I see you do." He sighed. "I assure you, I am quite sane. You see, I, ah, I thought you were someone else, and was trying to teach her a lesson." Even to his own ears the excuse sounded weak.

"How flattering." Her voice was sarcastic, but she unclenched her hands from the upholstery.

He ignored her sarcasm and said: "How came you to be in Bond Street with my nephew, Paul?"

Miss Ashley looked bewildered at this change of subject and glanced back at the carriage door handle. He could see she blushed so that even in the dim light of the carriage it was apparent. "I, I know now I should not have been there. But no one had told me, and I thought, when Paul—Lord Wrenton—recognized me just outside my cousin's house, that he could show me the quickest way to New Bond Street. I suppose he did not know a lady should not have been there either. There is a milliner's there where Lady Boothe has lately bought all her hats."

Lord Rothwick remembered suddenly that while there were no ladies' shops in Old Bond Street, some ladies of his acquaintance had mentioned a few milliner's and draper's shops in New Bond Street. He grimaced. He wished he had remembered it earlier; but then he mostly kept his activities to the older street. He gazed speculatively at the woman before him. Anyone could know about the new shops in the area, however.

"How came you to know Paul?"

"Why, he is Susan's, that is, Miss Wrenton's brother. We were friends in school, and he often came to escort her home during the holidays, and she introduced us." She paused. "He recognized me the day you saw us together and was kind enough to escort me on my errand until you came."

"What school did you go to?" He looked at her sharply.

"Why, Miss Brinkley's Academy for Young Ladies in Bath. I was four years ahead of Susan."

Rothwick pressed his palms against his eyes. Miss Ashley looked at him nervously and waited.

God, what a fool he was! He knew now without doubt that Miss Ashley had spoken the truth all along. It was very unlikely that any courtesan, however clever, would know of Miss Brinkley's, as it was an unknown, though excellent, school. Lydia had gone on forever about Miss Crosby's being most fashionable and tonnish, and he had initially intended to send Susan there, but the headmistress was fawning and obsequious, qualities he detested. He had seen Miss Brinkley's on his way out from Bath and thought he would look into it. Miss Brinkley was a no-nonsense woman, whose school taught much more than the dancing, drawing, and deportment Miss Crosby thought adequate. It was possible a light o' love of Paul's could have found out from him, but that was as likely as the Thames flowing backward. Paul never took much interest in family activities unless it affected him directly.

Rothwick lifted his head and looked at Miss Ashley. She seemed calmer now but still watched him carefully. "I promise I won't do anything to you," he said soothingly. "I believe you are who you say you are. I am sorry I did not believe it before."

"I am sorry, too, my lord." She looked at him curiously. "What made you decide I was not a, ah, fallen woman?"

Rothwick grimaced. "Ladies who are, er, used to entertaining gentlemen may put up a bit of a struggle if it is what they think the gentleman wants, but they do not protest with as much vigor as you did." He indicated the carriage door with a wave of his hand. Miss Ashley nodded, but he was not sure she fully understood. He preferred not to explain it further, however.

"Well," she said at last. "Perhaps all this can be

remedied. You need only return me to Lady Boothe's and . . ." She trailed off as she caught the look in his eye.

"Not likely, ma'am," he replied dryly. "It is late, much later than it would take anyone to go from Lady Boothe's house to Lady Strahan's. By the time we arrived at your cousin's door, they would have already missed you for some time. You would be thoroughly compromised. How would you explain your long absence?"

She looked a little frightened. "I—I don't know," she stammered. "Perhaps I could say I was lost."

"For almost an hour?" Rothwick replied sardonically. "It would take another hour to get back, you know." The lost look returned to Miss Ashley's eyes, and she rubbed them wearily. A faint pity stirred within him. "I think you had better come with me," he said. She looked at him suspiciously and glanced at the carriage door handle again.

"No, no!" he said, irritated. "I told you I don't mean to ravish you. I promise it—on my word of honor!" A wry smile twisted his lips. "My sister, Lydia, would comb my head with a stool if she found out I had injured a friend of her daughter's."

Miss Ashley still gazed at him warily but seemed to relax. "To tell you the truth, I do not know what I would say to my cousin," she said. She looked down at her dress, a little torn and rumpled from her encounter with the two drunkards. "I do not look at all respectable, do I?"

"As well as anyone can look after what you have been through." Rothwick pulled out his watch. "It is very late—past midnight, by the way. There is an inn close by. I think we should go there to discuss what we are to

do, and depart in the morning for my sister's house."
The earl caught her alarmed look and said testily, "And I
will also hire a maid to sleep in your room."

Miss Ashley gave him a determined look. "No," she
said. "I will choose the maid."

Rothwick let out an exasperated breath. "My dear
girl, surely you don't still think—"

"I do not know what to think of you," she said simply.

He felt his face grow warm and was glad the carriage light was still dim enough to hide the red he was
sure was rising in his cheeks. "Well, as you wish." He
sat back against the squabs of the carriage and looked
out the window. A light shone in the distance. Lord
Rothwick sighed. It should be the Lion's Stone, where
the innkeeper was known to be extraordinarily discreet, thank God. They would have to stay there for
the night.

3

Linnea felt sure she was in a nightmare. Though she felt she managed to cover it, confusion reigned in her mind, and her fatigue was such that she had no spark of energy left to speak or even to think. The carriage rumbled up to a well-lighted inn, and the innkeeper bowed and scraped until, she thought a trifle hysterically, that his round little body would burst. He gave her a curious look, but that was all; at his lordship's orders they were shown to a private parlour.

A knock on the door made her jump, and a yawning chambermaid came in with a food-laden tray. That heavenly scent rising from the covered plate—yes, it was pheasant, Linnea marveled as Rothwick lifted the cover. She was very hungry. Her cousin had given her so many errands the past two days, she had scarce time to dine. Her stomach uttered a protesting growl at her hesitation, and, embarrassed, she laid her hand upon it as if to stifle the noise. Linnea glanced at the maid, wondering if she could ask her for assistance in escaping this inn, but the girl's eyes only slid past her as she left the room. No help there.

The scent from the food tray called to her. Perhaps she would be able to think of a way to escape after a few bites. She could not think with a growling stomach, and when she did think of a way, she could not be fainting with hunger when she tried it. Linnea picked up knife and fork.

The bird melted deliciously on her tongue, and she ate far more than she thought she would under such upsetting circumstances. Linnea smiled wryly to herself. True abducted heroines would refuse all food and no doubt stab themselves with any sharp object available to escape the villain's clutches. She glanced at the earl, who concentrated on carving. Lord Rothwick looked more like a hero than a villain, with his clean good looks and strong frame. She sighed. This merely proved, despite all of her novel reading, that she was without any sort of sensibility and not romantic at all. Perhaps that was why her father let her read novels. He always did say he should have named her Prudence. Linnea sighed. She had not been prudent tonight.

The maid appeared again and removed the remnants of their meal. The earl and Linnea sat looking at each other for a few moments. For the first time she could examine his face in detail: in all, he was nothing short of handsome. His hair was a raven's-wing black, and his face was composed of sharp, strong planes from chin to cheek to high-bridged nose. For some reason she had thought his eyes were blue at first, but they were not such an insipid color. Slate gray they were, and set in his face like chips from that stone. She imagined they could be as hard; but they were not now. They gazed at her with a frustrated yet—could it be?—embarrassed expression.

"Well," he said finally. "Well. I think the first thing I shall do is take you to my sister's house. From there, we will see what we can do about you."

Linnea felt a rising anger. "I assure you, sir, you need not do anything about me at all."

Rothwick frowned. "And I assure *you,* Miss Ashley, that as I am responsible for your predicament, I need very much to do something about you."

She lifted her chin defiantly. "I could go back to Miss Brinkley's as a schoolmistress."

"And when it becomes known you disappeared and were in my company for a long period of time, how well do you think you will be received, even there?"

"I assure you, Miss Brinkley has always been very kind—"

"And I assure you it is not Miss Brinkley's kindness that will decide whether you stay or not. How many families, do you suppose, will send their daughters to a school which has amongst their faculty a man's cast-off mistress?" he said harshly.

Her hands clenched. "But I am not your mistress."

"It matters not." He sighed. "You have spent a considerable time in my company, and will spend the night in this inn—granted, with a maid, but society will overlook *that* for the sake of titillation. It is what they will assume, will you, nil you."

Linnea stood up abruptly then, feeling the heat of anger and frustration burning within her. She faced him. "So, you!" she said furiously. "You, who have effectively ruined my reputation and any means to

earn my bread—what do you suggest? What do I do
with myself, your high and mighty lordship? You have
left nothing for me. Nothing!" She pounded her fist
upon the table and turned her back on him, facing the
fireplace. She bit her lip, shaking with the effort to suppress her sobs.

She heard his high and mighty lordship draw a deep
breath. "You could always marry me, you know," he said.

Linnea whirled around again, almost stumbling
over a chair, and stared at him, astonished. There was
nothing in his face to deny the sincerity in his voice.
She sat down abruptly. "You must be joking."

He lifted an eyebrow. "I never propose in jest, my
dear. And it is a possibility you must consider *if*—and I
emphasize *if*—word of our, ah, situation becomes
known."

"But this is absurd!" she cried. "Why, you do not
even know me—you can't have fallen in love with me."

"No," he admitted. He smiled at last. "And I trust we
will not have to resort to such extremes. Yet I am not
without a certain amount of honor, and as you pointed
out, I have effectively ruined your reputation and owe
you at least my name. It is, therefore, important that
we—especially you—consider it. You would be provided for, and need not find employment, and your
reputation will not, frankly, be in shreds."

She eyed him in disbelief. "And how would *you* benefit from it, sir?"

The earl's voice was equally cool. "Of course, it is
not as if I had not an interest in the matter. My sisters
have often pointed out to me that it is time I considered marriage to, ah, secure the succession. You are a
gently bred young woman and quite attractive, which
makes my proposal much easier to make, believe me. I

think you are also quite intelligent, and thus we should get along quite well."

"Impossible!" Linnea shook her head. His bland tone and words nettled her—he spoke of her as if she were a brood mare!—but she contrived not to show it. "There must be some other answer—should our association be known, of course."

"Of course. But if there is, I would like to hear it," replied the earl. He looked at her with expectant politeness.

"I could tell my cousin I was kidnapped by a madman," Linnea ventured. She caught a derisive look from Rothwick. "Well, it would be not far from the truth, after all!"

"And she would believe you, of course."

Linnea knew it did not matter whether her cousin believed her. They had no real use for her except as an unpaid servant; they would throw her disgrace in her face every day until they were rid of her. Her present predicament would merely be a good excuse to use her harder than they had been or throw her out into the street altogether. "Oh, heavens. I—I cannot think of anything right now." Her shoulders slumped, then she looked up at him again. "I am sure there must be a solution to this mess."

"I am sure there is, Miss Ashley. As I have said, we shall see if we can find one when we arrive at my sister's house. If it is any comfort to you, I seriously doubt anyone of importance will come to know of our stay together. You must be prepared, though, to accept my proposal should we need to." He leaned back on his chair and clasped his hands around a knee.

"Absolutely not."

His face became morose. "Alas! I had not thought it! I am repugnant to you!"

Linnea put out her hand. "Oh, no! Not at all—that is to say—"

His expression brightened ludicrously. "Then you accept." He grasped the hand she had inadvertently held out.

"No! Really! I cannot—" She stopped then, for she had glanced at his face. His mouth wore a lopsided grin, his brows were raised in wistful hope, but his eyes danced with laughter. "You are laughing at me!" she cried angrily. "How dare you make fun of me by making me an offer!" She tugged at her hand, caught in his.

He held on firmly. "No, I was not making fun of you, merely seeing if the idea of marriage to me is really odious to you. My offer of marriage stands: I cannot do otherwise, in honor. But—you do not find me repugnant; can you not perhaps find me tolerable? There are many arranged marriages made with the partners actually disliking each other. We, at least, may come to like each other comfortably." He paused and looked at her downcast face. "Or am I mistaken? Have I sunk below any hope of redemption? Have my actions made me seem a monster in your eyes?"

Linnea did not know how to answer. What did she think of him? She had thought him odious at first, then mad, then kind, then mad again. . . . She did not know. She laughed tremulously. "You must acknowledge, sir, that your actions since I entered your coach were not of a quality to inspire confidence. Even if I were to pretend it had not happened, why, I hardly know you. For all I know, you may deem it a virtue to beat one's wife on a regular schedule."

"Come, this is better!" Rothwick laughed. "You now

have one less objection to my proposal: I can promise you upon my honor that I believe no such thing. I have always held it is better to kiss a wife on a regular schedule than to beat her."

She retorted, "Your own or someone else's?" before she could stop herself.

His eyebrow lifted, and Linnea's cheeks grew hot. She should not have said such a reprehensible thing, but were these not unusual circumstances? And what did she know of him, after all? She stared at him steadily.

"Since I have no wife, that question is really unanswerable, is it not?" he said, but he smiled. "I can tell you, however, that I have never trifled with what belongs to another."

Linnea believed him, but a faint dissatisfaction rose within her. She suppressed it out of embarrassment. What business was it of hers, after all? He was not proposing to her out of love. And she need not accept him; certainly there must be other solutions. She must think of another way out, but she could not think of anything now; her head ached with weariness, and she wanted only to sleep.

"I will take you to my sister's house tomorrow; it is but ten miles from here. If marriage with me is that repugnant to you, perhaps Amelia or Lydia or my other sisters can find a situation for you. Or would you rather I return you to your family?" His voice was gentle.

Linnea looked away from him, her hands clasping together tightly. The kindness in his voice almost undid her, for she could not bring any anger to bear against it. "I have no family—or rather, Lord and Lady Boothe are the only family I have. My father died five years ago, not long after my brother fell at Ciudad Rodrigo."

"I am sorry," replied Rothwick, but Linnea thought

she heard a note of relief in his voice. She almost smiled. No doubt he had little taste for confronting a justifiably enraged father or brother. "But you are tired," he continued. "You need not decide now. Rest, I think, would be best for you now."

Linnea looked at him gratefully. "Yes, I am tired. Perhaps I can think more clearly tomorrow." She glanced at him uncertainly.

"Ah, yes, the maid," he said, responding to her look. "And a room." He went out of the parlour and returned with two maids. Linnea selected a stout-looking girl, who then led them upstairs. She opened the chamber door, and Linnea went in.

However, when the earl did not go in as well, the maid looked at him in consternation. "Sir, are you not going in?" He heard Linnea close the door hastily, and he almost smiled.

"No, you are to show me to my room now," he replied with a hint of impatience.

"Oh, dear," the girl said, much flustered. "I cannot do that, yer lordship. There's not another room to be had!"

"You must be mistaken."

"Oh, no, sir! There's a cockfight nearby, and all the rooms have been let for the next few days. Mr. Chawleigh, he thought—"

"Yes, well, never mind that!" He looked longingly at the closed chamber door. He sighed. "Well, I must say, this will be a first for old Chawleigh." He left the hallway in search of the innkeeper.

Chawleigh raised his eyebrows at my lord's request and bowed his round little body again, regretfully. He disliked ejecting one customer for another, for even the private parlours below were full—but this was the Earl of Rothwick, after all, and. . .

Rothwick could see these thoughts reflected in the innkeeper's face and changed his mind. He had done enough damage for one night.

"Never mind, Chawleigh. I will make do in the common room."

Chawleigh's jaw dropped. "But, but, sir!"

"No, I insist!" The earl smiled his most charming smile. "It will be a novelty, and I dislike passing up such a chance as this!"

As he settled himself down on the hard bench, he smiled ruefully. He was just as surprised at his proposal, he was sure, as Miss Ashley had been. His honor had been at stake, however, and it was the first thing that had occurred to him. He was certain they would find another answer to their problem, certain he would not need to marry Miss Ashley. He grimaced as he turned on the hard bench. Well, perhaps the morning would bring better ideas.

Linnea closed the door on the earl and surveyed the chamber. Lord Rothwick had procured one of the best rooms in the inn. It was well lighted and warm with the fire burning merrily in the grate, and the bedsheets were white and soft. She held her hands out to the warmth in the hearth, for the night was chill and her grey cloak thin.

She shook her head in wonder. On one hand the nobleman seemed arrogant and brusque, and on the other full of enough consideration to command the best comforts for her. Surely the man was half mad. Impulsive, certainly.

She looked out the window to the courtyard below. The moonlight had turned the roadway on which they had just traveled to textured silver, but she saw nothing that told her where she might be. She gauged the distance from the window to the ground and eyed the bedsheets. They did not look long or sturdy enough to serve as a rope, and though her foot throbbed only a little now, she did not relish a broken neck.

Her fear had abated after Lord Rothwick had clearly shown he would leave her alone—and her practical mind dismissed the thought of escape through the window. If she attempted to escape, she knew she might well meet a worse menace than his lordship; better to "bear those ills we have than fly to others that we know not of," after all. Linnea recalled the context of that quote and shivered. She believed her foot was better, but that had little to do with it. She knew the dangers in returning to London alone; travelers unused to self-defense often disappeared.

She paced in front of the fireplace, chafing at the conclusion logic had given her. She wished she had something she could do, either escape or, or, even embroider, for goodness' sake! A slightly hysterical giggle escaped her. Embroidery, at a time like this! She sat on the bed. It was soft, the sheets fine and freshly clean, and Linnea realized she was more tired than she had thought. It would not hurt, surely, to rest just a little. Surely it would make her more able to deal with his lordship when she saw him again. The maid returned then and helped her remove her cloak—she could not afford to crush it more than it was already—and readied Linnea and her own small cot for the night. Linnea reclined herself gratefully on the bed and fell instantly asleep.

4

It was not because Sophia Amberley's trip into London had been so long and wearying that she planned to stay the night at the Lion's Stone Inn. She knew well, however, how important it was to make an appealing picture when entering the center of the ton. The inn was just close enough to the City so that she could get a good night's rest and arrive in a fresh and un-travel-stained condition. She drew a mirror from her reticule and surveyed her reflection with satisfaction. Travel never did seem to touch her blond perfection much, but one could never be too careful. Sophia brushed a pale lock from a smooth pink-and-white cheek. There. Perfect. She returned the mirror to the reticule.

The Lion's Stone Inn. Discreet, just off the main road, with a close-mouthed innkeeper, it was a perfect place for the ton to keep its assignations. The perfect place, Sophia had found, to pick up fresh-cut gossip—which could bloom into the latest *on-dit*—if one's eyes were sharp and on the lookout. The innkeeper might be close-mouthed, but his wife was not so reticent, and if information could not be had from her, why, the chambermaids were more forthcoming still, especially if there were a few shillings to be earned.

A loud snort interrupted the snores emanating from the young gentleman who sat across from Sophia. His sleepy gaze wandered about the carriage until it lighted upon his sister's fair visage. A discontented look settled upon his face. "Well, are we near London yet?" he asked abruptly.

"Dear Richard, do you not remember?" Sophia said gently. "We are to stay at the Lion's Stone Inn."

All sleepiness fled from the Honorable Richard Amberley. "No, I don't remember! There is nothing to remember! We were to go directly to Aunt Agatha's house from the last inn we were at."

"But dear brother, you know how I hate to be creased and travel-stained when I come into town."

Richard looked at her fresh complexion with disfavor. He fished for his fob and opened his watch. Disfavor turned to disgust. "It wouldn't matter if you came to Aunt Agatha's covered with mud. It wants but an hour and a half of travel to London and but an hour to darkness. You could put on a veil. No one would see you but myself and the servants."

Sophia pouted. "But I do not like veils. And everyone stays at the Lion's Stone."

Her brother shut his watch with a snap. "What the devil does it matter if everyone—" He stopped, a look of dawning horror creeping across his face. "No! By God, Sophie, if you are up to your gossiping tricks again—"

"Please, Richard! *Sophia.* Sophie sounds so much like some article of furniture. . . ."

Richard ignored her. "Look, my girl. You may wrap our parents around your little finger, but you can't do that with me! If you think we are going to stay at some rubbishing inn just so you can pull me into some nasty little escapade with your damnable blackmailing ways, think again."

There was silence except for a few sniffs coming from his sister. "And don't come maudlin over me, either," said Richard, very certain her eyes were as clear of moisture as a summer's day.

Sophia opened her reticule. "You have always been so very cruel to me, Richard."

"Ha!" He leaned back onto the carriage seat again, ready to catch a few more winks of sleep.

His sister pulled out a handkerchief, and a paper fell onto her lap. "Why, what is this?"

Richard closed his eyes, determined at least to look as if he were asleep.

"Oh, my, Richard, it looks like a tradesman's bill! What a silly thing I am to have it in my purse. I must have picked it up when I was looking for my notepaper."

A tendril of uneasiness unfurled within Richard's breast. He opened his eyes and a wary look crossed his face. "No doubt it is for one of your dresses again. I wish you would not bother me about such trifles." He turned a shoulder.

"But no, Richard, it is not one of mine! Why, I know I have never ordered a sapphire necklace and eardrops." Sophia's voice was the epitome of sweet concern.

Richard's uneasiness unfurled to open dread. "Perhaps it is one of Mama's, then," he said gamely. "If you will give it to me, then I will make sure to return it to her."

Sophia perused the bill further. "No . . . no, I fear you are mistaken, dear brother. It seems to be—why, it's yours! Now I wonder why you would be billed for a sapphire necklace?"

Her dear brother made a lunge for the paper and missed, but a second try caught her wrist. He tore the paper from her hand. "What the devil—it's blank!"

Sophia smiled kindly. "My little joke. It was such a large bill, you see, I did not want to carry it in such an unsafe place as my reticule. I put it away, oh, somewhere." She waved her hand vaguely toward the top of the coach where their luggage was tied.

"I don't believe you have it," Richard said flatly.

Sophia took out her mirror again and smoothed an eyebrow. "Mmm . . . Do you know, I think I saw such a sapphire set on someone once. Who was it? Oh, that actress, Therese de Montagne."

Richard shrugged. "Whoever the deuce she is."

"Your language, dear brother, please!" Sophia looked pained. "Your lapse is no doubt because of the low company you keep. It would sadden Mama and Papa to hear of it."

"There is nothing for them to hear!" Richard shifted himself uncomfortably. He watched his sister, wondering what was coming next.

"You know, I have often thought I would have been a very good actress, had I not been born to our station in life," Sophia mused. She delicately wet a finger and set one of her curls more firmly in place. She smiled at herself in the mirror. "But then, it is not a particularly comfortable life, is it? I hear the actresses' salaries are poor. Yet there is Therese de Montagne with a sapphire set. Now how is that?"

Richard eyed his sister with a certain fascination,

much in the manner a mouse might eye a snake. But he was a stubborn young man, and somehow all his sister's machinations through the years had not yet touched a core of optimism still in him. "No doubt she had a patron," he said in a bored voice. "Will you cease? I do not know what this has to do with me."

Sophia transferred her gaze from the mirror to Richard's face, her expression a study in sudden revelation. She set down the mirror carefully on her lap. "Why, that is it! That is where I saw her! I remember a night at the theatre, and between acts one and two, I saw you talking with Miss de Montagne. She was opening a case with—yes! I remember!—some blue stones in them!" She clapped hands her in delight. "I especially remember it because I needed to refresh myself with a stroll after the first act."

"You wanted to spy on me, is what you really mean!"

"I, spy?" said Sophia, her expression wounded. If Richard had not known her better, he would have felt as if he had just accused a newborn babe of murder. But he did know her better and thus knew he was at the end of her rapier thrust. He waited.

It came. A look of not altogether innocent wonder dawned on Sophia's face. "Why, Richard! Are you admitting you are Therese de Montagne's patron? How can that be? Did you not just lose your whole allowance at the races last quarter? I know Papa paid your creditors that time; what a scold he gave you, you naughty boy!" Sophia laughed merrily. Richard cringed. "But how is it that you had enough funds to purchase a necklace?" she continued. "I am afraid I am not very good at sums. I shall have to ask Papa."

"Tell Papa, and you will rue the day you were born, Sophie!" growled Richard.

"Do you know, I think I left the bill with Murphy," Sophia mused.

Richard groaned inwardly. Murphy, her abigail, was yet another who made up Sophia's adoring crowd. The woman would do anything for her mistress, he knew. He could not afford another of his father's scolds, for he was on his last legs until next quarter-day, and Lord Amberley was wont to withhold at least a portion of his funds with each scold. Though he was disillusioned by the Montagne woman and dismissed her when she clearly favored him no more than another despite his gift, she had been an expensive piece, and unless he was very lucky—or very conservative—he would not make a recovery in the immediate future.

"When are we arriving at this cursed inn?" said Richard.

Sophia's smile was beatific. "I knew you would like my notion of stopping there!" she said. "I think you are going to be the most helpful brother in the world!"

The morning broke differently for four individuals in the Lion's Stone Inn.

Sophia, recognizing certain crests on the carriages that came to the inn at the same time as her own, and satisfied with the large and very good mirror in her room, slept like the proverbial babe she was not. She woke with a sense of pleasurable anticipation. She had seen no fewer than three crests, and of those three, two of its owners were known to have reputations that bordered on the scandalous. Sophia sat up in bed, stretched, and looked in the chamber's large mirror. She looked like an adorable fluffy white kitten with her tousled blond hair and soft white lawn nightgown. She smiled with pleasure at the thought. She would have her breakfast in the common room downstairs. It would be quite proper, for of course Richard would accompany her.

The hapless Mr. Amberley, however, tossed and turned like a ship in a storm through the night. Ugly visions of moneylenders and tradesmen haunted his dreams. Richard dreamed of a school friend of his who was once sent to debtor's prison; the poor devil had contracted prison fever and had barely escaped with his life. Richard dreamed a monklike gaoler led him to his friend's cell, but when he came to it, it was not Jack there, but himself. He turned to the gaoler to protest, but the gaoler had laughed, and the laugh was horribly like Sophia's. He tried to leave the cell but could not, for the gaoler was reaching for him with clawlike hands. The gaoler's hood dropped back, and it was Sophia, yet somehow she looked very much like their father.

Richard woke up with a start and pressed a shaking hand to his eyes. He had to get that bill and find a way to keep his sister quiet. But how? One more confrontation with his father and he was stripped of his next quarter's allowance. He got up and gazed into the mirror above the mantelpiece. He groaned. He looked very much like he felt. He would definitely have his breakfast brought up to him. Breakfast. His stomach clenched, and bile rose in his throat. Perhaps he would not have it after all.

William, Lord Rothwick, awakened slowly and turned on his bench, almost falling off it. He righted himself and then looked about him with the usual disorientation one had when waking in an unfamiliar room. Ah, yes, the Lion's Stone. And then the events of the night before hit him, and the consequences of his actions rose up and mocked him.

Oh, Lord! Sophia! He had forgotten about Sophia last night. It must have been because their betrothal was so new. Or perhaps a part of him did not want to deal with any complications without enough sleep to fortify himself. Which all went to prove, he thought grimly, that things *didn't* seem better in the morning. He would have to make sure he and Miss Ashley departed unnoticed; otherwise he would have to do the honorable thing and lay his case in front of Sophia and Lord Amberley. It was lucky their betrothal was but a few days old and that his and Amberley's solicitors had not yet drawn up the marriage papers.

Rothwick did not think the interview with Sophia would be easy, though. The man and his wife doted on Sophia—sickeningly so, he had often thought. And he was not at all sure that Sophia would release him from their betrothal. Perhaps he could convince Sophia that she was better off without him. Perhaps she would break the engagement. Rothwick did not feel very hopeful this would happen. Well, then! He would have to be as discreet as possible when leaving this inn.

Chawleigh still did not have another room available. The innkeeper looked uneasy and clearly expected a reproof when he could not comply, but he did offer his own attic room for his lordship to refresh himself. Rothwick smiled genially and thanked the man, relieved that at least he could make himself somewhat presentable.

When he entered the innkeeper's room, the earl stopped and cursed softly. They had left his belongings in Miss Ashley's room! He rubbed his face, feeling the stubble on his chin, and frowned. He was damned if he was going to show himself in public in his present disheveled state!

Nicking himself with the innkeeper's dull razor did not put the earl in a better mood. A cut on his Adam's apple oozed blood. He searched for something with which to staunch it, but there was nothing—except his neckcloth. He sighed, cut a piece from it with the razor, and put the piece of cloth on the cut. He cursed again, loudly and long. The makeshift plaster looked grotesque, a cancerous-looking blob that no self-respecting throat should sport.

A neckcloth. He needed another neckcloth. An otherwise well-dressed man without a neckcloth was a very noticeable thing indeed. He looked around for a bell-rope, but there was none. He went down the attic steps, hoping to see a servant in the hallway. Neither hide nor hair of one. He would have to get a neckcloth himself.

Rothwick sighed and made his way to Linnea's chamber, looking around him first to see that no one was watching. God help him—and Miss Ashley—if anyone saw him going in!

He knocked, but no one responded. He crept quietly into the room. The maid had gone, and Miss Ashley was still asleep. One arm was flung over her eyes, stretching the material of her dress so that it outlined her bosom. It was a delightful bosom, reflected Rothwick. Certainly in that realm the change of fiancées should make little difference, if it happened. Sophia's was probably as delightful—he had not seen her for a few days, and he'd heard she had retired to the country for a while—but he was sure it must be since he had approved of the whole package when he first saw his betrothed.

He retrieved his neckcloth from a small carpet bag that had been brought in from his coach. He turned toward the door again to leave, but just as he put his hand on the doorknob, he heard voices outside in the hall. He grimaced. He could not leave quite yet, it seemed.

Sighing with impatience, he looked at the neckcloth in his hand. Well, he might as well put it on before Linnea awoke. He wouldn't want to shock her sensibilities any more than they had been, he reflected wryly. Not that he hadn't done that to the utmost already. He sighed again.

Linnea awakened slowly, easily, and stretched, like a swimmer reaching for the surface of a deep pond. She opened her eyes and was bewildered at being in a strange room, until the events of the past night rushed into her mind. She covered her eyes with a moan. The sound of movement made her uncover them again and swing her head sharply around. A man had his back to her, but she could see his face in the mirror he was using. Lord Rothwick. Linnea pulled the bedsheets up close to her chin. "My lord, how dare you—"

"Shhh!"

Linnea, startled by his abruptness, stopped what she was about to say and stared with surprise at his lordship in the mirror instead. His fingers seemed to be moving in an intricate pattern about his neck. They paused, hovering above a fold near the top, then dropped. Slowly Rothwick lowered his chin into the top fold.

"Mmmm, yes, it will have to do," he murmured. He turned and smiled at her. "Never, my dear, interrupt a man who is tying his neckcloth. Distraction has been known to ruin a dozen, at least." He paused. "And as for my presence here, I am sorry, but the innkeeper forgot to bring my clothes to my room. I intended to leave as soon as I retrieved it, but I heard people out in the hall, and deemed it unwise."

Linnea nodded, understanding. She looked at

Rothwick's intricately tied neckcloth. She remembered her father's care for his dress—for all that he was a vicar—and could understand Rothwick's wish to be presentable, but she thought such concentration on the mere tying of a neckcloth frivolous. She was much too polite to say so, however, so instead she said: "My lord, I thought on the matter last night. Perhaps you could take me temporarily to my former schoolmistress's home, and then recommend me to some one of your acquaintances as a governess. In that way, I would neither ruin her school's reputation, nor impinge on your . . . sense of honor."

"Miss Ashley, the tying of a neckcloth is not frivolous in the least—at least not when one must go about in society."

Startled, she replied: "I did not say it was!"

"No, but you thought it. Your expression revealed as much, you see. No matter. I am afraid I cannot do as you request. I have no acquaintances who need a governess, and if I did, I doubt they would hire you with my recommendation."

"Perhaps you have relatives, sisters . . . ?"

"All my sisters are older than I and are past the need of a governess for their children," he replied unequivocally. He picked up his jacket and brushed at it, shaking his head. He pulled it on carefully. "It is possible, however, that one of them knows of someone who is in need of a governess."

"Oh." Linnea absently smoothed a wrinkle from the bedsheet on her lap. "My lord, I cannot think of much else I may do. But wait! I can keep house very well, perhaps I can—"

"No, I think not. Ladies of your station do not become housekeepers."

"But now that you have ruined me, I do not think I can be called a lady, can I? So there should be no impediment in my seeking that occupation," she said practically.

Rothwick looked pained. "You are not ruined yet. You will be if we do not salvage this situation." He paused. "You are taking this very calmly," he said.

"Would you rather I fell into hysterics?" Linnea replied tartly. "I assure you I was very close to it last night! It would be a small thing to recall all that occurred and have the vapours this instant."

His hand flew up in mock horror. "No, not at all! I have a positive dread of vapours."

"Yes, it seems that most gentlemen do," she reflected. Smiling, she continued prosaically: "Well, then it would hardly be worthwhile for either you or me if I did have them. I would not be in a state to solve my situation, and you would be sorely discomposed, I am sure."

"Most sorely!" Rothwick replied with a hint of a laugh in his voice.

Linnea's eyes twinkled in response, but she said: "To return to the subject at hand. . . . Sir, I am sure I would do very well as a housekeeper."

"I am sure you would if you were given the chance." He held up a hand. "And no, it is not I who would deny you that chance. Think! Even the lowest of servants usually needs a recommendation, and if I were to give you one, what do you think would happen?"

"I would get hired, of course."

"The worse for you, too, if you did!" he said. "I could not recommend you to a female household, and those male households to which I could send you do not contain men who are made of ice! I think you an attractive woman, and they would as well."

"And they would try to—"

"Yes, they would!" Rothwick said hastily. "As I said, I will lodge you with one of my sisters, and see if we can find you a situation." He paused and looked at her curiously. "Is the idea of marriage with me, or marriage in general, odious to you? Have you even bothered to reflect on its possibility?"

Linnea was silent. She had not dared to think on it.

"I see you have not," he said. "Before you make any other plans, please do. If everything else fails, it is something you must consider." He sighed. "I am going to procure a private parlour for breakfast should one be available. It will take me a few minutes. While I am gone, reflect at least about what marriage with me might give you, and we can discuss it over the table." He walked to the door. "It would not be very odious, I promise you." He smiled at her before he left.

Linnea arose from bed and straightened her dress and hair as best as she could. She realized that she did not want to think of his lordship's proposal most probably because it seemed the perfect solution to her situation. Too perfect. She had dreamed of marrying for love, but living—no, working at her cousin Boothe's had shown her that marrying at all was only a dream. And now here was Lord Rothwick, handsome and no doubt wealthy, offering his hand, if not his heart. She knew she could not do better even if she had all the money and position in the world.

She could come to like him—for that matter, he was quite amiable now that all was explained, and she liked him a little already despite last night's events. Many men, she knew, would have done worse than he and not even offered any recompense.

But you cannot marry without love, Linnea said to

herself. *But most people do,* argued Miss Ashley. *But do you want what, say, cousin Boothe has?* retorted Linnea. Miss Ashley reflected on the formal distance between Lord and Lady Boothe and fell silent.

Linnea jerked at a wrinkle in her dress. What nonsense! She and Lord Rothwick would leave this inn, go to his sister's house, and she would find some employment. After that she would never see him again.

It was not long before Lord Rothwick returned. "Are you ready for breakfast?" She nodded. "But not for a discussion," he said, looking at her uncertain face. "Well, perhaps some sustenance will help. Come." He stopped. "Wait. I will go first. Count to ten, then go down to the private parlour. I should be out of the hall by then, and anyone who may see me coming downstairs will not think you are associated with me. Except the landlord, of course." He left.

As she counted, Linnea wondered if she could come up with another, better plan before breakfast was done. She doubted it.

Richard Amberley was not given the luxury of enjoying his misery in peace, of course. Sophia was quite ready to begin her day, but she knew well that she could not breakfast in the common room alone. When the chambermaid brought Sophia's freshly pressed dress—a lovely round dress of cerulean bombazine trimmed with pearl buttons and pink ribbon around the neck—Sophia instructed her to summon Richard.

The maid, yet another admirer won over by Sophia's charm, obeyed with alacrity. Richard eyed the maid with bleary discontent but made himself ready. He later overheard the maid wonder aloud to another chambermaid how such a lovely and charming lady could have an obvious ne'er-do-well for a brother.

"Such a pretty little place, don't you think?" said Sophia when Richard appeared at her door. Her abigail was putting the finishing touches on her coiffure.

Richard flushed in irritation. It was a thing he did easily, especially in his sister's company. She could be very close-mouthed if she chose. In fact, she could say anything she chose and their parents would take it as words from the pulpit; she always had been their darling and always looked so angelic. Richard himself had been a well-looking child born but two years before Sophia and was considered a fairly handsome young man now, but he had not the practiced charm of his sister.

"Richard, dear, do you procure a table for us in the public room, if you please." She added a smile to the request.

Richard looked at her suspiciously. It was customary to obtain a private room if accompanied by a lady and if one could afford it. Her gaze was guileless, an ominous sign; but he could think of no reason to refuse.

"Oh, and a pot of chocolate and a small repast as well."

Richard's heart rebelled, but his keen sense of self-preservation prevailed. "Oh, very well," he said petulantly, and stalked off, slamming the door only slightly.

When Sophia and Richard sat at their table she almost felt like hugging herself in sweet anticipation. She flicked quick looks from under her lashes at various other visitors to the inn and at the doors to the private rooms to see if she recognized anyone. Richard gazed studiously out the window.

A woman dressed in black entered the inn, but

Sophia caught only a silhouette through the veil over the woman's hat. There was something familiar about her. . . . The innkeeper directed the woman to the stairs. I shall simply die if I don't find out who she is, thought Sophia.

The maid approached with the chocolate, but Sophia rose and murmured a demure but obviously false excuse about needing to use the necessary, then followed the woman up the stairs.

Richard's eyes followed his sister's departure with dread. He closed his eyes for a moment. I do not care, he murmured to himself. She is only answering a call of nature, and is only going a different way. In fact, she isn't even my sister, I don't know her, she is only some girl who happened to be in the same coach and the same inn. This wistful but thoroughly wild flight of fancy soothed him somewhat. He resolutely returned his gaze out the window, as if the coming and going of coaches were his sole interest in life.

Sophia went up the stairs, in time to see a swath of black skirt disappear to the left. Close! Eagerly she rounded the corner and—

Came face to face with Lord Rothwick. "My lord!" gasped Sophia. The earl had just closed the door directly next to the stairs. An unreadable expression crossed his face, and then he smiled genially. Sophia felt the flicker of pique she usually did whenever she met her fiancé. For some reason she had always thought there was something she could not—ah, such an unpleasant word!—control in him. Perhaps it was that she could never tell what he was thinking. She could not quite pin him down, or always make him do as she wished, and this irritated her.

"Sophia! A pleasant surprise," said Rothwick, bringing

her hand to his lips. There was nothing in his voice to belie his words, but Sophia was uneasy. She was curious about his presence in this inn, for he had made no mention to her about removing from London the last time they had met; but for the first time she did not want to find out more than what appeared on the surface. *It would be so—so untidy,* said a voice in the back of her mind, *to find out more.* She ignored it.

"Most certainly, dear William," she murmured coyly, looking up at him through her lashes. "I had no idea you were removing from London. What brings you here?"

"I had heard the hunting was particularly good, and since I have a hunting box not far from here, I thought I should take advantage of it." He took her arm. "But come, perhaps you would like some refreshment." He started to lead her back down the stairs.

The door behind them creaked, and instinctively Sophia turned to look. A young woman—no, lady, her assessing mind told her unwillingly—emerged from the room Rothwick had just quitted. "Lord Rothwick, I thought you would already be—" The lady caught sight of his lordship's companion, faltered, stopped, and blushed.

An exasperated, half-angry look flashed across Rothwick's face, but then he sighed. "Sophia, may I present to you Miss Linnea Amberley. She is Lady Boothe's cousin, and a friend to Susan, my niece. I am escorting her to my sister Lydia's home."

Sophia did not believe this for one minute. Was she not *au courant* of all the foibles of the ton? And had not Rothwick's name been linked, however vaguely, with various ladies of the demimonde? But all that was to be done with—for after all, were they not betrothed? It seemed Rothwick did not think so. For the first time in her life, all of Sophia's practiced poise deserted her. She stood staring at the woman before her, numb with the realization that a man could actually prefer another besides herself, the beautiful, charming, irresistible Sophia!

The numbness faded quickly, however, for Sophia was nothing if not self-preserving. She looked at Linnea and knew with all the predatory female's instinct that she must take action swiftly, so Rothwick would realize his mistake.

Sophia gazed at Rothwick with eyes melting in sorrow. "Oh, Rothwick! How could you!" She lifted a gloved finger and delicately touched it to her eyelashes. "And we just recently betrothed!"

Rothwick made as if to move toward her, but Linnea was before him. "My lord! You never told me you were betrothed already! How could you, indeed!" She swept toward Sophia and extended a comforting hand. "My dear girl, it is not as it seems at all!"

But Sophia flinched from her. "Do not touch me, you sl—you horrid woman!" Linnea backed away, her face blanching. Sophia raised a weak hand to her bosom. "Oh, Rothwick, I swear my heart is breaking!"

But here Sophia made a grave mistake. Had she allowed Linnea to comfort her, the earl would not have been proof against the combined recriminations of two females. He might even have banished his idea of marrying Linnea, for Sophia had seemed truly unhappy. But Linnea's pale and stricken face reflected the realization of all the horrors of her situation at last and moved my lord to pity.

"Nonsense!" he said sharply. "You are indulging yourself in hysterics over a situation about which you know nothing." Rothwick glanced past Sophia and noticed a chambermaid peeking around a corner, totally absorbed in their altercation. "Further, this is not the place to discuss private matters. I suggest we retire to a private parlour, if we wish to do so."

"I do *not* wish!" cried Sophia, and stamped her foot. Things were not going the way they should. Rothwick should have been struck with her sad but appealing beauty, become abjectly apologetic, and abandoned that woman immediately. "Father will hear of this!"

"To be sure he will," Rothwick replied smoothly. "I shall send a letter requesting a meeting with him at once."

For the first time Sophia felt a touch of uncertainty. Perhaps she had misgauged the situation. She was not sure if Rothwick's proposed letter to her father would contain all that she would want it to contain. She would bring Richard into this. He was her brother after all, and it was his duty to put her interests above all else. "As for that," she said haughtily, "my brother can act for Father. Richard has accompanied me to this inn and you may speak to him as well as you would to Lord Amberley."

"Very well, then. If you will give me his direction, I will see him. But first, I desire breakfast."

Sophia stamped her foot again. "How can you think of breakfast at this time, you horrid man! The thought of food should be repulsive to anyone of delicate sensibilities!"

Linnea suddenly spoke up. "Indeed, my lord, I think it best if I did not accompany you to breakfast, and stayed within my—the chamber." She was still pale, but for all that she spoke with a certain dignity.

Rothwick paused, then said: "To be sure. I will, nevertheless, order a light repast be brought to you, for it would not do for you to be faint with hunger on the way to my sister's house." Linnea nodded and slipped back into the room.

"And what of myself?" demanded Sophia.

"Since you apparently have delicate sensibilities, I assume you will not be having breakfast," he said calmly. "However, I have often known persons of such delicacy to rest in a darkened room after an upset to their nerves. Perhaps you should do so." This last was said in as solicitous a tone as Rothwick could muster.

Sophia was not mollified, yet to remain would imply she did not, after all, have delicate sensibilities. Further, his tone reminded her that she had just had a shocking revelation, should be totally overset and in a weakened condition.

"Yes, yes, you are right," she said, her voice returning to a faint and heartbroken murmur. Sophia lifted a hand to her brow. "I am not sure how I will recover from this, this— Ah, I cannot say it!" She tottered away from Rothwick toward her room. She did not bother to tell him where Richard could be found. Why should she make it easy for him?

The earl clenched his teeth. It needed only this to make his situation complete. He opened the door to the stairs and nearly upset Mrs. Chawleigh, the innkeeper's wife.

"Oh, your lordship, I was only coming up to see if you needed anything. Perhaps a private parlour? My chambermaid was saying as how you might need a place to talk with your lady friends, private-like."

Rothwick gave a mental groan. No doubt the woman had been listening at the door, and between her and the maid, word of his and Sophia's altercation would very likely spread rapidly. "Your husband has already given me a private room, but I do need a breakfast, one for myself and one to be brought to the lady who accompanied me," he replied. "I would also be much obliged to you if you could locate Mr. Richard Amberley and send him to me."

Mrs. Chawleigh curtsied and hurried away down the stairs. Lord Rothwick followed more slowly. He rarely drank spirits and never in the morning, but somehow he felt a glass of fortifying brandy would not be a bad idea right now.

5

Richard Amberley pulled out his watch and looked at it for the second time. Sophia's chocolate was quite cold now, for its surface was congealing into skin. He wondered if something dreadful had happened to his sister and if he should look for her. The thought of being free of her machinations at last stayed him—for a few moments only, however. He rose from his chair.

"If it please you sir, would you be Mr. Richard Amberley?"

Richard turned to see the angular face of the innkeeper's wife, Mrs. Chawleigh. He inclined his head slightly in reply.

"Well, sir, Lord Rothwick would like to see you in his private parlour to join him for breakfast, if you haven't partaken, that is."

Richard blinked. Rothwick here! What would the earl want with him? Having breakfast with one's brother-in-law-to-be was not unusual, but their tastes were quite disparate and the circles in which they moved touched only tangentially. He rarely had anything to do with the man.

And how did Rothwick know he was here? Richard paled slightly. Sophia! He hurriedly dismissed Mrs. Chawleigh with the message that he would indeed meet with the earl.

As Richard walked to the private parlour he wondered what Sophia had got him into now. He frantically reviewed his past actions and wondered how his sister might twist them to vex his lordship. He could think of no way she could, but then he did not have the Machiavellian instincts she did. He could only wait and see.

Richard's first view of the earl was not encouraging. Rothwick sat at the table, grimly surveying his breakfast as if it had mortally offended him. At Richard's entrance he looked up, his face cleared, and he invited Richard to the laden plates before him. Richard let out a breath. So perhaps it was not he himself who was in trouble! Lord Rothwick's easy conversation and the fine breakfast before him quickly eased the young man's spirits, and he fell to dining with more optimism than he had felt for a long time.

At last Lord Rothwick pushed himself back from the table. A sigh escaped him, and Richard looked at him inquiringly.

"I suppose you are wondering why I asked you to join me," Rothwick said.

"Well, it was very kind of you to invite me to breakfast," replied Richard. "Not that you haven't been in the past, that is, but—"

"But I haven't put myself out to be more than pleasantly civil, is that it?"

"No, no!" Richard said, slightly alarmed. "Always up to snuff—I mean to say—we don't run in the same circles, after all!" He thought of Sophia again and hoped that whatever she had told her fiancé, it wasn't too incriminating.

His lordship raised a hand. "There's no need to say it. I have heard others say that I am a bit high in the instep." His brief smile was grim. "I saw your sister abovestairs a few minutes ago. We had some unfortunate words. She said I might talk with you in lieu of your father."

Richard blanched. Never before had Sophia referred to her brother as a figure of authority, and he was certain this new development was yet another twist in her schemes. He closed his eyes briefly. He was sure Sophia was trying to get him in trouble with Rothwick for some reason. If only he could see where this interview was leading!

The earl apparently took Richard's expression for something else. "Yes, it is a painful situation. It is one, however, that must be resolved quickly."

"I assure you, my lord, you needn't regard anything my sister says," Richard said desperately. "She doesn't always, ah, mean it." *She's a damned liar! I swear I didn't do whatever she said I did!* cried Richard's inner voice, but the rules of good *ton* stopped him. He ran a trembling finger under a neckcloth that was suddenly tight.

Rothwick shook his head. "I will be blunt. It is not anything Sophia has said. My presence here is not totally innocent, but I am trying to remedy that. Your sister found me with an unescorted—though respectable—lady, and thus that lady's reputation is now ruined. The lady's reputation must be saved. And yet here I am, recently betrothed to Sophia." Rothwick paused, and Richard thought he almost saw him wince. "You may not see it my way, and I will understand if you do not. I believe the least amount of damage would be done if we could hush up all of this. However, I am afraid our, ah, encounter was overheard and no doubt it will become well known. If Sophia could possibly find it within herself to break off our engagement, I would gladly take the blame. But I am not at all sure she will do it. And yet the lady who accompanied me to this inn is quite innocent and does not deserve a ruined reputation. You see my dilemma."

Richard's world whirled. It was not he who was in trouble, after all! An immense relief descended upon him, and then it hit him: Sophia might not marry Lord Rothwick! There was the distinct possibility that she was not going to be a countess, nor become disgustingly rich. For the first time in a long while a flicker of joy dared creep into his heart. He had been positively sick of Sophia's boasting that Rothwick had found her irresistible.

"Thank God!" blurted Richard.

Rothwick raised his eyebrows.

"What I mean is, thank God you aren't the sort of man who would abandon a lady after compromising her reputation," said Richard, recovering himself hurriedly. "I would be saddened, indeed, to think our family is that mistaken in your character."

The earl's eyebrows were still raised, but he gave an acknowledging bow. "I fear you flatter me," he said. "It's a damnable situation, and reflects badly on my judgment. I hope I can choose the course that will cause the least amount of scandal. There will be some gossip, but I will endeavor to see that your sister will not suffer any harm. You may be sure I will make it known the fault lies at my door, not hers."

Richard bowed in turn. "I have heard nothing that has not been honorable regarding you, sir. I am certain you will do all you can." An embryo plan suddenly sprang to life in his mind. "But . . . I think I may be able to convince Sophia to break your engagement, my lord."

Rothwick looked at him keenly. "You seem to be taking this quite calmly, Amberley," he commented.

Richard had the grace to blush. "Yes, well—that is to say—" He stopped and looked Rothwick straight in the eye. "Frankly, sir, after my first, ah, misgivings, I'm not all that sure Sophie didn't have it coming to her. She's—she's damnably difficult to live with sometimes."

The earl smiled disbelievingly. "Really? She seems charming enough to me."

"Of course," Richard replied bitterly. "*You're* not her brother. What's more, you're an earl. Easy enough to be charming to someone like you." He paused and came to a decision. "I'll tell you what, Rothwick: I think you are doing the right thing. I think Sophie is not really ready for marriage; but convincing her to end the engagement won't be easy. Father'll see your side of it; any sensible man would. But females aren't sensible. Sophie is sure to make a fuss over it, but—but I can do something about that."

Rothwick looked at him doubtfully. "Perhaps we should talk with your father."

Richard shook his head. "Oh, no! After all, it is not as if Sophia did not have an army of admirers. She will be speedily consoled." Privately he thought his father would have little effect on Sophia's actions. He believed he could make her break off the engagement, but a little doubtful part of him was sure his sister would even the score if he succeeded. But oh, how wonderful it would be to manipulate Sophia for a change!

Linnea's breakfast was taken from her chamber almost untouched. When Rothwick came to see how she did, he found her curled up on a large armchair by the fireplace. She had a faraway look in her eyes as she gazed into the fire, but it was a sad look as well—or so he fancied, he told himself.

Miss Ashley did not look up at him immediately when he came near. "You did not tell me you were betrothed," she said quietly, still staring at the fire.

"I did not deem it necessary," replied Rothwick. "The saving of your reputation was of more import than any social announcement, I think."

"That poor girl," said Linnea, and she finally looked at him. The flames in the hearth had far less heat than the anger in her eyes. She stood up. "I think she is well out of the betrothal, my lord, indeed I do! To carry off a woman with the intent to make her your mistress, just when you are newly betrothed!" She raised her hand to her cheek to damp a rising blush and turned away. "It is despicable!"

She did not know what to expect—excuses, protestations. Instead she heard only the crackling fire in the short silence between them, and then: "You are right."

Linnea turned back slowly, then searched his face for any trace of insincerity. There was none. Rothwick's eyes were grim, his mouth turned up in a self-mocking smile. "I am wholly despicable, am I not, for trying to separate my rich and gullible nephew from what I thought was scheming Covent Garden ware. And what a horrible beast I am, for trying to teach that bit of muslin such a salutary lesson that she would never manipulate a member of my family again."

"How could you mistake me for a, a— Surely there was nothing in my dress, or my manner, that could have, have—"

Lord Rothwick grimaced. "No, there was not, especially now that I look back on it. But my sister described an attractive young woman in half mourning, who was setting herself up as a widow—"

"You must have been mad to have carried me off on that description alone!" gasped Linnea. "Why, there must be hundreds of young women in half mourning in London!"

The earl had the grace to look uncomfortable but said: "Paul is not in the habit of escorting hundreds of young women in half mourning, and he had his usual besotted look that he gets when he is falling into calf-love. I assumed, therefore, that you were Cassey Pickens."

"You assumed! Could you not even have asked my name?" cried Linnea.

"I am not in the habit of conversing with courtesans in the presence of family," Rothwick replied stiffly.

"'You are not in the habit—'" Linnea stared at him, nonplussed. She felt for the armchair and sat down suddenly. She covered her face with her hands, and her shoulders started to shake.

"My dear Miss Ashley!" exclaimed Rothwick, and put his arm around her shoulders. "You have had some severe shocks, I know. But you must not cry. I know you are a woman of sense; your situation is salvageable, you know."

Linnea pulled away and to Rothwick's astonishment raised eyes full of tears of laughter, not of sorrow. "I think—I think," gasped Linnea, "I must be living in a farce. First you mistake me, a vicar's daughter, for a fallen woman; you then abduct me, and heap all sorts of abuse upon me; then, after you find out your mistake, your betrothed nearly calls me a doxy. And now you say you are not in the habit of conversing with courtesans—" She gasped again and went off into another wail of laughter. "All this because of one little 'habit.'"

Linnea put a hand to her mouth to suppress another hysterical giggle and finally managed to sober herself. "Oh, my, I never thought a virtuous habit could ever have such disastrous results, did you?"

She saw affront and then a reluctant grin on Rothwick's face. Linnea laid a hand on his sleeve. "You must not think, my lord, that I was laughing at you. I think—I think, if I didn't laugh at all this, I most surely would cry, and I couldn't do that, you see," she said simply.

Rothwick did see, and a spark of admiration for her flared in him. There were not many women who would have stood the rigors of what she had just gone through without succumbing to hysterics or the vapours, or at least casting a few sorrowful looks at him. But she was not one of those; indeed, he was not sure what sort of woman she really was. A superior sort, at least, perhaps.

"You are a most admirable lady, Miss Ashley," he said, raising her hand to his lips. The kiss was brief, but she blushed.

"Fustian, my lord!" she replied. "It is only that I have few sensibilities."

"Who told you that?"

"My cousin, Lady Boothe, for one. My father never

said it in so many words, but he often praised me for my practicality." She smiled wryly.

"A worthy virtue," said the earl.

"Mmm, yes, but hardly romantic," said Linnea, and waved a dismissing hand. "I am resigned to it. Certainly it is a more comfortable attribute than excessive sensibility."

"Most certainly!" Rothwick grinned. Then, sobering, he said: "I have talked with Miss Amberley's brother. We have agreed that his sister's and my betrothal should end."

"But, my lord, surely that is not necessary!"

"It is most necessary. I hope to brush through this thing with as little scandal as possible. He hopes to convince her to break off the betrothal because I am not worthy of her." He grimaced. That news should not be difficult to spread. It was already being bruited about by the servants, he was sure. It was awkward, damned awkward, and an annoyance. He had had his marriage and life with Miss Amberley fairly well planned out in his mind. Now it seemed he would have another bride. With any luck, his life would not change much. He continued. "If he is successful, I plan to retire to the country to, ah, nurse a broken heart and repent the consequences of my vices. Meanwhile, you will be staying with my sister, Lydia, where we ostensibly meet for the first time. After a suitable period, we will marry."

"And have I no say in what is to happen to me?" Linnea said quietly. Rothwick looked at her set face and felt perhaps she might have a point.

"I am sorry, but what else can we do? I have no doubt Sophia herself is thinking of the proper wording to end our formal betrothal even now." Or so I hope, thought the earl.

*   *   *

Indeed, Sophia was in a state of indecision: Should she make Rothwick come up to scratch after all? Or should she be the first to meet with her father and tell him what a horribly debauched man William was and that she wanted to break off their engagement? She knew Rothwick would only send a letter to her father requesting a meeting with him: her fiancé was enough of a gentleman to delay any explanations until her father arrived, at least. She ruminated on the vision of herself grandly rejecting an earl. How easy it would be to set it about that he had dealings in . . . Well, nothing of which a lady could speak.

Or perhaps she could make Rothwick drop that horrid woman and continue the betrothal. She paced her chamber in a tight line. How dare that hussy steal her prize from her! And yet what did she care? She knew she could have a duke if she wanted one. Indeed, she could have accepted the duke of Garston, except she had thought him a little overweight for her taste. Also, he was not as rich as Rothwick. She furrowed her brow in thought.

Richard. Sophia stopped her pacing and smiled. She always could decide what to do after talking with Richard.

Her brother did not take long to arrive at her door. Richard was used to her demands by now. Besides, there was always the faint possibility that Sophia might leave his jeweler's bill somewhere in sight. Very faint, but he still hoped.

"Oh, Richard!" cried Sophia, casting herself at his chest. Richard neatly sidestepped her embrace and helped her to a chair. His sister gave a brief moué of discontent but said: "Did you talk to that horrid man? What did he say?"

Richard paused. He had thought long and hard about what he would report to Sophia about his meeting with the earl. An innate sense of honesty warred with at least a decade-long need for revenge. He thought of the bill for the sapphire necklace. Revenge won.

"Sophia," he said solemnly, "I have never seen a man more heartless than the Earl of Rothwick."

Sophia's face brightened. "So, he is dropping that horrid woman after all!"

"No!" said Richard, flustered. "That is— What I mean to say is, he means to keep you both."

She laughed. "Silly boy, he cannot marry both of us!"

"That's not what I mean! He plans to marry you, and keep the other woman as his mistress!" He made his voice convincingly horror-stricken.

Sophia looked thoughtful. "I suppose that is tolerable. Just as long as he keeps her well hidden away."

Richard was aghast. This was not going the way he intended at all. He thought quickly. "Well, that's just it, Sophie. He is not going to keep her out of the way. He plans to leave you in the country and establish a house for her in London."

"What!" shrieked Sophia.

A little thrill of joy in Richard's heart threatened to make him smile, but he put it down manfully. "He specifically stated that you were to tend the estate at Staynes, and bear him strong sons to continue the line."

"No!" Sophia's face was set in clear disgust.

"But yes!" Richard shook his head. "You wouldn't know it to look at him, but I found him . . . well—"

"Vulgar," said Sophia.

"He said he preferred his light o' love in Town.

She's got the looks that are all the crack now." Richard had not laid eyes on the girl but knew Rothwick was always at the forefront of fashion. It did not matter what she looked like.

Sophia knew Rothwick was fashionable. She also knew Linnea had dark hair. The fashion for dark tresses had always been a matter of deep discontent with Sophia. It was unjust, something to which she had never been able to reconcile herself. And now she was to moulder in the country simply because her betrothed—former betrothed!—had the stupidity to prefer dark hair to her own wonderful blond. The vision of herself dramatically rejecting Rothwick rose again before her eyes.

"Richard, find me a pen, ink, and paper," Sophia said grimly. "I am writing to Papa."

Richard made a mental note to write a letter of his own. One could never be sure what Sophia would say.

Linnea looked out of the carriage window and gazed at the green hills of Wiltshire before her: a different prospect than she had known only a few days ago. She glanced at Rothwick, and he smiled at her.

"A penny for your thoughts," he said.

Linnea clasped her hands together nervously but said: "I have never seen such lovely country, my lord."

"Which is why you are tying your handkerchief into knots, I suppose."

Linnea looked down at her hands to discover she was indeed twisting her handkerchief all about. She smoothed it out upon her lap. "I shouldn't have agreed to this."

"Nonsense." Rothwick's smile turned from wry to

grim. "You have no other choice. My sister will welcome you with open arms, believe me."

Linnea looked at him. She was not certain of that at all. "You mean, do you not, that you will tell her to do so?"

Rothwick thought of the letter he had sent Lydia, requesting her at her country house near Bath. She would not like to do so as the Season was still in force in London, but he was sure he had been convincing enough.

"Not at all," replied Rothwick. "I have merely told her that I have some important information concerning Paul and Cassey Pickens."

Linnea eyed him with suspicion. "But I am not Cassey Pickens."

"I know."

"I think Miss Amberley is well out of the betrothal," said Linnea, irritated that he was not more forthcoming.

"I am sure she is," he said with a grimace.

He'd had a disagreeable meeting with Sophia the evening before, in which she had tearfully broken their engagement. She had not made much sense in her accusations—something about leaving her to moulder in the country—but he had let her speak and agreed that he was a veritable monster. He had been relieved to hear she had already written to her family, informing them she would never allow herself to be allied with one such as he. It needed only a letter from him confirming the end of their engagement.

"And I suppose you are not going to tell me what you wrote to my cousin?" Linnea said testily. "I would dearly love to know how you explained my abduction."

"I did not explain it at all, really," replied Rothwick. "Instead I wrote—in definitely shocked accents—that I found you strangely unaccompanied on Lady Boothe's errand. Doing the gentlemanly thing," he said, ignoring Linnea's gasp of outrage, "I took you to my sister's house, where she in turn invited you to stay with her in her country home."

"And of course my cousin will believe everything you have written." Her voice was sarcastic, her cheeks becomingly flushed in anger, and her dark eyes snapped.

"It does not matter what she believes," Rothwick said smoothly. "She will not want it bruited about that she forced a young relation of hers to be unaccompanied in the evening on a household errand. Furthermore, she would not want my sister, Lady Wrenton, to cut her, as she is already in jeopardy of it by being too encroaching at the last ball."

"You are a cynical man, Lord Rothwick." It was the only thing she could think of to say, for she could not deny the truth of his words.

"No, no, my dear, not cynical. I am merely a realist." He smiled at her, his eyes amused. "Now, then. I see you are feeling more the thing for a little sparring, as I thought you would. We shall soon be at my sister's house, and I think you will be better for some refreshment. Do you wish lemonade or ratafia?"

Linnea opened her mouth, then shut it. "Ohhh!" she cried in outrage. She recovered herself, however, and said with as much dignity as she could muster: "I shall require nothing but tea, thank you. Meanwhile, I shall sleep." She closed her eyes, determined that Rothwick should have no further communication from her. He had a most uncomfortable way of almost reading her thoughts.

"Come now, Miss Ashley. I saw you were anxious—I assume about meeting my sister. I knew any reassurances of mine would not help you recover your calm, or give me your confidence. I merely thought rousing your fighting spirit was far more becoming to you than pale nervousness. Your cheeks glow most charmingly, and your eyes become quite brilliant when you are angry, you know."

Linnea opened one eye. "You are a most provoking man, my lord." She opened the other and gazed at him sternly. "I think I must have been mad to agree to marry you."

"No, most sensible," said Rothwick. "Seriously, my dear, you know you have no other choice." He took her hand and patted it in a comforting manner.

But I do indeed, thought Linnea. A dismal one. She thought of going back to Lady Boothe's and the life she would lead there. She would be in disgrace, she knew, though none of it had been her fault. She thought of her cousin's weekly lectures to her household staff on the virtues of respectability—and yet she could not spare a maid to accompany Linnea on her various errands. Linnea had been lucky enough to escape being seriously accosted—until lately. She, too, was a realist. If she thought Rothwick's initial treatment of her shocking, it would have been nothing compared with another, less honorable man's treatment. She knew also her cousin would have been glad of any excuse to be rid of her.

She had been in a bad situation, her virtue compromised, and she knew she was incredibly fortunate to have Rothwick offer his hand, if not his heart. Yet a small, forlorn part of her wished it could have been his heart as well. Or any man's, for that matter, she told herself.

Linnea squared her shoulders. She was a realist.

Did not her father always say he should have named her Prudence? At the very least, she would do her duty as she saw it, now that she was promised to him.

"You are right, my lord," she said, looking at him straightly. "I will try to be a dutiful wife."

"I am sure you will be." Rothwick smiled.

He still held her hand. Slowly he took off her sensible York tan glove, sliding one finger off at a time. He raised her hand to his lips.

Linnea found her glove's removal strangely absorbing, and as he kissed her hand she discovered she was holding her breath. She blushed. She wished she had not let her maid (whom Rothwick had borrowed from the Lion's Stone) sit on top of the carriage with the coachman.

She had learned in the last two days of travel that Rothwick was an entertaining conversationalist. Away from the maid, they could indulge in talking of more than the commonplace, and this made their journey seem shorter. But this was the first time Linnea had felt the carriage's enclosure to be so intimate. Yet it was only a kiss on the hand.

She looked up at him again and saw he was smiling. There seemed almost a question in his eyes. He must be a practiced seducer, she thought, and removed her hand from his. And then she thought: I am to marry him.

She had to: she was sure the whole inn had known of the contretemps among Lord Rothwick, Miss Amberley, and herself by the time they had left. Her reputation was in shreds. If she wished to have any sort of decent life at all, she had to marry the earl. So when he had pressed her to do so one more time at the inn, she had agreed.

Rothwick still smiled, but the questioning air she

imagined was gone. "You might call me by my given name, you know," he said.

Linnea looked at him blankly, then recovered. "Oh, yes, well, I suppose since we are engaged . . ." Engaged. The word still seemed strange.

"William. Or you may call me Will."

"William, then." Linnea smiled. "You may call me Lin, if you would like. Mother used to call me Linnea, but Father called me Lin."

"A charming name," said Rothwick. "'Linnea,' then." He looked out the window. "Ah, yes, we are approaching the gate."

Linnea also looked and was favored with a quite spectacular view of Wrenton Park. It was—in comparison with most country houses—quite modest in size. To Linnea, used to the vicarage and Lady Boothe's town house in London, it was quite the largest house she had ever seen. The last generation of Wrentons had wisely restrained themselves during the rage for renovation. Instead of adding to the proportions of the house, they had chosen to preserve the exterior and enhance it with carefully landscaped lawns and shrubberies.

"It is beautiful," she breathed.

"Yes, quite," replied Rothwick. "But I hope you do not think me too partial when I say I believe you will like Staynes better."

Linnea was brought back to herself. She was to be mistress of a house as grand as Lady Wrenton's! She did not know if she liked this but reflected that it did not matter whether she liked it or not: Staynes was to be her home.

After ordering refreshment as soon as they entered the parlour, Rothwick inquired of the butler when Lady Wrenton was to arrive.

"Tomorrow, your lordship," replied the man, bowing. "Her ladyship did instruct that you were to arrive today. Your usual room is ready, my lord, and the blue room for the lady." The butler's gaze held just a hint of curiosity as he looked briefly at Linnea, but the rest of his countenance revealed nothing.

Linnea blushed, wondering what the servants must be thinking about her arrival. There will soon be much more to be talked of, I know, she thought.

A chambermaid led Linnea up to her room. Pink flowers dotted the wallpaper, and the window drapes and bed curtains were a lovely rose satin. The aspect from the large windows showed a large, palettelike green field with splashes of oak and ash throughout.

"I think I will like my stay here," Linnea said aloud. It gave her a bit of courage to say it. She washed her face, and the maid brushed the dust from her dress. She looked in the mirror. For all that she had gone through, she thought she looked remarkably well. At least, she thought, I no longer have those nasty dark shadows under my eyes. She then gazed at the worn fabric of her dress. For what that is worth, she thought, resigned. Linnea went down to the parlour again.

William Rothwick's temper—in expectation of his sister's arrival and admirably concealed from Linnea early the next day—was becoming more difficult to contain as the day wore on. It helped little that he brooded all the while upon the words he would have with Lydia when she arrived. As a result, when they heard coach wheels outside in the late afternoon, Linnea was surprised to see an almost savage smile upon his face. She could not think what would have caused it; they had been conversing most amiably for the last quarter hour.

"I think my sister is here," said Lord Rothwick.

It was a while before Lydia, Lady Wrenton, burst into the room. She had changed from her traveling dress to a charming round dress of pomona green.

"What is all this, William?" she said upon stepping into the room. "I meant to tell you at Lady Strahan's ball that Paul—" She stopped, looking at the expression on her brother's face.

"May I present to you, ma'am," he said, rising slowly to his feet, "Cassey Pickens." He bowed in ironic formality.

"But that is not—" said Lady Wrenton, confused.

"Exactly."

"What have you done, Will?" cried her ladyship.

"Absconded with Cassy Pickens, as you asked me to, of course," he said ruthlessly. "It seems Paul escorted this lady, who fit the description you gave me. I abducted her."

"Oh, but what a terrible mistake! And all for naught, Will! Why, I did not need to worry about Paul at all, I found. How silly I have been, to be sure!"

"What!" thundered Rothwick.

Her brother's state of mind finally dawned on Lady Wrenton. She took a step back from him.

"You see, Paul was not in love with Cassey Pickens after all. Well, he is, but only fashionably so—she's all the crack, although how such a low, vulgar creature can be in fash—"

"Why the *devil* didn't you tell me?" roared Rothwick.

"Really, Will, you needn't shout. And I was going to tell you at Lady Strahan's, but you never came! How can I be to blame for that?"

Linnea retreated unnoticed, sat on a chair well away from the battleground, and looked on in an interested manner.

"And I assume I am to blame for having the impression that Paul wanted to marry her?" Rothwick said through gritted teeth.

"Of course not, for it was what I had thought, too!"

"I will thank you, Lydia, if you would kindly keep your thoughts to yourself in the future. So far as I can see, they are clearly not based on anything comprehensible to rational humankind."

Silence reigned for a few moments while brother and sister glared at each other.

"Excuse me, but would either of you like some refreshment—some tea, perhaps?"

Two heads turned as one, and Lord Rothwick and his sister stared at Linnea as if they were only just aware that she existed. And that is not far from the truth, I am sure, thought Linnea, suppressing a giggle. She repeated her question.

A dull red flush crept into Lord Rothwick's cheeks, and he looked quickly away from her.

"You must excuse our ill manners, Miss Ashley," he said stiffly. "My temper was such that— But that is neither here nor there. You may be sure you will not witness any such again."

Lady Wrenton surveyed her brother's reddened cheeks with interest but turned to Linnea and said: "Please, do forgive us, my dear. How thoughtless of us! And we have not even been properly introduced!" Rothwick, belatedly, introduced them.

Linnea suppressed a smile, wondering if they made a habit of arguing before people to whom they *had* been properly introduced. She looked at Rothwick's stiff expression and decided not. "No doubt your travel here has discomposed you somewhat. I find that tea has a most settling effect on me," she said gently. "I do not want to presume, but perhaps you would like me to pour you a dish?"

Lydia, recalled to her sense of duty as hostess, declined Linnea's service and fluttered to the tea-tray. Linnea cast a look at Rothwick. His expression was neutral as he took and sipped his tea, but she could still sense a hint of anger in him. He put down his cup and turned to Lydia.

"You will be glad to know," he said sarcastically, "that my betrothal to Sophia Amberley is all but at an end."

"Oh, is it?" Lydia said brightly, then quickly changed her expression to one of deep regret when she caught Rothwick's fiery glance. "Oh, dear, I mean, how sad." She looked at him cautiously. "How—how did it come about?"

He told her. Linnea thought Lydia did not find it a bad thing at all that the betrothal was off, for her expression shifted from consternation to a barely suppressed joy. At the end of the earl's narrative, Lydia looked at Linnea with unconcealed approval.

"Well, there is nothing for it but that Will should marry you, Miss Ashley," said Lydia.

"But surely there is something else I may do," said Linnea. "Perhaps you know of a position available amongst your friends, one for a governess or a companion?"

Lydia looked at her regretfully and shook her head. "How would it be when your employer found out that you are related to Lady Boothe? They will surely ask questions, and then what will you do? No, no, the only thing you must do is to do as William says. Surely you can see it is your only solution."

"So Lord Rothwick has said," replied Linnea. "But I cannot see that it is right."

"No doubt Will has told you in a rag-mannered way," said Lydia, casting a scornful look at her brother. He opened his mouth to protest, then closed it, shrugging his shoulders. Apparently he understood Lydia was making amends by trying to persuade Linnea, and wisely he did not interfere.

"Come, my dear, we shall be private, so I may explain all to you. No doubt my brother can occupy himself in the library, perhaps." Lydia looked meaningfully at him.

Rothwick bowed. "Most certainly. But before I go, I must tell you that now you are here, I leave for London tomorrow."

A sinking feeling caught Linnea unawares. She looked at him questioningly, wondering when he would be back.

"Oh, Will, how could you!" cried Lydia.

"Very easily. I have business I must attend to if the formal ending of my betrothal to Miss Amberley is to go as smoothly as it should. And then, of course, I shall need to procure a special license. I shall not be gone much longer than a sennight, I believe."

"Oh, very well! But how intolerably dull of you." Lydia looked at Linnea speculatively. "I am sure we shall deal very well on our own."

Linnea swallowed the lump that had grown in her throat when the earl had mentioned the special license. She made herself smile, however, and held out her hand to him. "I have enjoyed our conversations, my lord," she said formally. "I am looking forward to continuing them."

Rothwick took her hand and kissed it slowly. She

wondered how he could make such an action so absorbing. He lifted his head at her and smiled. "I, too," he replied.

She blushed, looked away, and caught Lydia's interested eye. "Yes, of course," she said, flustered.

Rothwick bowed and left.

As soon as the door closed behind him, Lydia jumped up and crossed to Linnea, seizing her hands.

"Thank goodness he abducted you!" she cried.

Linnea looked at her, astonished.

"You cannot imagine how I have dreaded his marriage with Sophia Amberley. A more self-centered, selfish creature I have never seen in my life! When I heard that she was Will's choice, I think I must have cried every night for a sennight!"

"But, but, she is very beautiful, and—"

"Oh, I know *that* was a consideration for Will! It would be for any man—for what it is worth! Not that I think she is as beautiful as she or anyone else makes her out to be. Her nose, for example— But that is neither here nor there! I must tell you, she delights in mischief! She would have made Will miserable within a fortnight. No, no, anyone would be better for him than Sophia!"

"Thank you—I think," Linnea said dryly.

Lydia looked flustered. "Oh, my dear, I am sure you are not just anyone! Well, I have just met you, but I am sure you are entirely respectable, especially if you are to marry Will. Besides, I can see he likes you already."

"Oh, no!" It was Linnea's turn to be flustered. "He offered for me to save my reputation. I cannot think that he already—"

"If he does not, he should!" replied Lydia. "I think you will do very well for William." She gave Linnea an assessing look. "You must know your coloring is in fashion now. Do let me dress you! Oh, my, yes. You will be stunning."

"I?" said Linnea, taken aback. "I think I can say my looks are passable, but I do not know if I should be at all comfortable if I am to appear stunning. And I don't think it would be proper for me to accept clothes from you or Lord Rothwick."

"Nonsense! Of course it is proper. Am I not to be your sister-in-law? You will become used to it, I assure you! Now, there is a good seamstress nearby in the village. She will do for now, but later—it must be Madame Cerise in London. . . ."

Linnea let Lady Wrenton talk on, listening with half an ear. She rubbed the fabric of her worn dress between her fingers. Oh, it would be wonderful to have new clothes! She'd let herself be persuaded to this—frankly—rash betrothal; surely it would do no harm to accept a few dresses. She smiled wryly and sighed. In for a penny, in for a pound.

6

Sophia pulled at the sash around her bodice pettishly. Her rejection of Lord Rothwick had been as grand as she had envisioned it. She'd broken their engagement in fine form and had done it very prettily, she thought. Her dress of pale lavender had been just the right complement to her sorrowful demeanor, and she had made her hand tremble when he bowed over it in farewell. Her father and mother had commiserated with her and had told her she was well out of such a bad bargain.

Yet she could not help feeling she was not quite the victor in the encounter. That nasty Mary Frome had smiled at her at last night's ball, and it almost seemed her smile had been malicious. Sophia suddenly remembered then that she may have hinted to a few people of her impending betrothal to Rothwick. She bit her lip in frustration. No doubt Mary Frome had heard something of it. Sophia had comforted herself before retiring for the night, thinking of the stories she knew of Mary and what she would, justifiably, tell her beaux about her.

It was not so easy to deal with Rothwick, she found. It seemed society forgave a man for his indiscretions, the way it never would for a woman. He still appeared—properly humble, to be sure—at Almack's and at Lady Hassletine's, and it seemed no one snubbed him at all! Sophia gnawed her lower lip in vexation at the memory. Surely there was some way she could let people know—discreetly, of course—how seriously he'd insulted her. Or better yet, show Rothwick that he had erred, and erred badly.

She would think on it. Right now she needed to have her maid retie her sash and make the best possible entrance at Mrs. Rockwell-Jones's musicale. Sophia was sure to pick up a little information here and there. She would be going to the musicale with Alice Sharp and her mother, both of whom filled her with ennui, but it was better than being under her own mother's anxious eye. Mrs. Sharp had more interest in the card games in the provided card-room than in music, and Sophia could easily shake off Alice. She would be left to do precisely as she pleased. Sophia smiled at the thought.

Upon their arrival at Mrs. Rockwell-Jones's, Sophia noted the number of men in the room and felt the need to rid herself of her companions as soon as she could. Mrs. Sharp was already going in the direction of the card-room. Quickly Sophia introduced Alice—a shy child with mouse-colored hair—to a handsome Hussar and was rewarded with a grateful smile from the girl.

At least half of the gentlemen made their way

toward Sophia at her arrival. It was gratifying until she
noticed a gentleman she had never seen before. He
glanced at her and then did not bother to look her way
again. Yes, that was what was so annoying. He did not
bother, of all things!

Sophia smiled at one callow youth at her side, causing him to blush and stammer something unimportant.
She glanced at the man at the other side of the room. He
was not at all handsome—too much of a long-shanks for
that—and his skin was quite brown, contrasting oddly
with his sun-streaked hair. She chattered and laughed
at another unimportant tidbit that fell from the callow
whatever-his-name's lips. But there was something in
the way that man lounged against a pillar, the negligent
air with which he wore his finely tailored evening wear,
that claimed him for a man of fashion and taste. Yet if
he was a man of fashion, surely he knew it was required
that he pay attention to her?

The man looked up then and caught her eye. For
the first time in her life, Sophia blushed involuntarily
and looked away. Annoyed, she made herself look at
him again, but his gaze was on the musicians. She
allowed a small frown to cross her lips in frustration.

"Have I said something wrong, M-Miss Amberley?"
stuttered the youth at her side.

Sophia focused on him. Oh, yes. Jack Gordon. A second son of a viscount, with good connections and ten
thousand pounds a year. However, he adored her. She
gave him her second-best smile. "Oh, no, no! It is just
that—that gentleman over there gave me such a pecu-
liar look. I did not know what to think!"

Jack glanced in the direction her fan had waved.
"Oh, him!" he said. His voice was scornful, but Sophia
noted it was not without a touch of envy. "Pay no

attention to him or his glances. That is Sir James Marlowe. He may be a seasoned traveler, and it's said that he's as rich as Croesus, but he is known for a . . . well, I suppose I should not say. He is a mischief-maker at the very least. I am surprised Mrs. Rockwell-Jones invited him."

There was a general murmur of assent among the young gentlemen around Sophia, and a discussion of Sir James's supposed adventures—with respect for Sophia's shell-like ears, of course—ensued.

"Jealous, Mr. Gordon?" said a deep and musical voice. Sophia turned to find that Sir James had joined their circle.

Jack's ears turned an unfortunate red. He opened his mouth to retort angrily but was stopped by the look in Sir James's eyes. Sophia could not help but admire him then. The older man's expression was devoid of anger or challenge: instead a look of amused anticipation—as if Sir James were waiting for the denouement of a joke—slowly filled his large and sleepy-looking eyes.

Jack's cheeks matched the fiery color of his ears, but he straightened himself, saying with dignity: "Not at all, Sir James. We were merely relating some stories we had heard about your travels."

Sir James smiled genially. "My travels. How flattering." Sophia did not know how he did it, for his tone of voice was nothing but benevolent, but somehow the man managed to convey the impression that the young men had committed a social solecism.

He turned his gaze on Sophia. "And this is . . . ?"

Another young man, strangely impelled by the mild friendliness in Sir James's voice, made a hasty introduction.

"Most charming." He bowed over her hand, smiling.

Sophia felt piqued, for his voice seemed to imply that he had seen others more charming than she. It occurred to her suddenly that he had also been quite presumptuous in prompting an introduction to her instead of waiting for one.

He glanced across the room at the musicians, who were lifting their instruments in readiness. "Ah. They are about to begin. I believe the selection is to be a particularly intricate piece by Haydn. I have always thought it better appreciated at an appropriate distance." His gaze passed innocuously over Sophia's admirers.

Sophia did not know how it came to be, but she found her hand on Sir James's sleeve and was led to a chair closer to the musicians. She glanced back at her beaux and had to keep herself from laughing at their hangdog looks. She transferred her gaze to Sir James. How had he done it?

"Practice, my dear, practice," said Sir James. He looked down at her, an amused expression in his eyes.

Sophia stared at him—how did he know what she had been thinking? Surely her own expression did not reveal— She recovered quickly and said: "Yes, the music is very fine, is it not?"

Sir James gave her an appreciative look and agreed. The music washed over them for a few minutes while Sophia alternated her glances between her escort and the crowd. Her eyes lighted on a richly dressed woman in a round gown of puce, lavishly trimmed with point lace.

"Ah. Lady Ackleby—an interesting lady," said Sir James.

Sophia looked at him and saw that he had followed

her gaze. She raised her brows haughtily to depress his presumption.

A faint smile crossed his lips. "You are curious, of course," he said, deliberately misinterpreting her expression, she was sure. "However, I do not think a young lady such as yourself should hear . . ." Sir James paused.

Sophia bit her lower lip thoughtfully. She felt irritated that he assumed she was curious about Lady Ackleby—which was true, but he should not have assumed it. On the other hand, she *was* very curious about Lady Ackleby. She had heard only snippets regarding this lady's reputation, but no real details.

She laughed lightly, and her glance was amused. "Really, Sir James, you must know this is not my first Season! I have been about a little, you know."

"You amaze me! I would have thought you just out of the schoolroom." Sir James's smile was bland.

Sophia unfurled her fan just in time to cover her gasp of indignation. How dare he! She was well known for her fine sense of address, and here she felt he implied she was as gauche as a schoolgirl.

"You look so very fresh and . . . innocent, you see," Sir James explained.

She looked up at him. How was she to take that? If she took the compliment, would he tell her about Lady Ackleby? And that little pause before the word *innocent.* Was he implying that perhaps she was not? Perhaps she could turn back the conversation. She looked about her and noticed the music had stopped and the guests were going into supper. Sir James rose and held out his hand.

"And very lovely," he continued.

Sophia's fan fluttered and dropped enough to

reveal an innocent smile. "I am sure you exaggerate, Sir James," she said demurely. She laid her hand in his, and he placed it on his arm.

"Not at all. Surely you know you are the most beautiful woman in this room." He led her to a table at the far corner of the room. It was partially obscured by some ferns, Sophia noticed, but she said nothing about their destination.

"Oh, no. Not as attractive as, say, Lady Ackleby?"

Sir James paused, and an admiring glint appeared in his eye. "Many men have found her so—or so I would suppose, of course. Then again, it is said she is not a clever women. Some men find that attractive as well. Sir Daniel Scott, for example, or Lord Weatherby."

So, thought Sophia, delighted at this information. Sir Daniel and Lord Weatherby have been "involved" with the woman. She gave Sir James her most brilliant smile. "And you, Sir James, do you find clever women . . . attractive?"

"Mmmm, I find I do not grow bored with them as I do with women less clever. Beauty always adds to the attraction, of course." Sir James's eyes met hers, and he smiled.

He had a beautiful smile. Sophia felt a little breathless. How lovely it is to flirt with this man, she thought. So different from the much younger men who usually surrounded her. They were clumsy compared with Sir James.

"Although I understand the combination is not always appreciated by certain men," continued Sir James.

A little shiver passed over Sophia, and she pulled her shawl over her shoulders. He has heard of my broken betrothal, I am sure of it, she thought. I must make

sure he knows that it was I who broke it off because of
Rothwick's betrayal.

"Alas, it is true," she said sadly. "Who knows what
cruelty exists in a man's heart? It is better that a lady
break the connection when she learns of his perfidy
than to live with certain betrayal of the marriage
vows." Sophia had the talent to make her eyes fill with
tears without letting them fall, and she used it now.

It seemed almost as if Sir James's eyes took on a
look of amusement, but he said: "He must have been
mad."

Instead of being affronted by his directness, Sophia
found herself looking up at him. His gaze was intent . . .
compelling . . . and she found her heart beating a little
faster. "I do not know. Perhaps I am not as beautiful as
I have been told," she blurted.

She shocked herself. She had not meant to say that,
and what shocked her the most (though she could
scarce admit it to herself) was that it was the first
spontaneous remark she had made in many a year.

"No one lied when they said you were beautiful,"
replied Sir James.

Sophia looked at him, and his eyes were not mocking, but admiring. She felt much better, for his remark
restored her equilibrium.

"Some men merely lack . . . intelligence," continued
Sir James. "So easily . . . trapped." He smiled at her.

She sat up straight. She hadn't thought of that! That
woman had trapped Rothwick. Of course! And he was
known to be an honorable man. He would have no
choice but to marry the harlot, in spite of her own,
Sophia's, beauty!

Sophia turned melting eyes to Sir James. "How terribly sad that it should be so!" she said softly, a hint of

sorrow in her voice. "How horrid such scheming cannot be shown for what it is! One would think that right-minded people should work to show how badly people can be hurt by such duplicity."

Sir James's smile grew wider. "Most definitely, dear lady! I, certainly, would try." He raised her hand to his lips.

Sophia shivered with a certain joy. She smiled back at him. "I thought you might," she murmured.

Linnea smoothed her skirt, reveling in the muslin's newness. The dress was a deep royal blue, giving a pearly sheen to her skin, and the design was one that she had not seen before in a morning dress: it wrapped across her bosom, and a gold clasp fastened the bodice to the side of and just under her left breast. Bows of a clear white (matching the fichu at her throat) tied the dress firmly together. She had thought it a more modest dress than the others Lydia had ordered for her, for it was at least high at the nape, so she had readily assented to its purchase. But now that she had it on, she was not so sure. When she saw how low the wrap came in the front, she had felt it necessary to put on the fichu underneath. The wrapping effect at its high waist had none of the gathers she was used to, and the bodice hugged her bosom and waist with revealing accuracy. After all of Linnea's protests that had gone on before, Lydia had smiled mischievously when Linnea quickly agreed to buy it. Now she knew why.

The parlour door opened behind her and Linnea turned to see Lady Wrenton walk in.

"You knew!" accused Linnea, waving at the dress she wore.

"Knew what, my dear?" said Lydia, her eyes innocently wide. She reached up and pulled the bell to summon a servant for some refreshment.

"This dress! Why, it is almost as revealing as the others you insisted on!"

"Nonsense!" Lydia replied tartly. "I cannot see how you can say that. You can see yourself how it covers you from neck to heel—especially with that ridiculous fichu."

"Yes, but only look at it! It's so *close!*" cried Linnea.

Lydia surveyed her protégée from head to foot. "And a very nice figure you have, too, my dear," she said, nodding her head approvingly. Linnea blushed.

Lady Wrenton sat next to her and patted her hand. "I see nothing in your appearance at which to blush. You are well proportioned; it sets you off to advantage. How else will you catch my brother's interest?"

Linnea looked down and smoothed the dress again. "Is that necessary?"

Lydia was silent for a moment. "Yes . . . yes, I think so. I want him to be happy. He is wary of women, for all his popularity with them. You may imagine my dismay when he became betrothed to Sophia Amberley! A more insinuating little . . . Well, I shall not say more on *that* head! I wondered at him, indeed I did! How could he not see she was such a one? He is supposed to be a man of the Town, yet he could not even see—"

She sighed. "Well, I am happy that the betrothal

was broken, and I am glad Will did not seem to mind—"
She caught Linnea's raised-brow gaze and amended,
"That is to say, he did not mind as much as I thought
he might. He was not in *love* with her, you see."

Linnea did *not* see. She had seen Sophia's beauty,
and because it seemed Lord Rothwick could not see
past it to Sophia's nature made it clear to Linnea that he
was more affected by the break than his sister thought.

She looked up at Lydia, saying gently: "That is all very
well, ma'am, but even so, I am not in love with him."

Lydia smiled a little. "We shall see," she replied.
"Besides, I am sure you want to make the best of this
situation that you can—at the very least, I am sure you
can go along in this marriage in a friendly fashion."

"To be sure, I do!" returned Linnea. "But—"

"Well, then! It cannot hurt to look attractive, or
make yourself look pleasant, can it?"

Linnea bit her lip for a second in thought. "No, of
course not. But to take all these clothes—I cannot
wish to be beholden to either you or Lord Rothwick!"

Lydia shook her head. "No, no, of course you do not
wish to be beholden! And you will not. Listen to me: How
can you do your duty as a countess, and entertain my
brother's guests, if you do not dress the part? To dress
dowdily will not add to your credit, nor to my brother's."

The noise of coach wheels and horses stopped any
further protests from Linnea. She sat calmly on her
chair, but Lydia saw Linnea's eyes rise swiftly to the
window and her hand nervously smooth a stray curl.
Lydia smiled to herself and said: "That must be Will.
After all that traveling, he shall want some refreshment, I am sure." She pulled the bell-rope again and
requested the chambermaid bring additional pastries
and tea.

They could hear footsteps coming up the hallway outside the parlor. A mischievous look crossed Lydia's face.

"Oh, Linnea, my dear, do be still! There is an odd crease on the back collar of your dress. Let me flatten it—"

With a quick jerk Lydia pulled off the fichu from around Linnea's neck. Linnea gasped, the door opened, and Rothwick walked in.

There was no time for Linnea to do much but compose herself as best she could. Lydia noted with satisfaction that Linnea's cheeks wore a becoming blush and that Rothwick's first glance at his betrothed lingered.

He walked up and kissed Linnea's hand. "You look . . . well. And you, Lydia," he said, turning to his sister briefly. He gazed down at Linnea again.

He was surprised. He had almost not recognized her when he'd first looked at her, for the shadows were gone from beneath her eyes and her clothes fit better than they had before—much better. Her face glowed pink and white instead of the dull paleness she'd had before he left.

"For shame!" cried Lydia. "After all this effort we put in getting Linnea up to the mode, all you can say is that she looks well!" But Lydia was quite satisfied. Most certainly her brother noticed the change, for he still had hold of Linnea's hand and was apparently not aware of it.

"Ravishing, then," Rothwick said, and smiled at Linnea.

Linnea felt her face flame even warmer, and she pulled her hand from his grasp. She was not used to the polite but admiring regard of men, and it unnerved her. At best she had been ignored at her cousin Boothe's house, at worst leered at. And it had been a long time since she had been given the respect due her as a vicar's daughter. "I—I am pleased to see you again, my lord." She looked away and saw with relief that the chambermaid had brought in some more pastries and tea. "Some refreshment, my lord?" She glanced at him and saw his raised brows. "William, I mean."

"Yes, only a cup of tea, as I shall have to change out of my travel dirt soon." He smiled at her.

Lydia apparently saw she was not needed, for she moved quickly toward the door. "Oh, dear, you must excuse me! I have just remembered that Cook wanted me to approve this week's menus. I simply must go—"

Linnea rose, as did Rothwick. "But, Lydia—" began Linnea, but Lady Wrenton cut her off.

"Oh, I am sure you can stand hostess to my brother just as well as I," she said, and shut the door firmly behind her.

Lord Rothwick's brows lifted at his sister's departure, then he looked at Linnea. "You must excuse my sister; she is determined to throw us together."

She sat on the sofa and indicated that Rothwick do so as well. "She needs little excuse; she has been so very kind to me," replied Linnea. She shifted on her seat uncomfortably, for she saw him looking at her dress again. "You must be wondering at this dress. Your sister insisted on buying me a wardrobe of clothes, though I protested—at first. She said you would not mind. . . ." She looked up to discover that Rothwick had moved his gaze to her lips.

"You look charming," he said.

Linnea blushed and looked down at her hands in her lap, for she was not looking for compliments. "No, I, I, it is just that I do not want to be beholden to you in this way—"

"Beholden!"

Linnea looked up again and saw that his face was as astonished as his voice sounded. He took her hand and pressed it gently.

"I do not know what you are talking about. I abduct you, I treat you poorly, I ruin your reputation, and now you say you are beholden to me because my sister insists I supply you with some frippery dresses. It is the least I can do for you."

Linnea sighed, and her shoulders lost their tenseness, but she said: "Yes, but you are marrying me. It does not seem fit that I take clothes from you before I am married to you."

William raised his brows haughtily. "Nonsense. I will not have you wed to me in rags. It will not do for—"

"Your consequence?" she interjected.

"Exactly," he replied, and they both laughed.

Linnea's smile faded as she looked at Rothwick and saw he was gazing intently at her again, his look moving from her eyes to her lips.

"I have brought a special license," he said. "I procured it four days ago. We may be married as soon as you are ready."

"Oh," was all Linnea could say, and looked down at her lap again. She had thought she was resigned to being married to him, but a surge of uncertainty clenched her stomach. She felt a finger under her chin and looked up into Rothwick's eyes.

"Are you still not sure?" he asked. He moved closer, and she sat very still. "I promise I shall be a good husband. . . ." He leaned forward, and his lips moved across hers.

They were soft and gentle, and she relaxed after an initial stiffness. His hand at her waist pulled her closer, and she moved her own hand and grasped the lapel of his coat.

A sudden noise at the window made them part, startled, and she saw a bird looking quizzically into the parlour at them from the window ledge. The sun abruptly chose to shine through the clouds into the room, brightening the patterns on the carpet and casting a golden glow over the furniture.

"I think he is inviting us out," said Rothwick. The bird chirped as if in agreement. He turned to Linnea. "Have you been about the gardens much?"

"Only the ones closest to the house," she replied, glad of the interruption and grateful that Rothwick had changed the subject. Her experience in kissing was small, limited to her father's salutes on her forehead, her brother's affectionate smacks on her cheek, and the abortive assaults from the men who accosted her on her unfortunate errands. She tried hard not to flinch at Rothwick's touch—and succeeded far better than she thought she would. Her reaction bewildered her, and she almost despaired she'd ever understand this man or herself. She was not used to this. For all her straitened circumstances, she had always had a certain measure of control, at least over herself. Now she was not sure of herself at all.

"You are missing a great deal. My sister is a mistress of gardening, and designed the larger part of the outlay at this estate." Rothwick glanced at the ormolu clock on the mantelpiece. "It wants three hours until dinner. Perhaps I can show you the gardens in an hour and a half?" He waved a hand at his still dusty boots and grimaced. "I still must change from these clothes."

Linnea smiled. "Certainly, my lord. I would enjoy a walk, for I have been much too idle lately."

*   *   *

Lord Rothwick was surprised and pleased to see Linnea waiting for him upon his descent from his rooms. His experience of women—mostly his sisters—was that a man must wait at least half an hour past the appointed time.

In all, he was very pleased with her. She was certainly brave, practical, and more lovely than he had thought when he first saw her. She was wearing a deep cherry-colored walking dress that threw pink highlights into her cheeks. Very lovely indeed.

She had flinched when he kissed her, however, and he sighed mentally. He thought he repulsed her a little, and he wished he had not treated her with so much harshness when they had first met and when he had abducted her. He did not want an unwilling wife; he well knew he had made a mess of things, and that it was his fault.

But how else to remedy the situation? In London he had hit upon the idea of establishing her comfortably in the Americas, then rejected it as cowardly. Now that he saw her again, he was glad he had.

As they walked along the paths of Lady Wrenton's garden, he looked at her assessingly. Linnea seemed, despite her misfortunes, a very self-possessed woman. She had an air of reserve that broke only when she talked on a subject that interested her or when she responded to his funning. Then she sparkled, for her eyes lit up from whatever emotion she was feeling. But the rest of the time she seemed almost watchful, as if to see what his response would be before she committed herself to any communication.

It was his fault, he was sure. His mistreatment of her still must lie heavy in her mind; she no doubt wondered when he would commit another unpredictable act. He gazed at her as she smiled at a small joke he made and resolved at that moment that she would come to trust him. He would make sure of it.

They waited less than two weeks after the end of Rothwick's betrothal to Sophia and then married by special license. It was a quiet affair, for which Linnea was thankful. She would not have known what to do if Rothwick had invited all his friends and acquaintances. As it was, she found it difficult to face the curious looks from some of the few wedding guests. At least Rothwick's family seemed accepting of his marriage to her. For that, she was sure, she had Lydia to thank.

Lydia had spirited Linnea to one shop after another, choosing bride clothes and other, very fashionable dresses. She had also arranged the guest list as well as the wedding feast. By the wedding day Linnea was sure she would never wear all the clothes in the trunks she saw piled on top of the coach in preparation for their journey afterward.

When she finally put on the wedding dress, she looked in the mirror and scarcely recognized herself. She had chosen white satin silk for the bodice and skirt of the dress, having seen such a dress in a wedding her father had conducted when she was a girl. Tugging at the low décolletage, Linnea remembered Lydia's dictum that the low cut of her dress was in the height of fashion. Linnea did not feel quite comfortable with the bodice, which seemed to display more flesh than she was used to. And that was another thing. She was no longer so painfully thin, for the lack of daily errand running and tasks and the availability of food had added a new sleekness to her figure that she was also not used to. New clothes, new figure—and, soon to be, new station in life—she did not feel as if she were quite herself anymore.

Sooner than she thought, she was summoned to the church. She smiled at her escort, Sir John Grey, as he helped her into the coach next to Lydia's excited maid. He was one of Lord Rothwick's friends: a tall, blond, and somewhat rumpled-looking man. He was to give her away, as she had no real near male relative to do so. Her cousin by marriage, Lord Boothe, had not offered his services, and she was relieved he had not. She could scarcely bear Lady Boothe's sudden fawning change of behavior toward her, and she would rather not have to face Lord Boothe, either.

"You are in great good looks, if I may say so, Miss Ashley," Sir John said, smiling at her warmly. "If Will were not my good friend, I would be sorely tempted to run off with you."

Linnea laughed. "Then I am thankful you are his friend, for I have had more than enough of sudden—suddenness lately." She bit her lip and felt a blush rising in her cheeks. Good heavens, she had almost blurted out that she had been abducted! She wondered how much Rothwick's friends and relatives—aside from Lydia—knew of the circumstances of her marriage.

But Sir John only laughed. "Swept you off your feet, did he? That is Will all over. He was ever impetuous when we were at Oxford, and certainly never neglected the ladies—" He stopped abruptly, and it was his turn to blush. "That is to say, he was always a gentleman, of course—"

"Oh, you need not feel so conscious!" Linnea laughed lightly, though a forlorn feeling seeped into her chest at his words. "My own brother was always ripe for mischief before he went in the army."

Sir John's ears seem to perk up. "Oh, is he in the army? I am on furlough for the next few days, but would much rather be back on the continent. In what regiment is your brother?"

"He was in the Sixteenth Light Dragoons. He died at Ciudad Rodrigo."

"I am sorry." Sir John patted her hand comfortingly. "He must have been very brave. We lost many good men there, I know."

Linnea smiled at him. She felt her heart lighten at being able to confide a little about her brother to one who understood what the war was like. "You are very kind. I am sure he was not the only courageous one. He always commented about the bravery of his comrades in his letters, and his descriptions of their living conditions made me think he must have gone through just as much hardship."

Sir John nodded and went on to relate his own experiences in the Peninsular campaign. They conversed amiably in this way, and Linnea could almost put from her mind the reason she was in this coach. But then it halted suddenly, and she felt her heart rise to her throat. They were at the church.

Linnea drew the veil over her face and stepped out of the coach. Taking a deep breath, she went up the shallow steps of the church and entered, clutching Sir John's arm in her nervousness.

Looking neither to the right nor to the left, she walked slowly up the aisle. She could see Lord Rothwick at the altar, handsome in his black coat and pale fawn pantaloons and looking toward her expectantly. Her heart hammered and her knees felt weak. She had never fainted, but now she was sure she could manage it quite easily and was glad of Sir John's support at her side. She cast a look to either side of her, trying involuntarily to find a route of escape, then castigated herself for the thought. She was committed, and certainly she had nowhere else to go.

Her veil was a mist that made everything outside of it seem unreal. She hardly attended to the vicar's words; she had heard the service many times before in her father's church. Her responses came automatically to the rhythmic rise and fall of the words in the marriage vow; Linnea had said those words to herself many times when she was a girl, dreaming of a husband who would someday love her. She glanced at Rothwick's handsome face and wondered how he could look so calm. She knew, for herself, this wedding was far from the dreams she had had so long ago.

"You are now man and wife," the vicar said, and his words rang in her ears, startling Linnea from her cloud of thoughts. She felt her veil rise and looked up at Rothwick, his face suddenly in clear focus. He smiled at her and drew her toward him for a gentle kiss.

The kiss was not as long as Rothwick would have liked it to be, but he thought it best to restrain himself. It was not easy, however. Though her face had been concealed, Linnea's dress emphasized her form in the way the silk clung to and fell away from her limbs. And then when he lifted her veil at the end of the vicar's words, she had looked up at him with her large, lost, frightened eyes. He had smiled at her to give her some comfort, but when he bent to kiss her, he was startled by a surge of fierce possessiveness. It made him want to press her close to him and explore her soft pink lips tenderly, wildly, and far more intimately. He caught his breath and paused, then kissed her lightly. Later, he thought to himself. There would be plenty of time later.

Going down the aisle with Linnea on his arm, Rothwick smiled and nodded to the wedding guests to either side of them. He did it easily and automatically; as he walked he occupied his mind with the sudden impulse he'd felt at the altar. His smile turned a little rueful, for he was sure he knew what it was: Linnea had looked so lost and forlorn that his natural instincts had taken over. Since a child, he had always brought home this or that hurt or abandoned animal and taken care of it until it was well again. Linnea's anxious eyes had pulled this protectiveness of his to the fore. Indeed, it was the same impulse that had moved him to rescue her from those drunken louts in London, despite what he'd thought she was then. Rothwick sighed as he helped Linnea into the waiting coach. He should be more careful and not give in to his impulses. Look where it had put him, after all!

William. Linnea looked at her husband relaxing against the coach squabs and wondered if she would get used to saying his Christian name. Surely she'd had time enough to become used to it, but it still moved oddly on her tongue. She smiled at her thoughts. How very strange and unlike herself she felt. Where was Linnea Ashley, vicar's daughter, potential governess, and cousin Boothe's unpaid servant? Those things she was used to, could understand, and manage—with difficulty sometimes, to be sure, but she was used to them. There was something comforting in routine, even with the harsh treatment her cousin had given her, for it was a known thing, and she knew what her strengths and weaknesses were when she had to deal with them.

But now she had a husband, and she was a countess. She smiled wryly, thinking: What did the Beggar Maid do when she suddenly became Queen? Did she pine for the floors she once washed? Did she scatter ashes around her silken bed, so as to feel more at home? Linnea chuckled at the image. She glanced up to see William look at her inquiringly.

"Oh, it is nothing, really. I was wondering how King Cophetua's Beggar Maid felt when she went to live in the palace. If she was frightened, or knew instinctively—from her noble character, of course—what to do."

William smiled. "The latter, of course. That is how all fairy tales are, you know." He gazed at her intently, then said: "You will go on quite well, I am sure."

"Will I?"

"Of course. Lydia will see to that."

Lydia? And where would *he* be, pray? thought Linnea. She frowned.

"And how do you know I will do all that she says?"

His eyebrows rose. "Of course you will. You are my wife."

Of course again. Linnea pressed her lips together firmly. "And all wives do as their husbands and their families say, of course," she said, looking at him straightly.

"Of cour—" He caught her look. "Ladies of character, I should say." A small smile touched his lips.

Linnea laughed. "Piqued, repiqued, and capotted! And how am I to answer that? If I were to be contrary, I would not be a lady of character. Yet were I to meekly repeat every aye and nay that dropped from your lips, I think I would be as characterless as an empty stage in a play."

Rothwick smiled a devilish smile. "Of course."

A giggle bubbled behind her lips. She said severely, "Impertinence! Did not your governess teach you never to vex a lady?" She felt more at ease now—her brother Jack had often teased her thus, so long ago.

He opened his eyes wide. "What, are you vexed? I thought you were merely being contrary."

"Ohhh!" exclaimed Linnea, and furiously cast about in her mind for a stinging reply.

"I am afraid there is no ruler to rap across my knuckles here, and I am sure your reticule is empty of rocks," said William. "Ooof! Stop, you vixen!"

She smiled sweetly as she pulled back her arm for another blow with the small pillow she had found beside her. "But I have always been resourceful, sir."

Linnea found her arm grasped, and she was pulled suddenly into his lap.

"So have I," Will replied, and his mouth came down on hers.

This time it was different. Perhaps it was that he had taken her by surprise, perhaps it was that their mock fight had banished her nervousness. But this time she moved into the kiss, and her hand crept up to his cheek and opened to touch him, just as she felt she was opening herself to this new and sudden sensation of closeness and warmth and sweetness. A small voice, her own long-ago vicar's-daughter-cousin's-servant's voice cried out that this was not seemly; but the touch of his lips upon her mouth, her cheek, her throat, drowned it, and all she could do was gasp in reply. The touch of his fingers upon her skin was alternately soothing and exciting: first feather soft, then vibrant like a strong spring wind.

"I think . . . I think we should stop," murmured

Rothwick as his lips traced a fiery trail down the fine chain of her necklace.

Necklace. Oh, good Lord. Her pelisse was undone! Linnea straightened quickly, pulled her coat together, and scrambled back to the seat opposite the earl. She put up her hands to press down the heat in her face. What had come over her? She had never responded this way to the kisses pressed upon her in the past. She glanced up at his face.

His expression was cool, but the warmth she had felt from him was clearly reflected in his eyes. She looked away, confused. Was he, as Lydia had said, not really in love with Miss Amberley, then? Or were all men like this, easily amorous with whatever female was near?

"We are almost at Staynes, after all," Rothwick continued smoothly.

Linnea looked up at him again, and he smiled at her—a cat-in-the-cream smile. Her face flamed again, and this time it was not from embarrassment. "Do you always use such, such stratagems to gain your ends, sir?" she said, teeth clenched.

"Oh, no," said Rothwick. "The gentlemen of my acquaintance would not take to it at all."

"Well, let me inform you, sir, that they will not work with me!" She sat back on the squabs of the carriage, her spine straight.

"No?" he replied genially. She ground her teeth. "I hear that grinding your teeth like that is not good for them. You should be careful." He gazed out the coach window. "Ah, here we are. Staynes." In spite of herself, Linnea turned quickly to look.

If Lady Wrenton's house was beautiful, Staynes was magnificent. The grounds were lush with smooth-shaven grass and rose to a hill upon which the mansion sat. Rothwick's ancestors had not spared any expense to build upon the original, central part of the building, and their additions merged form and design to a seamless whole. On one side of the building was a copse of birch, beyond which Linnea could see part of an elegant summerhouse and a glimmer of water. The other side was densely forested, and she could imagine it held an abundance of game. Linnea admitted to feeling a bit awed by Staynes but was comforted by the landscape and what it offered. It reminded her of home a little, and of the times her brother had taught her how to ride, fish, and swim on their neighbor's property—long before Jack had gone to war and died.

Linnea gave herself a mental shake. All that was in the past. She glanced at Rothwick, then back at Staynes. She was married now and mistress of something she was not sure she could truly command. She took a deep breath. She would have to learn. This was her life now.

Rothwick took her hand, and she was glad of it, in spite of his irritating smugness earlier. His look was encouraging, and she thought perhaps he understood her nervousness.

They were greeted by Bartle, the butler, a tall, thin, sixtyish man with a countenance strongly resembling a bloodhound's. He was not at all as impressive as her cousin Boothe's butler, who had despised her as a poor relation. But Bartle was kindly and greeted the earl with both deference and affection. Bartle briefly introduced her to the senior staff (whose names she did not register). She suspected he kept the introductions short, for he had looked carefully at her face and murmured some words to a maid. When the maid returned she led Linnea up to her rooms. There she saw the bed turned down as if inviting her to rest.

The bedroom walls were a pale rose, and the bed draperies echoed the color with their rose pattern on cream brocade. Someone had arranged a small vase of flowers on a stand, and water and towels were ready for her use. She shook her head. She always had to ask for necessities at her cousin Boothe's and was given them grudgingly. Here, not only were they provided, but random touches of beauty had been included as well.

She washed and went to the window. Here she had a clear view of the lake she had glimpsed upon arriving. Willows waved their limbs gracefully over the water, and a path weaved its way around them. The summerhouse sat near it—a charming Grecian construction with vines climbing up the pillars. Linnea glanced at the clock sitting on the mantelpiece. It wanted two hours until dinner; she wondered if Rothwick—no, William—would be willing to escort her to the summerhouse.

The earl was very willing. As they left the house, he tucked her hand on his arm, noting her flushed cheeks and air of ease. She did not flinch this time at his touch, and there was a smile on her lips as she surveyed the lake and the summerhouse. She had a lovely mouth, he noted. The bottom lip was full, and the top lip curved down to curl upward at the corners. She looked up at him, and her expression was neither self-conscious nor wary.

"It has been a long time since I have seen a lake," she said. "I think the last time was before Jack went in the army. He was my older brother, and I remember thinking when I was a girl that no one could possibly have a better brother than I."

"You must have cared for him a great deal," said Rothwick.

Linnea smiled. "Yes. He was rarely cross with me, and taught me all manner of things: swimming, shooting—yes, I can shoot a pistol, but not well—and fishing." They stopped by the water's edge, taking in the reflected blue of the sky.

"A *Compleat Angler,* are you?"

"Hardly." She laughed. "I always seemed to slip and fall into the water—which was why Jack soon taught me to swim."

"Hmmm. Remind me not to ask you along when I wish to cast a line."

"No, I assure you, I have learned to be quite still, and have caught any number of trout."

"Ah. Then I shall know whom to blame if I find all my sport gone."

"You are a vexing man, to be sure! There is no pleasing you." Linnea stooped to pick up a rock.

Rothwick eyed it with mock unease. "I am very easy to please, ma'am. Especially when you are armed."

She suppressed a laugh. "I was *not* going to throw it at you! I was going to throw it in the lake!" she said primly. "There is something very gratifying about throwing rocks into water, you know."

"Is there?" replied the earl with just a hint of laughter in his voice. He shook his head sadly. "For a vicar's daughter, you are quite violent. First you abuse me, then my fish."

"I had cause, I think," Linnea said tartly, throwing the rock far out in the water. It landed with a satisfying splash.

"My trout are totally innocent, I assure you," he replied.

"As you were not, *I* assure *you!*" She picked up another, much larger rock.

Rothwick grinned. He wondered how she would throw it, for it was half again the size of her hand and obviously heavy from the way she bit her lip in an effort to heft it. He put on a pained look.

"*That* again," he replied. "I have tried to remedy my mistake, you know."

Linnea turned toward him impulsively. "Oh, I am fully conscious of it, my lor—William! I, oh, ouch, oh, good heavens—"

Will swiftly grasped her arm to support her. Linnea's face was pale with pain: in her haste to turn in his direction, she had stumbled and dropped the rock on her foot. The same foot, apparently, that she had twisted that night he had abducted her.

He led her to a small stone bench a few feet from the shore of the lake and kneeled down in front of her. She quickly tucked her foot beneath her, her face reddening even as she gasped with pain. "No, really, I am quite all right—so stupid of me! I don't know how I came to be so clumsy—"

"Nonsense! Let me look at it!" commanded the earl. He reached forward and grasped her ankle, ignoring her cry of mingled pain and outrage. Gently he eased her shoe from her slender foot. A touch of blood stained the stocking; the rock had cut it, but he could not see through the sturdy cloth to determine the extent of the injury. "You will need to remove your stocking so I can see if you have broken anything."

"I will *not!*" Linnea exclaimed. Her cheeks were becomingly stained with pink, and her lips pressed together tightly.

He grinned at her. "Missish, are you? You will have

to get over that, you know. We are married, after all. I have no compunctions about removing it myself, if *you* will not do it."

Linnea's cheeks grew redder still. "Oh, you, you—!" Quickly she swung her legs around to the other side of the bench so that her back was to him, and he was rewarded by a brief glimpse of a well-shaped knee before she tossed her skirts back down over it. She turned around again.

"There!" she said, and thrust her foot at him defiantly.

Will took her foot and examined it gently. It was oozing a little blood, not badly, but a large bruise was forming under the wound, and if he was not mistaken, her instep was beginning to swell. He moved her foot this way and that, and though she gasped at the pain, it did not seem that anything was broken.

"A sprain, I think—not bad, I hope, but you should stay off it," he said.

"And how would you know, O Doctor?" she said sarcastically.

Will stood up. "I have seen a few sprains," he replied, smiling. "I was used to follow after Dr. Grenwich—and I will send for him once we return—when I was young, always asking him this or that. I don't know how he bore with my incessant chatter, but he did. But come—" The earl held out his hand, which Linnea grasped.

Suddenly she found herself swung up in his arms. "Oh, for goodness' sake, do let me down! I hardly need to be carried!" She looked up at him and found his face unnervingly close to hers.

He smiled down at her. "True, but think what a sensation it will make when the servants see us arriving this way."

Linnea bit her lip to keep from laughing in spite of herself and her hurt foot. "Odious man! Do, do let me down! I am convinced I am much too heavy to carry!"

Rothwick appeared much struck. "I had not thought of that. And here I believed I was lifting nothing more than . . . oh, ten stone!"

"Ten stone!" cried Linnea. "I am hardly—how dare you—"

She was cut off by a kiss. This time it was deep and full and lovely, and she could feel the warmth of his body pressed close to hers. His arm shifted slowly from under her knees to let her down, but he still held her so that her feet only brushed the soft grass beneath them.

"Not fair . . . ," Linnea murmured as his lips moved just beneath her right ear.

"All's fair . . ." His lips moved farther down to the base of her neck. She gasped.

"And is this war?" she managed to say.

Rothwick gave a husky chuckle and let her down gently. Linnea balanced gingerly on one foot.

"I think we should go back. Dr. Grenwich should see your foot as soon as possible." He put his arm around her waist and took her hand firmly in his.

The sun had sunk a bit lower on the horizon as they turned back to the house. They exchanged no further conversation except scattered inanities about the weather or if she was experiencing much pain, for both were too preoccupied trying to wend their way back home. Growing tired, Linnea made only a token protest when he lifted her in his arms again, though she hid her blushing face in his chest when they went into the house.

It was with a sense of foreboding that the earl viewed Dr. Grenwich's examination of Linnea's foot, which was quite a bit more swollen now. The good doctor shook his head. No strenuous activities for my lady for a while, said he. A bad sprain and badly bruised, it was; he prescribed cold compresses, elevation of the limb, laudanum for the pain, and tincture of arnica.

Rothwick had looked forward to his wedding night with anticipation, but he had to be content with a chaste kiss on Linnea's forehead when they parted for the night. He dared not come any closer to her lips than that. Her lips had proved too dangerous and tempting so far, and if he lingered near them, he feared he'd not have the strength to stop in consideration of her injury. Long ago he'd once himself had a sprained foot and had later tried to please a mistress of his. Perhaps he had pleased her, but the act of lovemaking had too many vigorous movements to it for him to ignore the sharp pain that had lanced through his foot at the most inappropriate moments. No, it was best that he wait until Linnea's foot healed.

In his chamber he prepared for bed, but as soon as his head touched the pillow, he knew he would not drop off to sleep as easily as he had hoped. Rothwick sighed and rose again, putting on his robe. It would be a library-and-brandy night; a good book and one small glass of brandy often cured any amount of sleeplessness he had.

Once in the library he rang for Bartle for a fire to warm him and a bottle of brandy. He ignored his butler's speculative look and picked up a book at random from the shelf. He settled down on his chair, stretching out his legs in front of the fire. Bartle silently poured the brandy.

"You may go, Bartle—and leave the bottle with me."

Bartle's face was impassive. "Very good, sir."

Rothwick turned and looked at him. "And don't give me that look. I've known you long enough to know you don't approve of my hasty marriage—it doesn't suit your notions of what is due my station in life. But I assure you, your consequence as my butler won't suffer."

A brief grin cracked the butler's proper demeanor. "The thought never crossed my mind, sir."

"The devil it didn't," retorted Rothwick. "Well, off with you, and a good night. The lady is from a good family, you know."

"I always rely on your judgment, my lord," replied Bartle with a bow. He turned toward the door, but not before he noticed his lordship had already downed a second glass. He shook his head. Not an auspicious start, this marriage. Not auspicious at all.

8

Linnea closed her chamber door behind her and leaned against it. This was her wedding night, and all her fears and hesitant anticipations were for naught: her husband had merely kissed her on her forehead and left her at her door.

She did not know whether to be sad, embarrassed, or relieved. Well, embarrassed, certainly! What in heaven had caused her to be so stupid as to twist her foot and drop that rock on it, too? William must have thought her a regular nodcock, and she would not have blamed him if he had.

A knock at her door made Linnea wonder if it was William again, but no—Betty came in to help her undress. Linnea was soon ready for bed, her delicate lawn nightgown buttoned securely, her nightcap tied loosely under her chin. She winced as her maid helped her to bed. Her foot hurt, and the bedclothes pressing down on it irritated it. Linnea shifted herself this way and that, pulling the covers to the right and to the left of her foot. She sighed. She would have to bear the discomfort and have warm feet or uncover her foot and be chilled. Choosing warm feet, Linnea closed her eyes.

She could not sleep. She could not help being conscious of the fact that her room connected to Lord Rothwick's—her husband's—own chamber, that it was no doubt unlocked, and that someday it would open and he would come through it. She stared at it through the dark, trying to discern its shape. Useless!

Linnea fumbled with the tinderbox and, after a few tries, lit a candle. She would go to the library for a book. Perhaps she would ring for a little something to eat. *Then* she would sleep; reading at night always made her drowsy. She had been so nervous this evening that she had barely touched her supper, and the nervousness had not yet faded.

She discovered that putting weight on her foot still pained her dreadfully. Her eye caught sight of the medicine bottle on the side table next to the bed. She detested taking medicine; it always tasted horrible, and she always resisted taking it. Oh, drat! It was either lie awake in pain or take the awful stuff so she would be able to get to the library and select a book. Well, she would not take the full draught—just enough to take the edge off the pain, perhaps. She read the doctor's receipt and poured half the prescription into water and drank it. Ugh!

Slowly Linnea hobbled down the hall and the stairs, trying to remember where Rothwick had said the library was and trying not to let her candle drip badly. By the time she came to the library, her foot was not paining her as much as it had, although she felt a little light-headed. She noticed the door was ajar, and there was a light within. She pushed the door open hesitantly but did not see anyone. At the bookshelves, she scanned the titles. Fielding, Cowper . . . Ah. *Sense and Sensibility,* and there was *Pride and Prejudice* as well. Linnea hesitated. She had read and liked both and would be more than glad to read them again. But then perhaps she should try a book she had not yet read. . . .

"There is a new one by the same author, if you'd like to see it."

Linnea jumped, almost upsetting her candle. "For goodness' sakes, could you not give me warning before you send me into an apoplexy?"

Rothwick grinned. "You are too young to be apoplectic. I thought you must have known I was here." He was standing next to a chair that was facing away from the doorway. No doubt he had been sitting in it and its high back had obscured him from view.

"No, I did not," she said crossly. She had come to the library to get away from thinking of him in the room next to hers, and here he was again. What was more, he was in a magnificent dressing gown that showed off his shoulders to perfection, and she was acutely conscious of her own state of relative undress. She hoped the shadows in the room disguised her blush.

"Foot paining you, is it?" Rothwick asked solicitously.

Linnea shot him a fiery look, for his amused expression was in extreme contrast to his voice. "Actually, yes. The bedclothes pressed upon it in an irritating manner, so I could not sleep. I decided to get a book to take back with me."

"I am sorry you were uncomfortable." This time

Rothwick's voice was grave, and his face matched it. Then he smiled. "Come, sit. Elevating your foot should help." She sat, and he reached over to a bottle on a small table to the side of his chair and poured a small amount of golden liquid into a glass. "Would you care for some brandy, or perhaps some other refreshment?"

Linnea had never had any brandy before and hesitated.

"Please try it. It is strong, but quite good, and I assure you it should bring a bit of comfort to you this night."

Linnea took the glass and sipped it. The brandy coursed down her throat like liquid fire, and she coughed. A smoky-sweet taste flooded her mouth. "I, I think I like it." This time she took another, more cautious taste. She smiled up at him. "Yes, I do like it. Thank you." She drank a little more.

"You are welcome." He returned her smile and knelt at her feet, pulling up a footstool. He held out his hand and looked meaningfully at her foot. Linnea blushed, and he laughed. "My dear, it is much too late to be missish. I have already seen your ankle, and held your delightful little foot. As it is, it is covered in bandages. You are not used to the weight of them; I am merely offering to set your foot gently upon this footstool to forestall any painful knocks against it."

Linnea smiled at him and lifted her foot. It wobbled on the way up, and he lifted an eyebrow at her as if to say "You see?" He lifted it gently until it was over the footstool, then let it down carefully.

"Good." He sat down and picked up a book that lay next to the brandy bottle. "Do you like Gothics?"

Linnea did not want to admit she had a fondness for them, even some of the ones from Minerva Press. But

Reader Service.

the light-headedness had increased, and she said, "I do—the better ones, of course."

The earl's smile turned to a grin. "So do I, and *not* always the better ones. Here, I think you will like to take this one—" He opened the book and began to read:

"No one who had ever seen Catherine Morland in her infancy would have supposed her born to be an heroine. Her situation in life, the character of her father and mother, her own person and disposition, were all equally against her. Her father was a clergyman, without being neglected, or poor, and a very respectable man, though his name was Richard—"

Rothwick's voice was deep and expressive, and he read the passage with ironic seriousness until the last five words, when his tone changed to one of wistfulness.

"You, my lord, are a terrible tease." She laughed. "Even worse for me than for poor Miss Morland, my father's name was not Richard, but an undistinguished Lambert. Is this another book by Miss Austen, then? Do let me see it."

He handed her the book, and Linnea touched the title engraved into the leather binding. "*Northanger Abbey.* How intriguing! With such a promising beginning, I am sure I shall enjoy it." She stood up, then sat down again abruptly.

Rothwick rose swiftly from his chair. "Are you ill, Linnea?"

She put a hand to her forehead. "It is very strange, my lord. Though my foot has stopped hurting, my knees are at odds with the rest of me." Linnea stood up again, then wobbled back down to her chair. She giggled. "How very odd!"

Rothwick looked at the glass of brandy he had given her. It was empty. He had not thought he had given her much at all; surely she could not be tipsy! He sighed. First the accident and now this. Everything was turning awry today. Now he would have to help his bride back to her . . . bed.

He looked at Linnea smiling at him. Her eyelids drooped in a sleepy, almost seductive way. The pink tip of her tongue emerged to lick the last sweet film of brandy from her upper lip. Oh, God. And to help her to her room, he'd either have to carry her or have her lean on him as they walked up. The thought of her soft form against him for an extended period of time . . . Good Lord. He poured himself a dash of brandy and drank it in one gulp, then regretted it instantly. The drink flooded his body with warmth and gave him certain heat-making thoughts as well. Manfully he dismissed them. He would do the gentlemanly thing—escort her up the stairs and leave her at the threshold of her chamber.

Gently Rothwick put an arm around Linnea and helped her to her feet. She leaned heavily against him, and he could feel a definite lack of stays beneath her dressing gown.

"Oh, dear. I think I shall need your help, Will. My knees are quite wobbly. It must be because I hurt my foot. It is all connected around there, you know. But my foot does not really hurt anymore. How strange. How very, very, very strange."

"Yes. Well, here, put your arm around me this way," replied Rothwick. He maneuvered her arm around his waist and put his arm around hers. Linnea wobbled again, and his arm slipped upward. He found his hand grasping something warm, rounded, and firm. He groaned. Hastily he righted her, and both of them walked out the library.

"Most improper," remarked Linnea. She smiled at him and gave him a heavy-lidded look again.

"We are married, so it is quite all right, I assure you," replied the earl.

She shook her head. It made her nightcap fall off onto the floor. He made a mental note to pick it up later. Her hair tumbled down and flowed over his hand. It was soft. Very soft.

"You don't love me, though." She sounded sad.

He sighed and said patiently, "I could grow very fond of you, in time." They reached her chamber, and Rothwick opened the door.

"Really? That is very good of you." Linnea turned in his arms and rested her head on his chest. "There. My head feels much better. I think I could grow fond of you, too."

"That is very good of you, also." He rolled his eyes. Good God, how inane. It was getting harder to concentrate on getting Linnea where she belonged, especially with the way she clung to him. He managed to pull her along toward her bed, clenching his teeth against the feel of her body against his. *Control, Rothwick,* he thought. *You can control yourself.*

"You think so, too?" Linnea's nose bumped his chin when she looked up at him, smiling, and the tip of her tongue came out over her lip.

It was his undoing. His sigh was long, and as that breath left him, so did any resolve he had formed to respect Linnea's injury and leave her alone. His lips came down on hers. They were soft and sweet. Her arms crept up around his neck, pulling him closer, and he opened her mouth with a gentle pressure. At last he could feel that tantalizing tongue against his, experimental and tentative, sliding sensuously within. He pulled at the strings of her dressing gown. Surely the rest of her must be as sweet.

Through her sleepy haze, Linnea's rational mind raised an alarm, which she ignored. The dressing gown fell from her shoulders, and the cool air of her chamber drove her to the closest source of warmth—Rothwick. How pleasant. How pleasant and warm. And comfortable. She felt herself lifted and carried. How considerate of him to think of her poor foot and carry her to her bed like this, she thought. And he gave her a proper good-night kiss this time. Much better than a forehead one, much, much better. Although, Linnea reflected vaguely as she felt his lips mark a wonderfully warm trail from her ear to the base of her neck, perhaps it was not really as *proper* as one on the forehead. But oh, how pleasant. How very, very pleasant. She would like to do it again. They were married, after all. He said so. Abruptly she pulled him down to her.

Rothwick, who had drawn away from her to concentrate on getting out of his own clothes, suddenly found Linnea's lips on his again and her tongue mimicking what his had done to hers before. By God, this was incredible. He never thought this woman he'd married would be so responsive. He tore off the last inhibiting folds of his clothing, impatiently shaking a stubbornly adhesive sleeve of his robe from his hand, while Linnea, equally persistent, continued to explore his mouth with her own. He could feel her soft form pressing against him beneath the sheer lawn gown she wore. It was torture, for he knew it was the only thing that delayed the eventual meeting of their flesh. She moved and shifted under him, the thin cotton making soft susurrous friction between them.

Linnea felt hot, as if in a fever, and suddenly more

dizzy than ever. It was William's fault; his kisses were
making her too warm. She stretched languorously,
sleepily, unconsciously causing her body to lift and
rise against him.

Rothwick stared at her. Unbelievable. He knew
Linnea must be a virgin, as her first hesitant kisses had
told him. But now, her eyes half closed, she showed no
missishness, no shyness, but stretched her arms
above her head in a gesture so sensual that it took his
breath away. God save him, but he had to have her.

He bent his head to take her lips once more, and
then his mouth traveled down her neck and into the
valley between her breasts. He heard her murmur
softly and sigh. Encouraged, he continued the explo-
ration of her skin with his lips. Another, deeper sigh
followed, and then—

A snore.

Startled, Rothwick ceased his caresses and peered
at her through the dark. The single candle at the side
of the bed only dimly illuminated her face, but enough
to show him what he feared: Linnea was asleep.

With a groan he collapsed facedown into the pillow
beside her. Had he a pistol, he'd shoot himself and
mercifully put himself out of his misery. No one
deserved to suffer the agonies of frustration he had
encountered this day of all days. His wedding night. Ye
gods. And worse, he had broken his resolution not to
touch her. He'd forgotten her injury and had gone
after her like a rutting boar. Good God, he could not
even trust his own motives. He hoped, very much
hoped, that Linnea would not remember anything of
this. The earl was—as much as his pride would let
him—very close to despising himself.

Rothwick sighed. Sitting up, he looked at Linnea

beside him, still stretched out in that unconsciously sensual pose. He could feel himself growing warm again gazing at her, and he muttered a curse under his breath. Gently he rose and pulled the bedclothes over her, tucking them around her chin. He gave one last, wistful look before going through the connecting door to his room.

He could not sleep. Visions of Linnea in the next room, the way the pink tip of her tongue had hesitantly smoothed her lips, the way she had pressed herself against him, made him toss and turn, trying to find a comfortable way to sleep. Finally he flung himself out of bed, roughly pulling on his much abused dressing gown, and stomped out of his chamber.

Little Jack, the stable-boy, rubbed his eyes sleepily. It was dark still, but a loud creaking sound persisted in the stable-yard. Frightened, he paused, listening intently. It sounded like the water-pump.

Cautiously he peered out a window into the moonlit yard. Cor, it couldn't be! He crept to the door and opened it. His eyes widened. Gawd, nobody was goin' ter believe this, not in a hunnerd years, he thought. He shook his head. That was quality-make for you. You never knew what they'd take into their brain-boxes and fly with.

For there was his lordship, in the dead of a cold, dark night, clad only in his dressing gown, dumping freezing water over his head.

When Betty drew back the curtains, she knew her mistress was awake by the way she groaned. Betty was a good girl, and this was her first chance at being an abigail to a real lady—what's more, a countess—so she was alert to any opportunity to do her lady a service. So when my lady groaned—and a terrible sad groan it was, too—Betty did her best to tiptoe quietly about and do her duties as best she could and not intrude on her ladyship's notice. But then Lady Rothwick groaned again, and it near wrung the girl's heart to hear it. She was a country lass, and her mum always said she was the best-natured of her children. And . . . well, to hear her ladyship moan so, it was more than a body could bear.

"My lady?" whispered Betty. "Is there aught I can do for you? You sound mortal bad, ma'am."

Two hands appeared above the bedcovers and slowly slid them down until my lady's eyes showed. They were reddened, and if the exposed part of her face was any evidence, her ladyship was as pale as the sheets she lay on.

"I have the headache," Lady Rothwick said hoarsely. She cleared her throat. "Please . . . close the curtains."

"Of course, my lady. And I shall get some cool cloths for your poor head, too." Betty hurried to the windows. My, but her ladyship looked dreadful. She'd heard that his lordship had visited his lady last night, and from the looks of it, it hadn't done my lady any good at all. The maid shuddered. Thomas the footman had been giving her the eye, and after seeing what my lady must have gone through on her wedding night, well, it was enough to put one off, it was!

Linnea pulled the covers down to her chin. She did not know whether to be glad her head was hurting so or not; certainly, in comparison, her foot hurt not at all. She watched her abigail's movements about the room. "Betty, would you happen to know of a good remedy for the headache? I'm afraid I am not used to Dr. Grenwich's medicines."

"Well, I remember my grandmum giving us willow bark tea whenever we—me and my brothers and sisters, my lady—felt poorly, and it perked us up right and tight. Nasty tasting, though."

Linnea thought this over. Her stomach was not feeling much better than her head, but having one of her pains gone had much to recommend it. "I think I would like some, if you have any."

Betty bobbed a curtsy. "Yes, ma'am. I shall fetch it straight away. Oh, and I can sweeten it with honey, if you'd like."

Linnea summoned a weak smile. "Please." She sank down carefully into her pillows again and closed her eyes. She castigated herself for not thinking properly last night: she should have remembered to take only a quarter dose of medicine. She rarely could tolerate much medicine of any sort and usually only took a quarter dose. She groaned. It had been many years since she'd needed any medicine. How was she to remember?

A quarter of an hour later Betty came back in with the tea. Heartily refusing an offer of breakfast in bed, Linnea smiled her thanks and took a sip. The tea was, indeed, sharp and biting, but Betty had laced it liberally with honey, and it was not as bad as most remedies.

Two hours later Linnea felt much better. Perhaps she would even have a little something to eat. She summoned Betty again and selected a modest morning gown—which, after putting it on, was not as modest as she had thought. Linnea let out an exasperated sigh. Lydia again! The dress was a round gown with a pink bodice and frilly white skirt and covered her from chin to toes. However, the pink muslin bodice was only just a shade darker than her skin and fit her like it, too. Further, the silken fabric that extended from almost the crest of her bosom and foamed in lace-edged gathers about her chin was so sheer as not to be there at all. It clung to her when she moved, and her sleeves were of the same material, banded at elbows and wrists with pink muslin. Linnea gazed, aghast, in the mirror. She looked for all the world like some pagan goddess arising out of foam. Good Lord, what could Lydia have been thinking of?

She knew *exactly* what Lydia had been thinking of. Hazy images of Rothwick and the night before formed before her mind's eye, and Linnea felt her face grow hot. More edifying images floated through her mind, and she cringed. Had she really acted that way? What must Rothwick think of her? She pressed her hands over her eyes and groaned. She did not remember all of what passed, but it was enough to know he had been in her bed and she had acted with disgraceful wantonness.

"Is everything all right, my lady?" Betty asked.

Linnea let down her hands. "Oh, it's nothing, Betty, just a leftover ache in my head. It's gone now."

"Do you need more tea, perhaps, ma'am?"

"No, not at all. I am quite well now." Linnea turned to her wardrobe. The rest of her trousseau had arrived the day before yesterday. Surely there was something more modest than this!

She went through four dresses before she gave up and went back to the pink sea-foam goddess one again. Every gown she had picked when she went shopping with Lydia had been altered in a more dashing manner than the original in the fashion plate. Lydia! She would have a thing or two to say to her sister-in-law when next they met!

A glance at the clock on the mantelpiece showed her it was a few minutes to eleven. Well, at least Rothwick should be done with his breakfast by now and she need not see him—and be seen by him—this time.

But, of course, he hadn't finished breakfast and so was exposed to the full glory of her sea-foam morning dress. Rothwick was not in the best of tempers. Dousing himself in near freezing water last night had only temporarily cooled his heated imaginings, and he had tossed between that and self-recrimination at his weakness all night long. He was tired. He felt guilty. And having Linnea come down in a dress that clung to her bosom every time she breathed did not help. After one riveted gaze and a hastily murmured "Good morning," he abruptly put his newspaper in front of him and apparently became absorbed in an article about a new method of mulching.

Linnea swallowed a lump in her throat, and the food-laden table before her became less appetizing. So, she had embarrassed him and herself last night. Well, all she could do was apologize. She waited until the servants had left, then cleared her throat.

A corner of the newspaper flicked down, and Rothwick peered over it at her. "Yes?"

"I—I am sorry."

"Sorry?" Rothwick's brows rose.

"About last night. I am afraid I did not act as I ought." Linnea could feel her face grow warm, but she lifted her chin and looked her husband in the eye. "But I suppose we are irrevocably married now, and what's done is done."

"What *are* you talking about?" said Rothwick. He had put down his newspaper and he stared at her, his brows together in a frown.

Linnea pressed her hands to her cheeks, trying to cool the heat that rose higher there. "Why, I mean, last night, after we left the library—you came to my room, and, and . . ." She faltered and stopped.

Rothwick rose from his chair, put both hands on the table, and leaned toward her. "And nothing happened. Absolutely nothing." He sat down again and put up the newspaper.

"But, but, you were, well, in my bed, and you, ah, touched me, and, er—"

The newspaper came down with a snap. "You needn't throw it in my face, for God's sake, woman! For all that I was determined not to touch you, it *was* our wedding night, and the way you kept pressing yourself against me—it was more than a man could bear!"

"I *said* I was *sorry!*" retorted Linnea. "Besides, I did not know how my medicine would affect me." She sat up straight on her chair, glaring at him. Embarrassment fled, and chagrin and a sense of insult overcame her. Determined not to touch her! On their wedding night! She would not have known that from the kisses he had pressed on her by the lake, and, yes, she remembered far different kisses last night.

Rothwick's innate honesty warred with his temper. "Oh. You took some laudanum, did you? Well, that would explain it. I suppose I should have remembered what Dr. Grenwich said about it since you were not in a state to do so." He averted his gaze, and there was silence, broken only by the light, rhythmic tapping of his fork against his plate. "For that matter, I suppose I shouldn't have had as much brandy as I did. The combination of that brandy and that dressing gown of yours . . ." He grinned. "I am not a monk, you know."

Linnea blushed rosily. "It was Lydia. *She* chose most of my gowns for me, and altered some of the ones I chose. They are not at all what I am used to."

Rothwick's smile faded a bit as he mentally cursed his sister. If all of Linnea's dresses were like the one she was wearing now, he was going to have to make damned sure he was rarely alone with Linnea while her foot healed. He put up his newspaper again.

Linnea absently surveyed the table before her, selecting different foods at random. She stared at what she could see of Rothwick, wondering if she was going to face a newspaper at breakfast for the rest of her life. Certainly she had married a strange man—or were all men strange like this? First he is free with his caresses and kisses, and then he says he never wanted to touch me—as if I forced him to do so! Linnea shook her head. She thought it was proper for a man to kiss his wife— did not he say so himself? But now he said he did not want to! And men called women contrary!

She looked at the newspaper separating them again, then took a deep breath. Well, if she did not ask, she would never know.

"Excuse me, my lord?"

"Yes?" His voice sounded weary behind the paper.

"Why *is* it that you did not want to touch me?"

A groan issued from behind the newspaper, and it collapsed, tentlike, over Rothwick's head. He removed it, the edges crushed in his hands, and the gaze he bent on her resembled that of a dog, much tortured and abused.

"Because it was not the gentlemanly thing to do." His voice was as calm as tension could make it.

"Oh." Linnea felt even more confused. How did a gentleman perform his marital duties if he did not touch his wife?

Her confusion must have shown on her face, for after tiredly rubbing both palms into his eyes, he continued: "Not when your foot is still hurt and healing."

"Oh!" replied Linnea, much enlightened. She smiled at him, warmed by his consideration and thoughtfulness. "Actually, I do not remember it hurting much at all last night."

Rothwick gazed at her, conflicting emotions fighting for a place on his countenance. He looked at his newspaper, crumpled in his hands. A hole pierced the mulching article. Useless! Not that he wanted to know anything about mulching, but a torn newspaper was a ridiculous thing to hide behind—far more than a whole one. He grinned.

"My dear lady, the way you were sleeping, nothing would have roused you—foot, kisses, or anything else." He rose. "If you will excuse me, I need to see to some matters with the bailiff. Shall we meet again for dinner, or would you prefer to rest with a tray taken up to you?"

Linnea smiled at him, puzzled but glad of his change of mood. "I would like to dine with you, my lord. I detest meals in bed."

Rothwick bowed upon leaving the room and smiled with a certain satisfaction. Perhaps he could show her someday soon that a meal in bed was not to be despised.

9

Some days later, as soon as he had quit his business at the gatehouse with Mr. Potts, the bailiff, Rothwick knew he was developing a cold. It started as a little tickle in his throat and disrupted his interview with Mr. Potts. The bailiff was a meek, if competent, man and paused respectfully in his speech whenever Rothwick cleared his throat. Since his lordship needed to do so constantly, Mr. Potts interrupted himself constantly, and neither of them did get to the point of their meeting by the end of their appointed hour.

Rothwick gave it up. His throat was already sore, his nose tickled, and he was as tired as if he had not slept in days. It was that damned midnight dousing he had given himself, he was sure of it. Well, at least he would not be tempted to make love to Linnea while her foot healed; sneezing profusely somehow put one off any sort of amorous activity. He went into the house.

Intent on going up to his rooms, he walked up the curving staircase, and upon turning at the end of the landing, he found himself face-to-face with Linnea.

"Good morning, my lord, er, Will." She smiled uncertainly at him.

Once more Rothwick cursed his sister's choice of Linnea's clothes. He had prided himself on staying away from his wife for the last three days since that disastrous wedding night, trying to content himself with a kiss on her hand or her cheek. He now saw he would have to give up kissing her cheek. It was too close to her delectable neck, now emphasized by the delicate frill that edged the V neckline. It drew his eye downward: unfortunate, for as much as he tried there was something irresistible about the lines of the dress, and he did not think it was the fabric.

With an effort he raised his gaze to her face. "Do you not have any other dress more—more modest than this one?" he snapped.

Linnea's face became pink, and a spark gleamed in her eye. "I am sorry, my lord, but dresses like this one comprise nearly all of my wardrobe. I believe I informed you of this some days ago, so you need not bite off my head."

Rothwick's expression stiffened. "You must excuse me, ma'am. I have had a most trying morn—ahh, ahh—" He hurriedly pulled out a large handkerchief and covered his nose. "Achoo! Achoo! Achoo!" He shuddered, then eyed Linnea's suddenly sympathetic look with suspicion.

"Oh, dear, it sounds as if you have a cold!" she said kindly.

"And if I interpret that look in your eye correctly, ma'am, I suspect the next thing you will propose is some noxious remedy to correct the problem." He dabbed his nose one last time and moved to go past her. "I thank you, but no."

Linnea's eyes widened. "Why, how did you know?"

"You forget, my dear, that I have three sisters." He continued through a door and down the hall. Linnea hobbled after him.

"But what has that to do with anything?"

"Quite simply, it has to do with survival."

"Survival?"

"Of course. Envision yourself an only son, cosseted and beleaguered not only by a mother, but by three older sisters. I was rarely left alone to run about in the dirt, fall into the lake, or freeze myself in the snow as any other boy might have."

Linnea chuckled. "And?"

Rothwick gave her a woeful look. "You laugh, but it was a trial and a burden, believe me."

"Well, then, how did you . . . survive . . . this burden?"

"I watched them carefully. A softening of the lips, a smile, a concerned crease on the forehead, and I knew a noxious draught was on its way. When the look manifested itself on the faces of my mother or my sisters, I made sure to make my escape."

A short burst of laughter escaped Linnea's lips. "And did you enjoy your escape?"

"Very much." He paused at the door to his chamber. "Now, if you will excuse me, ma'am, I shall rest."

"Oh, but perhaps—"

"*No.* A rest is all I need." He closed the door firmly in her face.

Linnea sighed and turned away. How useless she felt! She was used to acting as her cousin Boothe's maid-of-all-work, making up menus, dusting fine ornaments, running errands, and instructing the maids on laundry day. She had wandered this house—her house, now— and looked for any occupation she might put her hand to. There was none. The house was well ordered—the mantelpieces and all decorations polished to a bright gleam, the menus all determined by the excellent French chef—and there were no errands to run. Finally, when she found Lord Rothwick with a putrid cold, she thought there was at last something she could do. She had often nursed her father's parishioners when they were ill, and she knew she was considered a fine nurse. But he seemed neither to need nor want her help.

Linnea winced as she walked to her own rooms. She felt more inclined to hobble than to walk properly, but if she were careful not to make sudden movements, her foot only ached instead of giving her a stabbing pain. Indeed, she was sure she was recovering, for the ache seemed to recede the more she exercised her foot.

When she entered her room, she went to the window. There she looked out upon the landscape, at the lake and the little Grecian summerhouse. Except for the vines climbing up its pillars, there were few flowers or shrubbery near the gazebo. She wondered what it would be like if there were. Yes. Perhaps a small garden encircling the building; short boxwood shrubberies enclosing beds of roses and peonies. A smile touched her lips. That was something she could do. Though she had supervised the vicarage's vegetable garden, it was true she did not know much else about gardening. However, she was willing to learn, and she was sure she could ask the gardener if she needed help.

A small weight lifted from Linnea's heart, and she looked through her wardrobe for a plain, service- able dress she could wear while consulting the head gardener. At last, she could make herself useful. Why, if she learned enough, perhaps she could even assist Lord Rothwick—Will—in some agricultural matters. It behooved her, then, to find all she could on gardening and agriculture in the library. She changed her dress for her plainest grey, round muslin gown, draped a shawl around her shoulders, and went to find the head gardener.

When dinner was announced, Linnea was surprised to find that she came down before Rothwick. Indeed, he did not appear until fifteen minutes after her entrance into the dining room, and a fierce sneeze preceded him.

"Achoo!" He pressed his handkerchief to his nose, glanced at Linnea, and bowed briefly. "You bus escuze be, ma'am, but I am afraid I will nod be good company this evening."

"Oh, dear, you do sound quite ill! Are you sure you do not want—"

"No!"

"I have it on good authority that lemon-barley tea will do wonders for a cold, and as for dinner, my lord, I do not think you should partake of anything more than a light broth in your condition." Linnea looked at him, concerned. Lord Rothwick's nose was a decided red, his eyes watered, and he coughed a little. She shook her head.

"I ab quite all right—recoverig—*recovering*, in fact."

"Forgive me, my lord, but—"

"Will, Linnea. Do remember thad I hab a Christian name." He gave her an impatient look.

"Will, I have to say that you do not at all sound as if you are recovering," Linnea said firmly. "You sound worse than you did earlier today. I strongly advise you to rest in your rooms. It is an easy enough thing to have the broth brought up to you."

"Thang you, doe—thad is, no!" He gave her a fierce glare and bent to his dinner.

What a stubborn man he is! thought Linnea, poking her fork ruthlessly through a piece of roast beef. She was only advising him for his own good. What use would it be if he caught lung fever from this? She watched him smugly as he winced, attempting to swallow some food. His throat was probably quite sore. He looked up at her.

"Well? What is it?"

"Nothing at all, Will," she said sweetly.

"You are rejoicing in my bain—*pain*—I can tell."

"*I?* Never. Nothing of the kind." Linnea sliced an apple and put it daintily on her plate.

"Oh? Then why were you looking at be in thad manner?" he said slowly and distinctly.

Linnea almost smiled. He was trying hard not to sound congested. "I was merely reflecting on how stubborn you are."

"Oh, were you?" He sneezed once again and blew his nose.

"Yes. Here you are with a putrid cold, and an obviously sore throat, but you absolutely will not take any sort of remedy for it. Where is the sense in that?"

"My dear Linnea, I am more than ten, believe be, and habe taken care of myself in the past. If I wanted to be coddled and cosseted, I would habe taken up residence with one of my sisters." He gave her another impatient look and bent himself once again to his dinner.

Silence. Then: "My lord, is there no way I can be helpful?"

"Helpful?" Rothwick raised his eyebrows. "You are my wife. You may do as you please here."

"But there is nothing to do!" Linnea cried. "Your household is orderly, your menus made up by a most excellent cook. Your servants never need correction, and your tenants are well cared for and healthy. You even have a village school, taught by competent teachers!"

The earl's lips turned up in amusement. "I habe neber thought these were things to be complained about."

Linnea could not help smiling, albeit reluctantly. "Of course they are not. But it leaves me nothing to do but sit and be idle."

Rothwick looked at her measuringly. "So you would rather be id London, amongsd the ton and amusements?" His voice was cool, indifferent. "I can arrange that, if you wish."

She gazed at him uncertainly, suddenly feeling as if ice had closed around her heart. His face was still and expressionless, but his eyes stared into her own, as if he were looking for something. Was this the beginning, then? The beginning of going their own way, of having separate lives? She had agreed to his terms, to be sure, but she had thought perhaps they might come to know each other first and not be complete strangers. Indeed, it seemed they were on far more familiar terms than she had ever thought they might at first. And yet now, abruptly, he had become distant. Was it, perhaps, something she had said? She shook her head and sighed.

"No, my lord. It is just that I wish to have some occupation. I have always had something practical to do; I ran my father's household when my mother died, and even before that, I helped care for the needy. When I stayed at my cousin Boothe's house, I was given errands to run, and other household chores. I was busy, and at least at my father's house, content."

Rothwick grinned, and this time a hint of laughter appeared in his eyes. "So, the former Beggar Maid wishes to scatter some ashes upon her palace floor, just so she will feel at home?"

Linnea chuckled. "Yes. Or better yet, I wish to do something that will actively help you."

He gazed at her in a thoughtful manner. "Have you thought, ma'am," he said slowly, "that perhaps you might want to know what a life full of amusement, idleness, and . . . pleasure, might be like?"

"I—that is, I have never. . . I, I don't know. I have always been busy with something useful. I have never had the time . . ." She looked at him, nonplussed, and, remembering the abortive wedding night, blushed.

A lazy smile grew on his face. "Perhaps you should learn. I could, of course, teach you." Suddenly he sneezed three times and pressed his handkerchief to his nose. Linnea was hard put not to laugh.

"But, alas, not right now," she said, and rang for Bartle.

When the butler entered, she smiled at him. "Bartle, please have Cook prepare some sustaining broth for Lord Rothwick. He has a sore throat, and cannot eat this most delicious dinner. Indeed, he may even be starting a fever," she said, looking at the earl's reddened face.

"Bartle, my lady does not doe of what she speaks," Rothwick said pleasantly, casting a chilly glance at Linnea nevertheless. "I— Achoo! Achoo! Achoo!"

A small smile hovered around Bartle's mouth but disappeared swiftly at Rothwick's black look. The butler turned to Linnea and bowed. "As you wish, my lady," he said calmly, and left the dining room.

"Bartle! What the deuce do you think—" Lord Rothwick began, but it was too late. The door had already closed behind the butler. The earl turned and looked at Linnea's laughing face. "I suppose you think this is exceedingly humorous."

"Oh, yes, I do," Linnea replied. She pushed herself away from the table. "Just like a little boy who will not take his medicine." Lord Rothwick watched her speechlessly as she moved to the door, affront and irritation flashing across his face. "A most delicious meal, my lord. I am so sorry you are not able to appreciate it fully. I expect I shall not see you after dinner, as you are going directly to bed, are you not?"

As Rothwick's answer was more like a snarl from a caged lion than anything that may have issued from a human throat, Linnea clapped her hands over her ears, laughed, and quickly left the room.

She had not much cause to laugh the next day, however. Rothwick had grown feverish, and fearing it could be influenza or worse, Linnea sent for Dr. Grenwich. The good doctor had shaken his head and recommended that the earl stay in bed until fully recovered. Barley tea, lemonade, good hot broths were all the patient should drink.

Dr. Grenwich shook his greying head again upon leaving Rothwick's rooms, and Linnea felt a chill clutch her heart.

"Is . . . is it influenza, sir?" she whispered.

The doctor raised his grizzled eyebrows and smiled. "Yes, but it may not become at all severe, my lady. Your husband has a very strong constitution. He will be up and about in less than a week's time *if*—and I emphasize *if*, Lady Rothwick—he heeds my warning about arising before he is completely well! *And* if he takes the saline draughts as I have prescribed, as well as his medicine."

Linnea bit her lip and looked at the doctor doubtfully. "I do hope he will do as you direct. I have found Lord Rothwick can be a very stubborn man, Dr. Grenwich."

"That, too, has been my experience," he said, smiling wryly. "He was ever such as a lad, always dogging my heels, never mind I shut the door on him time and time again. He would climb in a window, like as not, so I soon gave it up and let him follow." The doctor sighed. "If he were not a nobleman, my lady, he would have made a fine apprentice and physician." He shrugged and smiled.

"But, but how am I to make sure he does not throw out all your medicines?"

Dr. Grenwich's smile turned wide as he picked up his bag. "My lady, you are newly wed, are you not? I depend on your considerable charm to persuade him otherwise. Good day to you, ma'am." He bowed to her and left.

Linnea watched the door close behind him and gnawed her lip. She was not at all sure she could charm anyone. She sighed. She would have to try.

Lord Rothwick took a turn for the worse. His valet, who had been watching over his master while Linnea was at supper, anxiously requested her presence just as she put down her fork.

"What is it, Potter?" said Linnea, her heart sinking at the servant's pale face.

"It's his lordship, my lady. He's not talking any sense, and doesn't seem to know me."

"Oh, heavens." Linnea rose hurriedly and followed Potter to his master's chambers.

Lord Rothwick's eyes were closed, but he moved restlessly and had kicked off the bedsheets. He had no nightclothes on except for his underbreeches, and thus Linnea was exposed to the full glory of his naked torso. She had not remembered how his body looked on their wedding night, for it had been dark, and she had been too sleepy. But now the candlelight outlined each muscle as Will strained against the fever. His shoulders were broad, and his lightly furred chest looked as hard as slabs of granite. She wanted to touch him, to see if his chest was indeed as firm as it looked. She could feel herself blushing and sternly reined in her wayward thoughts. She turned to the valet. "Potter, has he no nightshirt?"

It was the valet's turn to blush. "I am afraid, my lady, his lordship does not. He has never liked them, and thought them a waste of money. He prefers to sleep, er, as you see him."

"I see," she said. "It is just as well; he will need to be sponged to keep down the fever. And we will need extra quilts and blankets, for when he gets chilled. And cold water and cloths for his head. Except . . . Wait! Potter, does Staynes have an ice cellar?"

The valet looked at her curiously. "Why, yes, my lady."

"If possible, have someone cut some ice from it, and put it in a bowl. We must cool his head to keep down the fever. And tell Cook to prepare some lemonade if possible."

Potter's face brightened with hope. "Yes, my lady! I shall do so straight away!" He hurried out the door.

Linnea pulled the bedclothes over Rothwick again.

She put her hand to his forehead. Good heavens, he was burning up! She was glad she had thought to ask about the ice cellar.

Rothwick moaned and moved his head toward her. A lock of his hair tumbled across her hand, and she brushed it back gently. He sighed. She touched his hair again, tentatively. It was soft. She hadn't thought it would be, for it was black, thick, and usually impeccably styled. A tendril of warmth curled up around her heart, and she let out a long breath. Absently she continued stroking his hair, running her fingers through the thick waves. Rothwick sighed and seemed to relax. "Mother," he whispered.

Linnea smiled widely. Now was that not the way of it? It seemed most men still had a little boy within them that wanted coddling—bluster and complain as they might. Why even her father and brother had sometimes turned suddenly meek when they were ill. Then, however, she knew she had to worry, for that meant they were quite ill.

She sobered. Her husband, she feared, was very ill indeed. A knock sounded on the door, and she turned. Potter entered, carrying a large block of ice in a bowl, towels draped over his arms.

"Here, my lady, is the ice you wished for." The valet hovered indecisively next to the bed.

Linnea smiled at him reassuringly. "Thank you! On the washstand, if you please."

"Do . . . do you think his lordship will recover?" said Potter in hushed tones. "I . . . I have never seen him this ill, my lady, not in all the fifteen years I have served him."

"You need not worry, Potter. It is always such with men who have strong constitutions. They are rarely ill, and when they do become so, they have it worse than weaker souls." The valet looked relieved. Linnea only wished she were as sure as she sounded. Her father had also had a strong physical disposition, but he had finally succumbed to the influenza when it had developed into lung fever. And she had worked so hard to make him well!

Linnea pressed her lips together firmly. But her husband was young, not old like her father. That, certainly, was in his favor. And he had ceased coughing. That must be a good sign. Potter cleared his throat, and she was recalled from her thoughts. She looked at him. "Yes?"

"Is there anything I can do, my lady? To help Lord Rothwick?" He looked uncomfortable and uncertain. "I shall do everything in my power to make him comfortable. Perhaps I can watch him during the night?"

She smiled at him. "No, Potter, I shall watch him tonight. Dr. Grenwich has given me remedies that must be administered at precise times tonight. Believe me, your master will be safe in my hands. I have nursed many people in my father's parish and was known as a good nurse."

"But, Lady Rothwick . . . !"

"I see you are anxious about His Lordship, and believe me, I do appreciate it. What I—and Lord Rothwick—need from you is for you to get your rest, so I can rely on you later, should he become any worse."

The servant's eyes widened, and he nodded. "I understand, my lady. And please do call for me should you need any help."

Linnea smiled. "You are a good man, Potter. I shall make sure Lord Rothwick knows of your devotion."

The man blushed and disclaimed, but she could see he was pleased.

"Now, do go and finish the rest of your duties, and make sure you are well rested." She waved him away.

"Yes, my lady." The valet left.

It was going to be a long night, thought Linnea. She sat on the chair next to Rothwick's bed, read a book, then did some needlework by the light of the candles. After several hours she yawned and looked up at the clock on the mantelpiece. Eleven o'clock! She went through the connecting door to her room and rang for Betty to change into her nightgown so that she might be more comfortable. But when she returned to the chair by Rothwick's bed, the nightgown's sheer softness and the warmth of her robe only made her feel sleepy. Determined to stay up, she refreshed herself with some tea kept warm by a stub of a candle underneath a pot in Rothwick's room.

Rothwick grew no better. His forehead remained hot despite the ice-cold cloths Linnea put upon his head. Soon he was moving restlessly again, and then it turned to an ague. He shivered uncontrollably, and this seemed to wake him.

"Linnea!" He stared at her in apparent incomprehension.

At least he seemed to recognize her. She went to him immediately. "Yes, Will, I am here."

"I am so cold. . . ." He closed his eyes again.

Linnea glanced at the clock on the mantelpiece. It was time for another of Dr. Grenwich's medicines. "Here, my love, you need to drink this." A shock went through her. "My love." Dear God. Why in the world had she blurted that out? She bit her lip. Had Rothwick heard?

He opened his eyes again but said nothing. She put the cup to his lips and he drank, his teeth tapping against the glass. He sank back into bed and appeared to sleep, but she could still hear his teeth chattering together, and the bed shook with his shivers.

She clasped her hands together anxiously. This was no time to think of faux pas; Will's illness demanded attention. How to stop his shivering? She had given him medicine, had tried to keep him warm with not only his bedclothes, but some of hers from her bed as well. Then a dim memory came to her of her mother, long ago. It was when Linnea had been a little girl and dreadfully ill. She, too, had had the shivers, and her mother had taken her into her own bed. She remembered how comforting it was and how it seemed she felt warmer immediately and soon left off shaking.

Linnea looked at Rothwick and blushed. She could hardly carry him into her own bed; it meant that she would have to go into his. She bit her lip. Well, as brazen as it was, she was married to him, after all, and this was for his health, not for . . . anything else.

Blushing all the while, she took off her robe and slipped between the sheets. She moved toward him so she could put her arms around him. He sighed and reached out to her, gathering her close. He shivered violently against her but was still hot. She was glad of the warmth, however, for her feet had become cold while she'd sat in the chair. She dared nestle close to him and put her hand on his chest. It was firm, but not at all hard. His skin was softer than she had thought it would be. She put her head upon it; it felt quite comfortable. She could hear his heart beating, and it seemed that his breath slowed a little. Indeed, it seemed he did not shiver so much now. He sighed once again. "Linnea. . . ."

"I am here, love," she said. He relaxed once again, and his arm went slack.

Linnea's eyes drooped. He shivered much less now,

just a few tremors now and again. Perhaps . . . perhaps it would be all right if she just closed her eyes, just for a few moments.

And in a few moments she was soundly asleep.

The sunlight peeping through the curtains struck Rothwick's eyes and woke him. He kept his eyes closed, but the light persisted in turning the insides of his eyelids bright red instead of leaving them pleasantly dark. He turned over and moved closer to the softness next to him. He must have tossed all of his pillows about on his bed last night, he thought drowsily, so that they were at his side instead of properly at the head of the bed. No matter; he would put his head wherever the pillow was. He was too tired and still too racked with aches to rearrange his bed.

Moving his head against the pillow, he pushed at it with his hand so that it would plump up a bit. But instead of giving way softly, the pillow felt quite firm and stayed where it was. Rothwick opened his eyes. There, in front of him, was a lovely, full, rounded bosom. He sighed and closed his eyes again. I am dreaming, he thought. A deprived and suffering man's dream. He moved his hand up from where he had laid it and felt the definite shape of thigh and curving hip.

He opened his eyes again. Oh, God. The bosom was still there. It was a long time since he had seen such a thing, covered by the sheer fabric of a nightgown. Come to think of it, it was on his wedding night, when nothing had happened. He pushed himself up, even though his head ached at the exertion, and gazed at the owner of the bosom. Linnea. Ye gods.

Her arm was flung up above her head, her face turned

away so that he could see her delicate profile. Her hair was charmingly tousled about her shoulders, and one strand curled provocatively around a breast. She might as well have not worn her nightgown; it hid little, for the thin silken cloth clung to her as if it were wet.

Rothwick groaned and fell back onto the bed again. Here was the opportunity, but there was little he could do about it. His head pounded, his limbs ached, and he was exhausted. He was a man of reasonable appetites, and he usually had a good deal of stamina. But though he felt better, he knew he was still ill. Were he to try consummating his marriage now, he would tire long before he could give Linnea any pleasure—or himself, for that matter.

He turned and gazed at her resentfully. It was supremely unjust, and there was no reason for her to be in his bed that he could see. Surely she understood he was not well enough to exert himself?

Perhaps there was something in his bitter, concentrated stare that somehow impinged itself upon Linnea's sleeping mind, for she turned over slowly and locked eyes with him. A blush suffused her cheeks, and Rothwick noted with a long-suffering sigh that it crept down her neck to her breasts. She grasped the bedclothes and drew them up to her chin.

"G-good morning, my lord," she whispered.

"Why are you in my bed?" he said abruptly.

"I—I, it is not what you think, truly."

"Oh, and what am I thinking?"

"That . . . that I wanted to, to . . . But I did not, really!"

"You didn't?" Rothwick felt offended. Damn it, if she was going to insinuate herself into his bed, at least her intentions could be flattering.

"You needn't look at me that way! I did it for your own good, if you must know!"

"For my own good," Rothwick said bitterly. "And what good did it do me to have your deuced bosom encroaching upon my visual landscape as soon as I opened my eyes, pray?"

Linnea blushed more red than ever, but this time clearly from anger. "My bosom does not encroach, sirrah! How dare you say something so . . . so vulgar!"

"Vulgar, am I? Well, let me tell you that bosom of yours has been displaying itself in all its bounteous glory ever since we came to this house!"

"It has not. And I resent you speaking of my—my bosom as if it were something creeping about on legs. I have told you I cannot help what my dresses look like, and since you mentioned it some days ago, I have always been wearing my fichu! Encroaching indeed!"

Rothwick looked at her in frustration. How could he tell her that her fichus were as nothing: diaphanous, wanton creations, made to hint and entice—which was far more seductive than blatant revelation? I will strangle my sister, he thought venomously, for getting these dresses.

"Well, you are not wearing one *now,*" he retorted.

Linnea smiled scornfully. "Oh, my, and I thought you quite the ladies' man. Surely you know that fichus are not worn with nightgowns."

"They dam—dashed well should be!" Rothwick grew warm with irritation. He never cursed in front of ladies, but he was coming very close to it.

"You odious—"

Just then a knock sounded and the door opened to admit Potter. He was carrying another set of cloths, which he dropped from apparently nerveless hands when he glanced at his master and mistress. Rothwick noted the valet—mouth agape—took in the rumpled state of their dress and bed; an admiring and respectful light grew in Potter's eye as he regarded his master. It was clear he thought they had engaged in conjugal matters of some heat. Rothwick groaned inwardly at the thought.

"I—that is, I am happy that—" The valet cleared his throat. "I am glad, my lord, to see you wholly recovered and that you have regained all your strength so quickly." His eyes widened at his own words, and his face flushed to his receding hairline. "That is to say—"

"Never mind, Potter. Just pick up the cloths, and I will take care of Lord Rothwick," Linnea said, her haughty voice muffled by the bedclothes that she had pulled up to her eyes. The valet seemed to choke.

"And some breakfast, if you please," Rothwick said as calmly as he could.

"Of toast and tea for His Lordship, Potter," Linnea interjected.

"Of kippers, eggs, and sausage, Potter." Rothwick glared at Linnea, who ignored him.

"Toast and tea, please. I am sure we do not want Lord Rothwick to suffer a relapse."

"Yes, my lady. No, my lord. I mean to say—" The valet clasped the cloths anxiously to his chest and gazed, confused, at the couple.

"Just *leave!*" roared Lord Rothwick.

Potter sprinted out of the room with all the energy of a young hare pursued hotly by hounds, scattering cloths as he went.

Linnea sat up and put her fists to her hips indignantly. "How could you be so *rude* to the poor man? He was only trying to be of service! But that is what you do to people who try to aid you, is it not? *I* certainly have had little thanks for *my* efforts, *if* indeed you have noticed them at all!" She gave a tense shrug of frustration.

But Rothwick was not attending. She had dropped the bedclothes, and her shrug had dislodged her nightgown from one shoulder, revealing an untrammeled expanse of white, soft-looking skin. He went breathless at the sight and knew it was not from influenza. He tore his gaze away and met Linnea's eyes. She was blushing but looked at him uncertainly, not moving.

No. He could not, absolutely he could not. With an agonized groan, Rothwick buried his face in his pillow.

"My lord! William! Are you in pain?" Linnea cried anxiously, her voice full of guilt.

"No," came the muffled reply.

"Is there anything I might do to help you?"

"No. Yes. You may leave me. Please."

"Perhaps you have a headache?"

At the suggestion, Rothwick's head began to pound severely. "Yes."

"Ah! That is it, then. I shall go and ask Potter to bring some willow-bark tea."

"Please do." He felt the mattress move and heard the door close. He pulled his head from the pillow. Linnea was gone.

Rothwick rolled over and gazed at the canopy above. What a farce this marriage was! He had thought a marriage of convenience would be just that—convenient. Well, this one had become damned inconvenient. Married for almost a week, and nothing had come of it. All they wanted now was some uninvited guests to drop in to make their honeymoon a travesty—not that it wasn't already.

He sighed. Oh, Linnea's reputation had been saved,

she had acquired a better station in life, but *he* certainly did not benefit at all. This was not going according to his plans or what he wanted for his life: marriage, an heir or two, a parting of the ways to enjoy his life as it had been before the wedding vows. That was what a marriage of convenience was, after all! Well, he had done the first, but God only knew if he was ever going to get around to the second.

He thought of the purpose of his marriage: the begetting of heirs. The thought of it made his loins twist with frustration. He had looked forward to it; yes, he admitted that the longer he was around Linnea, the more he desired her.

Rothwick knew a twinge of guilt. She was certainly not as beautiful as his former betrothed, Sophia. But Linnea was no antidote and never irritated him with frivolous idiotic chatter. He knew, suddenly, that it would have been a mistake to have married Sophia. She would have bored him in a few weeks; Linnea, he felt, would never bore him. She was intelligent and lovely and could laugh at herself, which he had never known Sophia to do. Linnea had even caused him to laugh at himself, and he had taken no affront at it. He had never known Sophia to laugh, easily and unconstrained, as Linnea did.

Fatigue washed over him, and he closed his eyes. He was, he thought sleepily, coming to care for her, perhaps. That was not a terrible thing, after all. How much better life would be if they went along amicably. But how did she view him? He surfaced from his near drowse at this question. He had no idea what she thought of him . . . well, other than she thought him odious and vulgar. *That* was not very promising, was it? No doubt she showed concern for him because she thought it her wifely duty. He sighed and sank once again into a drowse. Perhaps . . . perhaps he could remedy that somehow. Perhaps she needed to be courted. He would do that . . . as soon as he was well. . . .

By the time Potter came up with Rothwick's tea and toast, the earl was soundly asleep.

As soon as Linnea told the butler to procure some willow-bark tea for his master, she went into her sitting room. It seemed empty for some reason. Perhaps it was, she reflected, that for the whole of last night she had been with Rothwick, and now she only had herself for company. She sat at the window seat and looked out the window. The morning was bright, and the sun shone its way through wispy clouds, illuminating the rolling landscape before her. But Linnea did not see it, for she had turned her mind's eye to thoughts and images of herself and Rothwick walking, conversing, and, yes, sleeping in the same bed.

She did not know quite how it had happened. Oh, not the sleeping in his bed—that was to rid Will of those terrible chills. But she had called him "love" and "my love" the night before, and she knew indeed that he was her love. Linnea reviewed the months past, from the beginning when she thought him rude, arrogant, and impulsive. But later he had shown a different side of himself: he could be kind, generous, and honorable—or as honorable as a rakish sort of man could be. He was also intelligent, had a good sense of humor, and could even be charming. And then, of course, there was his undeniable handsomeness.

Perhaps she would have fallen in love with any man who treated her kindly, but she doubted it. A few gentlemen had come to call at her cousin Boothe's house and, being grudgingly introduced to her, had treated her with respect and kindness. However, she had experienced no tendre for any of them.

In any case, she was married, and though she did not know how, she had slipped from suspicion and dislike to liking and now to love. They had entered into a marriage of convenience, and Rothwick himself had said that he expected little of her except to be his wife and to bear him heirs. She had agreed to it, for it was that or a life of poverty and disgrace. Yet now she felt differently and wanted more.

Linnea's gaze was caught by a sparrow flitting across from one tree to another. In one sense she was as free as that bird, for Rothwick had given her carte blanche to do as she wanted, within reason and decorum. In another sense, however, she was not free at all.

For the thought of loving him and not having that love returned made a dull ache go through her heart, as if steel bands had suddenly squeezed tightly around it. She wondered if she could exist a lifetime, living with him, knowing that perhaps he was fond of her at best, that never had he loved her. Linnea shook her head. No . . . yes . . . perhaps. She did not really know but dreaded thinking the answer might be "no."

She had seen his former betrothed, Sophia Amberley, and knew she, Linnea, could not hold a candle to her in looks or grace of movement. How could he care for her? A despondent ache grew in her chest, but she bit her lip and dismissed it firmly. What could not be made to happen had to be lived with. That was all there was to it.

Yet she could not help wishing, wistfully, that somehow her husband would come to love her.

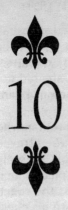

10

Sophia could not help feeling a little anxious. It was afternoon, they were nearing Rothwick's estate, and the coach did not seem at all as if it were going to break. She was not sure how a vehicle should feel when it was about to collapse, but she thought it should be less comfortable than this. It was all Rothwick's fault, she thought, twisting her new lace handkerchief about in her hands.

"He and his interest in new innovations—I am sure he is behind this stupid—what is it called?—macadamed road! Why, it has been almost entirely smooth since our last stop," she grumbled under her breath.

As she gazed out the carriage window, she turned over her problem in her mind. Perhaps she should have had the axle sawn halfway through instead of only one-quarter of the way through. But the wheelwright had been such a bore when he'd demanded almost all of her pin money to do it, and she'd felt just a trifle uneasy when his arguments had begun to draw attention from outside his shop. Then again, she did not want the coach to break down *too* soon; how awkward it would be to walk a great distance!

She cast a discontented glance at her brother, who sat across from her, sleeping as usual when traveling—indeed, with great comfort on this stupidly smooth road. She felt a terrible urge to pinch him if only to evoke some response; but at last the coach gave a huge lurch, and she was flung onto his chest with such force that his response was everything she could have wished for in the last boring hour.

"Gaaaak! Huuuuh!" wheezed Richard. His eyes bulged, and he gasped for breath.

Sophia scrambled off him, but the coach listed in such a way that she moved with far less than her usual grace. She shrieked as her hand encountered broken glass. "Oh! Oh! Richard! Now look at what you've done!"

"Haaak! Whaaah . . . What the devil do you mean, *I've* done?" snapped her brother, his lungs having finally recovered.

"If you hadn't been so beastly as to—to *sit* there making stupid noises instead of *moving,* I would not have cut my hand, and, and oh, oh, oh! I am *bleeding* on my pink muslin!"

"Well, get your handkerchief and staunch it," Richard replied unfeelingly. "And as for it being *my* fault—let me tell you, Sophie, that if you hadn't insisted on making this harebrained journey into the country, we dashed well never would have had this accident in the first place!" Gingerly he reached past the scattered glass and pushed open the coach door.

"Where are you going?" cried Sophia.

"Out of the coach, of course! We can't sit here like a pair of loobies. Lord, but I hope Bobs hasn't been hurt."

Richard stretched his long legs out the door and clambered out inelegantly. The coachman was nowhere near the coach that Richard could see, and the carriage was badly wrecked, not the least because of the horses' frantic bucking. Quickly he went to their heads and soothed them before they did any more damage. When they quieted, he looked about him. A low moan came from a ditch but a few feet from them. Bobs was indeed hurt.

"It's right sorry I am, Master Richard," whispered the man when Richard kneeled beside him. The groom closed his eyes in pain, then opened them again. "I don't know how it happened. We were going merry as you please, and then—"

"Never mind that, man!" exclaimed Richard. "Where are you hurt?"

"My leg, sir." Bobs smiled weakly. "I'm in a mort bit of pain all over, truth to tell."

Richard looked down at the man's legs and paled. One was bent at an unnatural angle, and blood smeared both. "Good God, you need a doctor—and as quickly as we can find one. And Lord only knows when that'll be." He looked back at the coach, where he could hear his sister complaining. "Damn! I wish I could leave my brat of a sister and get you to a doctor, but my father would have my head on a platter if I did."

"I'll do fine, Master Richard—"

"None of that nonsense, Bobs! I've known you since I was first breeched, and I know when you're pitching it rum. Come now, man, I'll help you." He did his best to make his servant comfortable by putting a carriage blanket around him and then turned back to the carriage.

He hesitated a minute before extending his hand to pull Sophia through. For just one moment he savored the idea of leaving her in the coach. But no. He remembered that little bill from the jeweler's for the sapphire set. Sophia still had it somewhere—which meant she still had him securely in the palm of her hand.

As witness this coach ride. Suddenly Sophia had had a desire to travel the roads, and of course Richard—dear brother!—simply *had* to accompany her. Certainly she could not travel alone and defenseless—it was not seemly! Richard privately thought his sister was more than a match for anything she might come across on the road, but then she had mentioned how the night sky reminded her of sapphires. Richard had sighed and given in.

As Richard pulled Sophia from the coach, he braced himself for an onslaught of recriminations, for her expression was one of extreme discontent.

But Sophia said nothing. Richard dared look at her again, and instead of the petulant glances she had been casting him, she was looking over his shoulder in positive delight.

"Oh, Sir James! Sir James Marlowe! How wonderful that you should be on the same road as we! Oh, please help us! We are in a terrible state!"

Richard turned around and saw a horseman riding at an easy pace toward them. When he came near, the man descended from his mount with effortless grace, and Richard could see he was indeed Sir James. Richard was not sure whether to be thankful or vexed, for though he was glad of any aid, he was not at all certain he wanted Sir James to be their rescuer. He eyed the man uncomfortably, for there was something about him that reminded Richard of Sophia, and Richard never felt comfortable around his sister—ever. Marlowe, meanwhile, was bowing over Sophia's hand.

"What is this, fair one?" he asked softly. "It seems you are in considerable distress." He put a quizzing glass to his eye and surveyed the wreckage.

"Oh, Sir James! It is quite vexing! I have cut my hand and bled upon my muslin dress, and the carriage axle broke!" Sophia gazed up at him, her round blue eyes filling slowly with tears.

She did this well, Richard thought disgustedly, for her eyes never reddened, and she always managed to let but one teardrop gather on her lower lashes and fall tastefully upon her cheek. A thought occurred to him, and he stared suspiciously at his sister. How did she know the axle had broken? She had not yet come around the carriage so that she might see the axle. Anyone else would have assumed the wheel had come off and caused the accident, since it was the wheel that was within her sight, not the axle. His hands clenched. By God, if Sophia had orchestrated this accident, he'd, he'd . . . He sighed. He'd do nothing. She still had that bill for the sapphire set. But he was beginning to think it was not worth all this mayhem.

Sir James was gazing at Sophia, an amused half smile on his lips. "A fortunate thing . . . that I came along, of course," he said softly.

Sophia felt that he was about to say something else but was obscurely glad he did not. She was unsure if she should be vexed with him or not, for his voice sounded quite genial, yet the *way* he said things . . . But then Sir James smiled a very charming smile, and Sophia could not help smiling back.

"May I be of service to you, dear lady—and to you, sir?" he said, including Richard in his gaze.

"Well, sir, our groom here is badly injured, and either I must go and leave Sophia here with him while I get a doctor, or we must leave poor Bobs alone here—neither of which would do, you see," replied Richard. He decided that he would have to make do with what was offered him. For all there had been rumors about the man, he never had heard of anything outright scandalous.

Sir James surveyed the scene again with his quizzing glass. "Quite," he said. He returned his gaze to Richard. "Unfortunately, we are far from any inn I know of; we will have to appeal to the good nature of a local landlord or cottager. Unfortunately, again, I am familiar with only a handful of persons in this area."

"There is Staynes," said Sophia.

Richard looked, horrified, at Sophia. No. She wouldn't—she didn't— But he recognized the mulish set of her chin and knew without doubt that she had indeed planned this accident. After she had broken the betrothal, surely she couldn't think she could— It seemed she could.

"Staynes is but a few miles from here," continued Sophia. "We could go there and ask for help."

Sir James's look was bland. "Ah," he said. "I am sure we could."

Sophia's face grew pink. "Well, what else *can* we do? I, for one, do not intend to stay here the rest of the day. And, and—" She looked at Sir James's raised eyebrows and hesitated. "And Bobs *must* be attended to. We cannot spend the time searching the countryside for a doctor when someone at Staynes must know where we can send for one quickly."

"Quite right," replied Sir James, and smiled at her again.

Richard stared at his sister. This was the first time he had ever heard her even imply concern for someone other than herself—much less a servant. He regarded Sir James with more respect.

"Well, then, who should go?" asked Richard. "The left leader is rideable, so I suppose I could take that one." He went to the horse and began unhitching it.

"No, Sir James and I should go," said Sophia. "I know the way to Staynes, it is only a mile away after all, and Bobs would not feel comfortable with a stranger."

Richard was wont to protest, for *he* did not feel comfortable allowing Sophia to leave with Sir James. But she was quite right to a point: she did know the way to Staynes, for she had visited it in the past, where Richard had not.

"Very well, then," Richard replied shortly. "But I will go with you, Sophia, not Sir James." He looked at Sir James apologetically. "I regret imposing on you, sir, but if you would stay with Bobs until I come back, I would be truly grateful."

"But *I* wanted to go with Sir James!" protested Sophia.

"I am flattered," replied Sir James, smiling at her kindly. "Alas, Miss Amberley, my horse is not at all used to carrying two riders." He shook his head regretfully and turned to Richard. "It would be no imposition at all. I will stay here with poor, er, Bobs."

Sophia looked confused, as if she were trying to decide whether to be insulted or pleased. Richard had a delightful feeling that in some manner his sister had been neatly put in her place. He did not know quite how Sir James had done it, but he allowed himself a fleeting sense of bliss in the thought that someone had the upper hand over Sophia.

He nodded his head. "Very well, then, sir," he said. Richard turned to Sophia and tried not to smile at the consternation in her face. He easily led his sister to the horse he had unhitched, for she kept glancing at Sir James.

Sophia was silent during the ride, speaking merely to direct Richard to their destination. For the first time in her life, she was uncertain and unsure of herself. She had had it all planned: The accident, placed conveniently near Staynes, made it necessary they seek help there. Rothwick would be forced by the rules of hospitality to offer them his home for their stay until they could get their carriage repaired. She only needed a little time to show him he had erred greatly in preferring That Woman to her. After all, she was not as beautiful as Sophia, despite her fashionably dark hair. Why, she was a thin, drab creature after all! How easy it would be to show Rothwick the error of his ways when they stood side by side.

She was also sure, when Sir James came upon them, that he had done so in pursuit of her and that he would easily fall in with her plans. But had he? He looked at her in *such* a way when he kissed her hand—it sent shivers down her back—she was sure he had followed her out of town. But then he was *not* accompanying her to Staynes. What did he mean by it? And yet he had told her she was beautiful before—surely he admired her?

Sophia tossed her head. Sir James could pursue her or not; it did not matter to her. *Her* purpose was clear: she *must* make Rothwick see he had made a terrible mistake. Sophia smiled as she pictured it: Rothwick, on bended knee, begging her forgiveness. Rothwick, casting that wretched woman out into the desolate wilderness. And finally, Rothwick avowing his love for Sophia—only to have her spurn him as disdainfully as he had spurned her. Sophia smiled gaily. That Bobs needed special help was fortunate in the extreme; she would make sure they had to stay until he was well enough to move. It would mean she would have more time in which to relish it all.

It was just after an errand to the head gardener that Linnea looked up to see a horse, carrying two riders, coming toward the house. She was certain they had received no notice of visitors; indeed, guests would hardly arrive riding two-a-horse. Perhaps there had been an accident on the road beyond the estate's gates. Hurriedly she instructed a passing maid to take away her gardening basket and went to her rooms as quickly as her still aching foot would allow her.

There Linnea rang for Betty, washed, and made herself as presentable as possible. She was glad, now, that she had all the dresses she needed; how awkward it would be if she had to meet her callers in her old dress!

She heard a knock on her door.

"Enter!"

Bartle entered and bowed gravely. "My lady, there are two young persons requesting Lord Rothwick. I understand his lordship is indisposed at the moment. Shall I refuse them?" His face was a study in stiff formality, and Linnea had come to know this expression as one implying extreme disapproval.

She shook her head. "No, of course not. Please take them to the parlour. I shall meet with them, instead of

Lord Rothwick. I am afraid he is not in a state to see anyone." Will was much better today than he had been last night, with only a headache and fatigue. Indeed, he had been most truculent about taking his medicine, which told her he was well on his way to recovery. However, he need not be bothered with something so easily dealt with as helping travelers. Well, she would go to the two people downstairs and see what she could do.

When Linnea entered the parlour, she recognized Miss Sophia Amberley at once. Miss Amberley's widened eyes and pale face showed clearly that she had not expected the new Lady Rothwick to greet them. To Linnea's dismay, the girl burst into tears.

By the time Sophia entered the front door of Staynes, she was in an extremely poor mood. Sitting two-a-horse was uncomfortable, the road had been dusty, Richard had barely spoken to her the whole way, and she was tired. She noted a mirror on one wall of the parlour, which revealed a most dismaying picture: her muslin dress did indeed have two bloodstains on it, her hair was in disarray, and there was a definite smudge on her nose. This was not the appearance she wished to present to Lord Rothwick. It did not fit at all with the vision she had of drawing him inexorably to her side and then spurning him in her grandest manner. Although there *was* the possibility she could make herself look exceedingly woebegone and gain the earl's pity, thereby drawing him to her in that way.

One look at her hostess entering the parlour, however, had dashed all her dreams to pieces. That *woman* was here! And the ring on her left hand showed she was married—to Rothwick, she was sure. How could it be?

She had not seen any banns published in the *Gazette*, nor any announcement of their marriage. Sophia's face went pale. A special license. They must have been married by special license. And if she had not seen it in the newspaper, it must have been done recently.

To make matters worse, it was just as Richard had told her—the new Lady Rothwick had fashionably dressed dark hair and looked even better than Sophia had thought she had at the inn. It was not fair. It simply was not fair! To her own horror, Sophia's eyes stung, and giving a decided hiccup, she allowed the tears to rush down her cheeks.

"There, there," said a soothing voice close to her. A hand patted her back, a handkerchief was given to her, and she was led to a chair, where she sat automatically. "Do tell me what has happened."

Sophia looked up in astonishment. The woman was actually trying to be kind to her. Or was it kindness? She looked searchingly at Lady Rothwick's face and saw nothing but concern there. Perhaps, thought Sophia, she was just very good at acting sincere when she was not. Yet Sophia felt oddly comforted by the apparent kindness in her hostess's voice, which, to her dismay, made her cry all the harder. How disobliging this woman was to act so very amiable, to be sure!

Richard spoke up. "I am sorry, ma'am, but you must excuse my sister. I am sure she has suffered a shock."

Sophia noted just a hint of doubt in his voice. Well, really! How could he be so unjust! She cried harder.

"We have had a bad accident to our carriage," Richard continued, "and our poor groom has been hurt severely. We have left him with a chance-met acquaintance, but we need to find a way to transport him to a place where we might find a doctor for him."

"Well, you must bring him here, of course!" Linnea said instantly.

Richard looked uneasy. "No, I did not mean—that is to say, we should be quite comfortable at the nearest inn. If you would be so kind as to lend us some servants and a coach or wagon—"

"Nonsense! I understand the closest inn is quite fifteen miles away. We have plenty of room here for you and your servant, until such time as he will be well enough to be up and about."

Sophia stopped crying. Well, it was turning out the way she wanted it to, after all! She managed to smile through her tears, dabbing at her eyes with Lady Rothwick's handkerchief. "Oh, you are so very kind! We would be very happy to visit until poor Bobs is well enough to be moved."

"Dash it all, Sophie—"

Sophia turned a sad and rebuking eye toward her brother. "Richard, I never thought you would put vanity and pride before the welfare of another human being."

"I didn't! That is to say, we can't . . ." A hopeless look came over his face. "Oh, very well. I suppose it is for the best."

Linnea smiled at him. "I understand how it is: one never likes to be beholden to another, is that not so? But if your servant is truly in a bad way, he should be cared for in the best manner possible. He cannot do well if he is jolted for another ten or fifteen miles."

Richard looked at her gratefully. "Thank you, my lady. It is just that—it must be awkward for you at this time to have visitors. . . ." He glanced at Sophia, then trailed off miserably, his face flushed.

An answering pink tinged Linnea's face. "Well, that is of little matter compared to your accident." She pulled the bell-rope. "I shall have Bartle escort you to your rooms, and shall order a large coach to convey your groom here."

Sophia suddenly thought of Sir James Marlowe. She wondered if perhaps she should return to the broken carriage—to see how poor Bobs did, of course. "Lady Rothwick, perhaps after refreshing myself, I should go with the coach—to make sure that our poor Bobs is all right. Also, your coachman will need to know where our carriage is. I could direct him."

She could see Richard eyeing her uneasily. Really! He had no need to look at her that way. She smiled sweetly at Lady Rothwick. "We left a friend of ours there to stay with Bobs, and I would like to thank him for his help."

"I think perhaps I should go along also," said Richard.

"Oh, I don't think so, dear brother," Sophia replied. "After all, you have already expressed your *indebtedness* to our *jewel* of a friend, have you not?" Richard paled, and Sophia was glad to see he had taken her meaning.

Linnea looked from one to another, clearly puzzled. "Whatever you wish. I will make sure a groom accompanies you to help, of course."

"I shall stay here," said Richard, eyeing his sister much in the manner a mouse might eye a snake.

Sophia did not take long at tidying herself. Bobs, after all, should not be kept lying by the road when he could be getting the help he needed. And then there was the intriguing Sir James. She had not really, truly thanked him as she ought.

Rothwick's horses were swift and the large barouche well sprung, so that Sophia arrived at the accident site far sooner than she expected. She looked about eagerly for Sir James but did not see him. Well,

she would have to see to Bobs first, after all, she
thought. A spark of disappointment flared within her.

She alighted from the coach and went to where Bobs
was lying unconscious. Her eyes widened. The groom's
head was resting on a pad made of fine cloth, and a large
swath of what used to be impeccable white linen was tied
around a splint on one battered leg. Sir James's work?

"Yes, I think I managed it quite well, if I say so
myself," said a voice close behind her.

Sophia jumped, startled. She turned to find Sir
James smiling at her. "Oh! It—it is you! I did not see
you. . . ." Miss Amberley found, much to her surprise,
that she could not continue speaking, for her breath
was quite taken away. Sir James stood near her, without his coat or his neckcloth. Sophia had never seen a
gentleman in such a relative state of undress and could
not help staring. His shirt was open, and she could see
that the brown of his skin extended down past his neck
and under the curling brown hair that peeked through
the shirt collar. He had rolled up his sleeves, and his
arms were also sun-darkened—and sinewy, too. His
shirt was tucked into breeches that fit his long, lean,
muscular legs quite well, she saw, now that they were
not obscured by his coat. He must have gone about
without his shirt at some time in his travels, thought
Sophia, to have got so sun-browned . . . all over. . . .

She looked up at him and saw that he gazed, smiling, at her, his eyes amused. She could feel her face
growing quite warm and averted her eyes for a
moment. "I . . . it must have been you who made Bobs
comfortable . . . your coat, and neckcloth. . . ."

Sir James's lips twitched upward in a wry smile.
"Not very comfortable, I am afraid, but at least there is
perhaps less of a chance that the man will be crippled."

Sophia looked back at Bobs. "Of course. How thankful I am you stayed here with him! We—my brother and I—reached Staynes, and Lady Rothwick has offered us her home until Bobs is recovered." Quickly she signaled the Rothwicks' groom and footman to carry Bobs to the barouche.

"How kind of her." Did she only imagine a rebuke in his tone? Sophia glanced at him through her eyelashes. His expression was bland, and there was nothing to indicate what his feelings were.

"Yes, yes, it was kind," she replied. If there was a defiant note in her voice, she did not care. What right did Sir James have to rebuke her, Sophia, after all?

"Do you think, Miss Amberley, that her kindness might extend to my poor self at all?"

Sophia raised her eyes and stared at him. A small, self-deprecating smile hovered about his lips.

"Why, why, I—I do not know. . . ."

"I could repair to the nearest inn, but in my present state of disarray, it would make for a very off appearance, you see."

Sophia's gaze was drawn once again to his open shirt. She did not think he looked at all odd, but perhaps innkeepers did not take well to men without coats.

"I am sure I could ask," she replied. She was rewarded by Sir James's wide smile. She looked toward the barouche. "Perhaps you could ride with me? In case Bobs should fall from the seat, that is. You could tether your horse to the carriage."

"How very thoughtful of you."

A blush rose in Sophia's cheeks. "Not—not at all."

Sir James helped her up into the carriage and then sat down beside her. She had not thought of that—that he would be sitting next to her, even though it obviously had to be, since Bobs occupied the whole of the opposite seat. The groom was pale and unconscious, but she noted he breathed regularly. She felt a twinge of guilt, which she quashed hastily. At least he was alive, thank goodness. Riding in a coach with a dead man would have been quite daunting. She glanced up at the man sitting next to her. Although perhaps with Sir James riding with her, it might not be so horrid. He seemed a very resourceful man; she only had to look at Bobs's leg to see his handiwork. She wondered where he had developed his tan—that is, his talents and his resourcefulness.

"How did you—know what to do? For Bobs, that is?" Sophia felt as if her eyes were drawn magnetically to look at his chest. It was the contrast of white shirt and brown skin that did it, she was sure. Contrasts, she knew, always attracted the eye. She dropped her gaze and caught sight of his hand, lax against his thigh. His hand was also brown—an elegant but strong hand, large and hard looking, but tapered delicately at the fingertips. His fingers looked sensitive, as if they were used to weighing, sensing, touching . . . She made herself glance up at Sir James's face again. He gazed at her, his look almost assessing.

"I learned in India."

"India?"

"Yes. It is a beautiful land, full of mysteries and knowledge, luxury and deprivation, light and dark."

"Contrasts. . . ."

"Quite so." Sir James grinned widely at her, his teeth white against his browned skin. "One learns to be ready for any . . . contingency." His gaze fell to her lips.

Sophia drew in a breath and bit her lip. Perhaps it was a mistake to have asked Sir James to ride with her. She had thought that Bobs—unconscious, to be sure, but undeniably present—would lend respectability to their situation. Indeed, she knew even the highest of sticklers would not object to this mission of mercy, for not only was Bobs in the coach with them, but a groom and a footman accompanied them as well.

Yet the coach had suddenly become very small indeed. Though Bobs was lying directly across from them in the barouche, she thought it would make not one whit of difference to Sir James, whatever he might have in mind. In fact, what *did* he have in mind?

She said nothing, for she felt spellbound, as if the man next to her were an Indian cobra and she his prey. He continued to gaze at her, and her lips. Sophia felt a gentle caress as his fingers traced a line from her earlobe to her chin. His smile faded, and it seemed that an intent expression grew in his eyes. Suddenly his hand was gone from her face, and she felt the absence as if a chill had come upon her.

"And who knows," he continued softly, "what dangers might arise in such a land?"

"D-dangers?" Sophia stammered. She quite forgot what they had been talking about. Oh, India. Yes, they had been talking about India.

"You need not be afraid, Miss Amberley. I learned much while in India, and never did come to any harm. Others did, however, which is how I came to know what to do about your servant's injury."

"Oh, yes, of course." Heavens, what was the matter with her? It was not as if she had never been in a carriage with a gentleman before. But here she was, stammering like a skitter-wit. Sophia gave herself a mental shake. She had come to Staynes for one purpose only: to make Rothwick sorry he had chosen another woman over her. That Sir James had decided to accompany her was fortuitous in the extreme: if she thought through her plan carefully, she could have him play a part in it. She thought of Lady Rothwick and smiled. Ah, yes. Most certainly he could play a part.

She peeked at Sir James through her eyelashes. He seemed to admire her, and that was agreeable. Perhaps she could amuse herself by flirting lightly with him during her visit, in addition to executing her plan. She smiled at him charmingly.

"So tell me, Sir James, are the Indian ladies as lovely as I have heard?"

"Oh, many are. But I found I missed their fairer sisters in England." His gaze flowed over her like the warmth of the sun. Sophia's smile grew more brilliant.

"It was your homesickness, no doubt, that made you think so."

"No." He flashed a wide, white smile at her.

"Ohh . . . Oh! There is Staynes!" Thank heavens, Sophia thought. She did not know how she was going to maintain any control in the conversation if he kept . . . Well, she did not know what it was he kept doing, but it disconcerted her, and she did not like it. Situations, conversations, felt far more comfortable if she held the reins. Sophia slanted a look at Sir James, but he was gazing toward Staynes. She bit her lip. She hoped it would not be difficult to persuade Lady Rothwick to extend her hospitality to Sir James.

It was not difficult at all. When Linnea examined the splint, she eyed Sir James with approval.

"Of course you must stay as well. You cannot continue your journey clad only in your shirtsleeves!"

Sir James bowed. "I thank you, Lady Rothwick. You

are most kind. I will only visit so long as I am without my coat; as soon as it is laundered, I will leave."

Linnea saw Sophia cast Sir James an anxious glance. She almost sighed in relief. It seemed Miss Amberley had formed a tendre for the man; possibly this meant she was at least somewhat recovered from her broken betrothal to Rothwick. She hoped it would make their situation less awkward.

For indeed, Linnea felt the awkwardness acutely. Here was Rothwick's former betrothed, a beautiful young lady, thrust into her, Linnea's, company by a dreadful accident. Linnea would not blame the girl if she thought of her as an interloper, a horrid person who had taken away her former betrothed. She was sure that it was not only the accident that had caused Miss Amberley to burst into tears upon seeing her. What a shock, indeed, it must have been to come upon the woman who had caused so much trouble in her life—and that after less than a month's time.

But if Miss Amberley had an interest in Sir James, perhaps it would not be a bad thing at all to have him stay. Linnea bit her lip guiltily. She was trying to distract her guests, just so she would not have to deal with any unpleasantness. Oh, but she would much rather not have any unpleasantness right now, not with Rothwick recovering from the influenza. Linnea's uneasiness grew as she thought of Rothwick's possible reaction upon finding he had guests. And what if he still had some feelings toward Miss Amberley? Linnea's heart contracted painfully at the idea. She thrust the thought away. These people were in difficult straits. They needed help.

So she smiled at Sir James and said, "Oh, if your business is not urgent, surely you can stay a little longer? I am afraid Miss and Mr. Amberley would feel

quite dull here, for my hus— I have been nursing Lord
Rothwick in his illness, and I would be a sorry conversationalist for you all, rushing back and forth from
sickroom to parlour. Your presence, sir, would add
leavening to our company, I am sure."

Sir James bowed again. "I am honored, ma'am."

"Oh! Is Lord Rothwick ill?" A look of consternation
flashed across Miss Amberley's face.

"Yes, but you need not worry," Linnea replied, and
smiled at her reassuringly. "He is recovering, and I am
sure he shall be up and about in a few days." If, she
thought to herself, he behaves as he ought and does
not arise from bed too soon. She rang the bell for
Bartle and smiled at her guests. "I shall make sure
your rooms are ready for you. Did you have trunks on
your carriage, Mr. Amberley?"

Richard looked up, apparently startled from a brown
study. "Trunks? Oh, yes! We did, just two, I believe."

"Very well, then. I shall have them brought to your
rooms. Meanwhile, do feel free to roam the house and
the estate as you will. There is some fishing to be had
in the lake, and our stable is at your disposal."

After Bartle came to escort them to their rooms,
Linnea slumped down on a chair by the fireplace and
rubbed her eyes wearily. Perhaps she could delay
telling Lord Rothwick about the guests while he stayed
within his rooms. How very awkward it was, to be sure!
Oh, but this marriage of convenience was far from
being convenient. She sighed. Lord knew this honeymoon—if it could even be called that—had not been.

Linnea made herself sit up straight and squared her
shoulders. Well, she would just have to do the best
she could with it, that was all. Certainly nothing worse
could happen.

11

"I beg your pardon?" Rothwick's gruel-filled spoon paused halfway to his mouth, and he stared fixedly at Linnea.

"I . . . I invited the Amberleys and Sir James Marlowe to stay with us for a while," Linnea repeated.

He put down his spoon, gruel untasted. "Why, pray, did you do that? And why did you not ask me first?" The earl's voice was chilly.

Linnea clasped her hands nervously on her lap. The chair in her husband's chambers suddenly felt uncomfortable, and she moved to the edge of it. She looked at Rothwick, sitting up in his bed, a tray in his lap. He did not look pleased. Well, she had not been, either, at first, so she did not blame him. But really! He did not need to be so autocratic. This was her home, too, now, was it not?

"I did not think I needed to ask your permission, my lord," she replied stiffly.

A flash of irritation crossed his face. "This is my home. I should at least be made aware of anything that goes on under its roof. As my wife, you should have told me who was at our door before making any decisions about who is to come and go here."

"If you will remember, my lord, you were asleep yesterday. Their carriage suffered a bad accident, and their groom was badly injured. Sir James sacrificed his coat and neckcloth to make the servant more comfortable, and had no other coat with him. What else was I to do? Tell them to go fifteen miles farther to the nearest inn? I think not!"

Rothwick broke his gaze briefly, and a tinge of pink settled on his cheeks. "Ah, I see. Well, I suppose there was no helping it," he said gruffly.

"No, there was not." Linnea's voice was subdued. She did not look at him. He had made it quite clear, she thought. It was *his* home, not hers. She was his wife and, as such, must consult him on all things and decide none. It rankled, to be sure. She had thought she had left autocracy at her cousin Boothe's house, but she had not, really. Ah, whom was she trying to fool? It was not his arrogance that rankled—she had dealt with that before in other people, and it never left her in the doldrums even if she did not like it. It was the thought that she was here on sufferance, that this was not her home, and that she did not really have a home unless he pleased. And how different was it, in spirit, from her cousin Boothe's house? She thought she had done well here, not interfering—much—in his life. Indeed, she had thought they were rubbing along quite well and had hoped they could become friends.

She bit her lip. Friends. No, more than friends. She had come to love him. He had been kind to her in his way. He was generous with her and gave her more pin money than she could ever use. He had done the honorable thing in his mind by marrying her. Linnea glanced at him, taking in his handsome face—pale from the tail end of his illness, to be sure, but handsome nevertheless. Of course she was attracted to him. Who would not be? Holding him in affection would be an easy thing to do. Affection? No, loving him. Admit it, Linnea, she thought.

She turned so as to hide the blush she was sure had crept to her cheeks. She rose from her chair and took three steps to the chamber door before his voice stopped her.

"Linnea. Don't go."

She turned back. "Is there something you wish?"

"Come here." Rothwick held out his hand to her.

Her eyebrows raised.

"Please."

"Of course." She went to his side.

"I am afraid this gruel has made me quite irritable," said the earl, looking at her with an ingratiating smile.

"Gruel? I doubt it, my lord." Linnea could not totally suppress her own smile, for his had turned quite mischievous.

"Indeed it has. I detest gruel. Therefore, it has made me quite out of sorts, and I proceeded to snap at you for no good reason at all. I would much prefer a good breakfast of ham, eggs, toast, kippers, and perhaps coffee or tea."

"But gruel is *good* for you, my lord." Linnea widened her eyes innocently.

"But it is not *good* for my frame of mind. I could very well become so irritable that it inflames my constitution to the point of fever. In fact, the taste of it has already given me the shivers." He shuddered eloquently. "You see?"

Linnea laughed. "You are as bad as a little boy! Inflame your constitution to a fever, indeed!"

"I do think I am getting worse. . . ." With trembling hands he moved the breakfast tray to the table next to his bed, then slumped down upon his pillows. "Perhaps . . . perhaps you should feel my forehead. . . . Is it warm? Hot, even?" He took her hand and put it to his head. She tried to pull away but was held in a firm grip.

"Oh, good heavens, William! I do not think—"

"I see it all, now. You do not care whether I live or die. . . ."

"Of course I do not want you to die! And how can you be as ill as you say when your hand is holding mine so firmly?"

"It is the rigor of impending death, I assure you," Rothwick said solemnly. He pulled her closer to him and drew her hand to his lips. Eyes twinkling, he took her other hand and dragged her to him until her face was but a few inches from his.

Linnea blushed furiously. She was well nigh on top of him now and could feel his hard body underneath his robe. It made her think of the first night he had been fevered, when she had seen him without any nightclothes. She looked down from his intent gaze, but it only made matters worse. She could see his chest between the collars of his robe, and what she did not see, she could imagine. She looked up at him again.

"I want to express my gratitude for your care of me in my illness," he said, smiling. His breath whispered warmly upon her cheek. "It was very kind." He released her hands and held her waist instead, caressing it lightly.

"I—it was n-nothing, truly," Linnea stammered. The

expression in his eyes was warm and held her spellbound. She could almost imagine some tender feeling existed there—but no, of course not. Pressing her hands against his chest, and trying not to notice what she felt, she pushed herself away.

Or tried to. He pulled her down again.

"It was more than most would do, Linnea. Certainly no one would else would feel obliged to keep me from shivering with the warmth of her own body." Linnea doubted this. She felt his finger trace the contour of her cheek to her lips. It made her breathless, scattering her thoughts.

"Of course she wou— That is, I—I remembered my mother caring for me in a similar way, so I thought perhaps it would help you also."

"And how right you were." Rothwick's eyes grew meditative as he gazed at her. "I do not have a fever now, it seems."

"Yes. . . ."

His finger drew a line from her lips to her chin and down toward her neck. She shivered but could not look away from him. "You do care for me a little, do you not, Linnea?"

"Yes, no, I, I had thought we might become friends, perhaps," Linnea managed to say. "But that was all."

"Friends. How amiable of you." Did his voice grow cool? She was not sure.

"Yes . . . ," she murmured.

"After all, there is no reason we should be at daggers drawn with each other." His finger moved back up her neck again.

"Oh, no. . . ."

"Much better to be friends, don't you think?"

"Oh, yes. . . ."

Suddenly he pulled her fully onto the bed and rolled over. Caught unawares, Linnea found her arms trapped beneath his chest. "I would very much like to be your friend, Linnea."

He smiled at her, and she felt even more breathless. "W-would you . . . ?"

"Yes. I think gratitude for your care in my illness is a good start, is it not?" He dipped his head and kissed her lightly on the cheek.

"Yes. . . ."

"And I am very, very grateful. . . ." Another kiss touched just beneath her ear. Linnea closed her eyes.

"Yes. . . ."

"Grateful that I am getting well again. . . ." The next kiss went lower to her neck.

"Yes," she breathed. She could feel his lips move up again, leaving a tingling trail behind.

"And stronger. . . ." Rothwick's mouth moved to her cheek again, at one corner of her lips.

"Mmmm. . . ."

"Much, much better. . . ." And finally, finally, his lips touched hers.

Linnea sighed, and her hands clutched the lapels of his robe. The kiss was soft and tender and deep, and she wished it would go on forever. But he moved from her mouth, and his lips explored the tender flesh just under her chin and her throat.

"So much better, my dear . . ." Rothwick moved aside the fichu of her morning dress, kissing the skin he uncovered.

"Yes. . . ."

". . . that I think I could certainly manage a good breakfast of ham, eggs, and kippers," he whispered.

"Yes. . . ."

"I am glad you agree," he said softly. With a last lingering kiss on her lips, he rose and moved off the bed.

Linnea blinked and sat up abruptly. Rothwick was straightening his robe, and at her movement he grinned at her. "I would welcome your presence at the breakfast table, of course."

"But, but, you cannot—"

"Of course I can. You see me on my feet, do you not? I am not faint, nor do I tremble from ague. Ergo, I am quite well, and need no more coddling."

A fiery light flared in Linnea's eyes. "You, you—"

Rothwick smiled kindly at her. "Yes?"

"Ohhhh! You odious man!"

He furrowed his brow, apparently concerned. "You have said that before. Do you truly find me odious?"

"No. Yes! Yes, I do! How dare you kiss me just to get kippers!"

The earl shrugged helplessly. "You behold a man desperate in his hunger. What could I do? You were a veritable dragon, keeping me from my rightful comestible treasures. I only used what poor weapons I had."

"You think you can overcome me with your kisses, do you?"

Rothwick gazed at her, seeming to consider this. "Yes," he said after a pause. "I do."

Linnea gasped in outrage, leaped off the bed, and stumbled when she felt a protesting sting of pain through her injured ankle. She straightened herself and tried to ignore it. "And this is what I receive for nursing you back to health—"

"Yes, it is," Rothwick cut in, gazing at her lips and smiling wickedly. Linnea felt her face flame. "I said I was grateful, did I not?" He pulled the bell-rope. "It will feel good to dress in a civilized fashion again, I think."

She stared at him, frustrated. It seemed he would do anything to get what he wished, will she, nil she, and never mind what she thought or felt. She turned and hobbled furiously toward the door.

"And do tuck in your fichu properly," he called after her as she grasped and turned the knob. "It is all askew."

Linnea went through and slammed the door.

As soon as Linnea left, Rothwick sat down on a chair by the window. Ye gods, but he was as weak as a kitten. He was better, however, and not nearly as tired as he'd been the day before. And he'd be damned if he was going to stay abed when they had guests! Especially when one of them was Sophia Amberley.

To tell the truth, he'd liefer stay in his chambers than confront her again, for he did not want a repeat of their last encounter. But if her reaction at the inn was any indication, it would be best that Linnea not have to face her slights alone. After all, this had not been her fault. And who knew what Sophia's influence on the other two guests would be?

Then, too, he was bored staying in bed, with nothing to stare at but the four walls and a windowed landscape with which he was now all too familiar. There was a limit to the number of books he could read, and there was nothing else he could do while in bed. He grinned a little, thinking of Linnea. Lord, but he had put her in a tizzy! There was something about her—perhaps her seriousness and wariness—that made him want to tease her unmercifully and bring a smile or laugh to her lips. Rothwick's grin turned wry. Well, he hadn't made her laugh this time, to be sure!

And there was the trouble. He wanted to make her

trust him, but every time he was at the point of doing so, a devil seemed to take his tongue and either give her a prosy lecture or tease her to the point of wrath. Well, perhaps it was partly her fault, after all, and certainly Lydia's! If his sister had not chosen all those tantalizing gowns, he would not be so inclined to want to take them off Linnea as soon as he saw her. And if Linnea had not insisted on keeping him in cotton-wool, he would be much less irritable and much less inclined to tease her or give her a lecture against which even he would rebel.

Rothwick sighed and stood up, this time slowly. His head had stopped aching today, but he needed to move with care. The sudden movement from the bed earlier had brought on a dizziness that had nearly overset him.

When Potter came in—upon Rothwick's answer to his knock, and cautiously this time—he smiled at his master in apparent relief.

"The dark grey jacket, the blue waistcoat, and a black neckcloth, I believe, would be appropriate today, Potter."

"Of course, my lord, very good." He looked at Rothwick expectantly. "And a shave, sir?"

The earl felt his chin ruefully. "Most definitely a shave."

Potter grinned. "Yes, my lord, I shall do so straight away!"

As the valet went to get the shaving implements, Rothwick sighed. He thought about his guests. For all that he was glad to be up and about, he wished he did not have to see anyone except perhaps Linnea. What a damned inconvenience it all was!

*   *   *

Walking upon the garden path with a frown upon her brow, Sophia paid only absent attention to the ordered rows of flowers and shrubbery. Her mouth pouted in discontent as she thought of her plans. How inconvenient it was that Rothwick was ill! There was little she could do until he appeared, and how tedious it was to have to wait until he was well. But she was fairly sure that Bobs's broken leg would take longer to heal than Rothwick's influenza. Did not Lady Rothwick—That Woman—say he was recovering?

Lady Rothwick. . . . Sophia gnawed her lower lip in thought. Perhaps there was something she could do in that direction. Perhaps if Rothwick were shown what a scheming adventuress That Woman no doubt was, then he would be even more repentant when she spurned him at the end. Sophia's face brightened. Yes, of course! He would be miserable tied to that woman and regret for the rest of his life that he had once preferred Lady Rothwick instead of Sophia.

Sighing happily, Sophia bent her mind on how to accomplish it. Well, there was Sir James Marlowe. She hesitated for a moment, feeling uneasy, then dismissed it. Sir James would do as she wished, she was sure. Did she not have a special charm over men, after all? She rarely had any difficulty at all getting gentlemen to do as she wished. Requesting Sir James to focus his attentions on Lady Rothwick should be easy. Having a great deal of finesse, he could easily move into her good graces, and he would . . .

What would he do? The conclusion to which Sophia came made her feel rather odd. He would run off with her, of course, thereby showing Rothwick that his wife was unworthy, no more than a trollop. Sophia bit her lip again, this time in consternation. Surely she did not

have to sacrifice Sir James to such a thing? Perhaps
Richard could do it. But she shook her head. No. He
was a graceless gudgeon and had no finesse whatsoever. He would botch it, and all her plans would be for
naught. It must be Sir James. She sighed, shaking her
head. How unpleasant pursuing justice was, to be sure!

"A sigh, my dear Miss Amberley? In such a lovely
garden, too."

Sophia whirled around. She had thought herself
quite alone in the garden. "Sir James! You startled me."
Her heart was beating quite fast—with surprise, she
was sure. "I thought you might have left already, for I
had heard your clothes have been washed and
mended." And indeed he was looking quite handsome
in his newly cleaned clothes—or would have been, of
course, if he were not so brown. But it was not his fault
that the Indian sun was so harsh.

"I am sorry, ma'am," he said, but his voice was
more caressing than apologetic. "I cannot seem to
break my habit of walking quietly. All that hunting in
India, you see."

"Yes, yes, of course," Sophia replied. "But this is not
India, and I think you must change your ways a bit."

"Ah. Shall I stomp about, then, ma'am, before I
approach the prey—er, person?"

Sophia laughed. "Prey, am I? Well, let me tell you,
sir, I am not so easily caught!" She cast a glance at him
through her eyelashes. "And why is it that you see me
as something to be hunted?"

"Sheer instinct, of course. The Hindus believe that
one lives many lifetimes in the form of animals of
increasing intelligence, until one becomes human. I
think my last life must have been as a hunter of some
sort." He flashed a wide white grin at her.

Averting her gaze, Sophia thought that he must indeed have been a hunter—a large cat, perhaps a tiger or, better yet, a panther. A silent panther.

"So you think of people in general as prey of some kind?" she replied.

"No, not all. I am afraid I am quite particular in my tastes."

They walked along the path, silent for a few moments, for Sophia could not think of what to say. She was flattered that he should think of her as someone to be pursued. But as prey! She shivered. She did not know if she liked that—it was, to say the least, unsettling. It made her feel as if Sir James would suddenly pounce on her, and she was not sure if she would like this or not.

"Perhaps we should return to the house," Sir James said in a solicitous voice. "It seems you have a chill."

"Oh, no, I assure you I am quite warm," Sophia said hurriedly, for she did not want him to leave just yet. "And walking in these lovely gardens is so very pleasant on such a day as this, do you not agree?"

Sir James smiled at her, and an admiring look appeared in his eyes. They had stopped by a rosebush, full of flowers that scented the air with their perfume. He picked one and held it to his nose, then held out the flower to her. "Very pleasant indeed, Miss Amberley."

Sophia smiled and relaxed, deigning to take the rose, and began to walk again. What nonsense she was imagining today! Comparing Sir James to a panther, indeed! He was quite ordinary —except for his tendency to flirt (and that was not a bad thing, after all) and his resourcefulness. She paused before saying: "And what particular sort of people would you . . . pursue? What of someone like, oh, Lady Rothwick, for example?"

The man beside Sophia bent a thoughtful gaze upon her. "Oh, I suppose she might do. I would have to cultivate her acquaintance before I knew."

"Poor lady! I am afraid she must feel quite alone, despite being newly married, and no doubt feeling full of ennui. It cannot be pleasant to have Lord Rothwick ill, and the house so scarce of company. What is she to do in such a large, empty place? I am certain the neighbors have not come to call yet. I cannot help thinking she must be wanting some company. Indeed, perhaps it was a fortunate thing for her we happened on Staynes at just this time." She noted they were walking toward some tall hedges, and a sense of unease rose in her. As they were now, they were in plain sight of the house, and thus she needed no chaperone. Perhaps they would not approach the hedges.

"Yes, I imagine it should be fortunate," replied Sir James.

Sophia looked at him suspiciously, distracted from her unease. She thought she had heard just the slightest tremor in his voice. Was he laughing at her? But his expression was quite bland, and he only raised his eyebrows questioningly in response to her gaze.

"What Lady Rothwick needs," continued Sophia, "is companionship. Do you not think so?"

"Unless one is a hermit, one usually prefers the company of others."

"Well, then! Perhaps you should think about cultivating hers."

"I?" Sir James turned and looked at her in apparent astonishment.

"Why not? You are a personable gentleman. I think she would welcome your attentions."

He stared at her for a few moments, an indecipherable

expression crossing his face. "I am gratified you find me personable, Miss Amberley. But, alas, I am afraid you forget I am soon to leave. Cultivation of anything is most difficult from a long distance."

Sophia felt her heart sink. "Are . . . are you going far away, then? I thought . . . I thought you might stay near for a while. Oh, not here at Staynes, to be sure, but not so far that you cannot come to call."

Sir James smiled slightly. "I suppose I could be persuaded."

"What . . . what would persuade you, then?" Sophia said, looking down at the rose she held in her hand. His voice had been intimate, and she was suddenly afraid of looking at him. She felt a finger under her chin, making her gaze rise to his.

"A kiss, Miss Amberley." His smile had widened, so that his teeth showed white against his sun-darkened skin. It left her breathless, at once alarmed and excited.

"I, I—No. Really, Sir James, what you suggest is quite beyond the bounds of propriety," she said as primly as she could. But somehow Sophia could not take her gaze from his face. There was an intent, almost feral look in his eyes.

"I am afraid I am quite unfamiliar with the bounds of propriety. The lack occurs, you know, when one has been away from one's home country for so long."

"D-does it? I . . . I suppose you should learn, then, Sir James."

"Perhaps you can teach me."

She should have moved away from him, but she felt she could not. Convulsively she clutched the rose in her hand, and a thorn pushed through her glove to her skin. "Oh! Oh, I am afraid I have hurt myself!" There, she thought, half relieved that the pain had cleared her mind. That should distract him. He cannot want to kiss a lady who may bleed upon his freshly washed clothes. Sophia was finally able to look away from him and noticed that they were behind the tall hedges, quite hidden from the house. She really should not be here with him. What if someone should notice?

"I am sorry." Sir James took her hand in his, turning it so that she could see the blood staining her York tan glove. Slowly, carefully, he pulled off her glove. He slipped one finger off at a time, and Sophia could not help staring at him as he did so. He pulled out a handkerchief and dabbed the cut. His clasp was warm as he wiped the blood away. He lifted the palm of her hand to his lips and kissed it. He smiled at her. "It is the least I can do, is it not?" He kissed again, this time on the inner, soft part of her wrist.

Sophia watched, unwillingly fascinated. He lifted his head, looking at her, and there was something compelling in his gaze. He had green eyes, she noted. Green like a cat's.

"Kiss me, Sophia."

She said nothing as he came closer and then could not say anything even if she chose. Sir James's lips were soft upon hers, then more firm. She gasped, and his kiss grew deeper. Sophia had allowed a few select admirers to kiss her before, but never had she been compelled to—or at least felt she was compelled to take a kiss. And those past kisses had never been like this. *You shouldn't, oh, you shouldn't,* whispered a conscience she had forgotten some years ago. *Oh, no, you definitely should not,* her mind echoed, and her arms finally responded. She pushed against his chest, but he did not let her go until her arms weakened at last and she succumbed once more to his lips. Only then did he draw away from her.

Putting her fingers to her lips, Sophia stared at Sir James. He smiled at her, but his gaze settled upon her lips, as if he thought to kiss her again. No. She could not let him do that again. It was not in her plans. And if word of this ever got back to anyone in the house, she could not follow through with her scheme to make Rothwick regret anything at all. She put up her chin.

"Are you persuaded now, Sir James?"

For one moment Sophia thought an angry look sparked in his eyes, but it was so fleeting she could not tell. There was only his smile, and she could not discern anything from that.

"Persuaded? I think so."

"And you will come to call, and cultivate Lady Rothwick's acquaintance?"

His smile grew wider. "Why not?"

She gave her most brilliant smile in return. "You are so very kind, Sir James. Lady Rothwick will appreciate your attentions, I am certain." She took his arm, and they turned away from behind the hedges. Sophia looked about her and saw that there was no one near, nor did she see anyone at the windows of the house.

"Am I kind? You flatter me, my dear Miss Amberley."

Sophia glanced up at him, but he only gave her an amused look. He must know she wanted him to ruin Lady Rothwick's reputation, and she was sure he would do so—was she not expert at making others do as she willed? She gazed at the rose she still held in her handkerchief-wrapped hand. But somehow she felt perhaps that there was more to Sir James than she had thought at first. He would need watching. She smiled at him. She would watch him carefully, herself.

*   *   *

Sir James patted his horse on the neck and absently gave the gelding a little piece of sugar. He gazed out of the stable, and he could see Sophia going into the house. He grinned. The little witch! He did not remember the last time he had been so entertained. He had been on the point of returning to India not so long ago; he'd been bored to the point of pain for the year he had been in London. Oh, he had thought he would welcome the return, for this time he was no longer penniless but a rich man. There was far more with which to amuse oneself when one had a great deal of money.

But there was little excitement to be had. India had been different. It was hot, wild, and one had to use one's wits to the fullest to survive. There was a certain electric edginess on which he thrived when he hunted the tiger or other wild beasts. It was not the kill he enjoyed, but the hunt itself—indeed, he often regretted the sacrifice of these savage and wonderful animals. Even more exciting than that was using one's wits to maneuver around the animal. It was not unlike the hunt for fortune and using one's wits to outmaneuver one's competitors. As a result of his keen business insight, he had amassed a goodly fortune and enjoyed himself all the while.

But now the only amusement he had been able to find was the hunt known as the Season in London. The tables had been turned on him; once the society matrons and their marriageable daughters got wind of his fortune, he had become the prey instead of the predator. This had amused him greatly. He had admittance to Almack's by his subtle and not-so-subtle flattery of the patronesses. Quite aware that he was entering the portals of the marriage mart, he had let himself be lured by the flutter of an eyelash and learned the messages the movement of a fan could send.

Never, of course, to be trapped. He had gained himself a slightly rakish reputation after a few bold damsels had learned that while he was quite adept at lovemaking in secluded places, he was just as adept at avoiding a compromising scene. He was diverted by the lady of the day, and when the next day arrived, there would be another. But he was becoming bored with that, as well.

Until now. Now there was Miss Sophia Amberley, who laid no traps for him at all, or if she did, it was for her own tortuous and vengeful plans rather than for marriage. He had at first thought she was yet another lovely but insipid little debutante, with her halo of golden-blond hair and large, kittenlike blue eyes. Indeed, he had almost not bothered to strike up her acquaintance, until at the musicale she'd given him a look so full of offended hauteur that he'd been intrigued. He'd learned she was a vain creature, but she had an excuse, he thought. She was extraordinarily beautiful, even at close range. And then he found how delicately she could flirt and manipulate at the same time, and he'd become intrigued. It had been enormously amusing to watch her trying to get him to tell her about Lady Ackleby. He had relented and told her of the lady's liaisons, of course, for she deserved some reward for her cleverness.

As he gave his horse a last pat and left the stables to seek out his hostess and take his leave, Sir James felt he must pursue Miss Amberley's acquaintance further. Though he knew full well she intended to gain some revenge on her former betrothed, he had felt a sudden spurt of anger at her proposal that he—in effect—seduce Lady Rothwick. He smiled at himself ruefully. Perhaps he was becoming vain himself; he had dallied with so many ladies since his return to England that he wholly expected Miss Amberley to cast out lures in his direction as well. But she had not. She had only used her wiles with the thought that he would do as she bade. He was surprised at his sense of chagrin at the thought, then chuckled. Ah, perhaps he was getting to the age when a man had thoughts of settling upon his own estates. But if he was, they were thoughts only. He had no intention of marrying some insipid little debutante from Almack's—or anyone else, for that matter. Seduction, however . . .

Sir James's grin grew wider. Miss Amberley needed a little lesson. The kiss he had pressed on her, he felt, was not enough. Certainly it was not enough for him. He chuckled to himself again. He could not help admiring her determined recovery after their kiss, but she was too used to having the upper hand. One needed only to look at her hapless brother, and the bedazzled and anxious faces of her suitors in London, to see that. Oh, yes, definitely he would pay a good deal of attention to Lady Rothwick and see how Miss Amberley liked it.

"Lady Rothwick?"

Linnea jumped, startled. She turned to find Sir James Marlowe bowing gracefully to her. She had been absorbed in sketching a plan of the little Grecian gazebo—more absorbed than she thought, for she had not heard him come up behind her.

"I am sorry if I startled you, ma'am," he said politely.

She smiled. "I was only a little startled, so I will readily forgive you, Sir James. Is there something I may do for you?"

"I am merely here to take my leave, my lady. I am afraid I must retire to my hunting box, as I have promised a few friends some sport there."

Linnea felt a little vexed, though she did not show it. Though she knew he did not have any real excuse for staying, she had hoped he would be inclined to set forth perhaps the next day. Now there would be one less gentleman to entertain Miss Amberley.

Oh, of what use were her hopes, after all? She knew that since Rothwick so stubbornly insisted on rising, he would be available to entertain guests, so there was no sense in thinking another gentleman would be needed to keep the number of dinner guests even. She admitted to herself that she could not stop the natural course of things. A sense of despondency crept into her heart. This was a marriage of convenience, regardless of what Will said about becoming friends. She had heard that spouses often agreed to go their own ways in such a marriage, often in a friendly manner. Linnea dismissed these thoughts from her mind. This was not the time to mull over what was no doubt a foregone outcome. She looked up at Sir James with a smile.

"We will be quite sorry to see you leave, to be sure. You have been of such kind help to Mr. and Miss Amberley. Of course, you must see to your guests. However, I hope you will come again to call."

"You are most gracious, Lady Rothwick. My hunting box is a mere fifteen miles away, so I would be pleased to call upon you . . . and your guests." He bowed once again, this time over her hand. He held her hand for longer than Linnea felt comfortable. Just as she was about to pull away, he released her hand, rising, and it seemed that the assessing glance he gave her looked deep into her soul. Then he smiled once more, and

Linnea let out a breath she was not aware she had been holding.

Heavens, but she was becoming fanciful! His smile now was merely courteous, and his eyes held only a friendly expression. Yesterday he had in passing said that he had lived in India for a long while; no doubt he had forgotten the proper length of time to hold a lady's hand.

Linnea inclined her head politely, and with a wider grin, he took his leave. She followed him with her gaze as he left, a perplexed frown on her brow. The man was something of a puzzle, she thought. He did not say much, but there seemed to be a world of meaning behind what he *did* say. She shook her head. It was not her concern. If Sir James came to call, he would come, no doubt, to see Miss Amberley. And that, she was sure, would be a relief.

12

Relief, however, was not the emotion that passed through Sophia's heart as she gazed at Sir James taking leave of their hostess. She had come up to her chambers to wash her face and cool her heated cheeks after her walk with him, and she could easily look out the windows and see him below with Lady Rothwick. She knew it was proper for him to bow over Lady Rothwick's hand when taking his leave. But it seemed to her that he held his hostess's hand a trifle too long for mere politeness.

Sophia lifted her chin in defiance. Well, he was doing what she wanted him to do. In truth, she was glad he had taken to carrying out her instructions so quickly. Not only that, she thought even more truculently, but she would be ecstatic when he carried off Lady Rothwick and proved to all and sundry that the woman was not worth the title she bore. Oh, she was not yet absolutely happy now, but that was only because her business had not come to its inevitable conclusion.

In fact, she hadn't seen Lord Rothwick yet. Sophia frowned. She should find him. He had yet to see her in her ravishing periwinkle-blue gown. Perhaps he would appear at supper, but the sooner her plans were put into action, the better it would be. Yes. She would definitely seek him out.

After a last look in the cheval mirror in her bedchamber, Sophia emerged, satisfied that she looked absolutely beautiful. Now where would Rothwick be?

Ah, the library. He was fond of books, she knew, and if he was just recovering from his illness, he would most likely not go about his estates much. It would be the perfect place for him to stave off boredom and rest at the same time.

Sophia was quite right.

Lord Rothwick had intended to take a walk in the gardens for some fresh air but found that walking down the long hall and down the stairs made him frustratingly fatigued. Muttering a curse as a wave of dizziness came over him, he closed his eyes and leaned against the wall. He took a deep breath, opened his eyes again, and noticed that he was right next to the library. Well, the library was a bright room with comfortable chairs. At least he could open a window and read for a while until he revived. And *then* make his way to the gardens.

He had just selected Fielding's *Tom Jones* and settled onto his favorite wing chair when he heard the door open. He suppressed a sigh. Perhaps if he made no sound and sat quietly, the intruder would not notice he was there and go away.

But of course not. The intruder came around the chair, and he saw it was Sophia. She saw him, smiled, and he let out the sigh he had suppressed. Well, there was no escaping it, Rothwick thought. Better to get over the initial awkwardness now and try to establish a foundation of civility.

"Oh, Lord Rothwick! I am sorry if I have disturbed you! Shall I leave?" Sophia looked at him wide-eyed.

Suppressing an urge to say "Yes," the earl made himself rise from his chair, bow over her hand, and say: "No, no, not at all. Did you wish a book to read?"

Sophia raised her eyes to the shelves of books that extended from floor to ceiling. She shuddered and pulled her shawl over her shoulders.

"Not at this moment, thank you, my lord. I . . . I had heard the library windows opened to a excellent view of the lake and surrounding landscape, so I thought perhaps I would see for myself what it looked like."

Rothwick went to the window. He pulled back the curtains and gazed out at the landscape, dim now, though the sun was trying to fight its way through the clouds. "It is pleasant. I am quite used to it, so it has no surprises for me. However, I have whiled away many hours here, alternately reading and looking at the lake, blessedly solitary." He stopped short and cursed himself. Implying that he wanted to be alone—regardless of his preference for solitude —was positively boorish. He had become so used to speaking freely in Linnea's company that he'd forgotten one must be forever complimentary to Sophia. He turned back to her with an apologetic look.

Sophia looked at him and pouted. "Ah, my lord, I see you have not been truthful to me. If you wished me to leave, you should have said so."

"I am sorry, Miss Amberley. But do stay. There is little excuse for my words except that I am still rather fatigued from my recent illness." He smiled and put as much persuasiveness in it as he could muster.

A dimple appeared in Sophia's cheek, and her eyes brightened. "Oh, I thought that must have been it. I am so sorry that you have been ill. It must have been exceedingly tedious—and lonely—for you."

"Not at all. I have had a good nurse in Lady Rothwick, to be sure."

"Oh, nursing! I daresay Lady Rothwick did only what she should have in repayment for your saving her reputation."

Rothwick caught himself before he snapped at her and made his voice fairly neutral. "As distasteful as it is for me to mention it, it was not her fault that she almost lost her good name."

Sophia smiled up at him. "You are so kind, my lord. Most gentlemen, I am sure, would not have been so generous."

He gazed at her coolly for a long moment before turning to look out the window. "You flatter me," he said.

"Oh, no, my lord. I have always known you to be a kind gentleman."

Good God, thought Rothwick. And to think he had been within aim's ace of marrying this chit. She was as shallow as a birdbath. She had not one thought that perhaps it was up to him to make recompense to Linnea and not the other way around. Yet she had certainly thought he was grievously at fault for her own injury when she had found him at the inn with Linnea.

He had thought of marrying Sophia with the purpose of getting heirs; she was young and had many childbearing years ahead of her. But the earl had not thought of how he would spend his time with her or that it was wholly possible to have but one person for company for more than a few days.

He thought of Linnea, but five years older than Sophia, and how different they were. He glanced at the girl beside him and acknowledged that she was beautiful; but beyond that, what else was there? He reviewed the many times he had danced with her, or taken her into supper many months ago, and could not think of anything she had said worth remembering.

With Linnea, however, he felt he would never be bored. If he wished to talk of serious matters, she would do so and with a certain wit and depth of insight. If he wished some levity, why, then he need only tease her out of her seriousness and make her laugh—or run off in a high dudgeon. He smiled to himself at the thought.

"I see by your smile you must be feeling better. Shall we see you at supper tonight?" Sophia had a hopeful look on her face.

"To be sure, I would not miss your company for the world," he replied as gallantly as he could, and bowed over her hand. He heard the door creak.

"Oh!" came a voice at the door.

Both Rothwick and Sophia turned to look. Linnea stood at the threshold of the library, gazing at them in consternation. Her face quickly became smooth, and then she smiled.

"I am so sorry! I saw the open door and I did not think anyone was within. Please excuse me." She turned to leave.

"No, Linnea, please stay," said Rothwick, extending his hand. Linnea turned back—reluctantly, it seemed.

She gazed at him attentively. "I was just telling Miss Amberley that I shall be joining you all at supper tonight."

"There will be no gruel at supper, my lord," Linnea replied gravely. "You shall have to do without."

"Thank heavens." Rothwick laughed and was rewarded by a small smile that lifted his lady's lips momentarily.

Sophia gazed from one to another. She could not help being aware of the ease between them, as if—as if they had been married a decade rather than a week. How had it come about? The woman was not as beautiful as she, Sophia, was. Oh, she had dressed herself finely, and perhaps she did not look as pale as she had before, but there could be no comparison! Rothwick should not have looked at the woman as if he *liked* to look upon her; his attention should have been on Sophia instead.

"How fortunate it is that I was able to persuade Lord Rothwick to join us tonight," Sophia remarked.

The two turned to look at her, as if surprised to see her still there. Why, it seemed they had forgot her very presence for a moment! Sophia could feel her face growing warm with affront, but then she noticed the suddenly unhappy glance Lady Rothwick cast at her husband and the look of frustration on Rothwick's face. Well, Sophia thought, gratified. Things were not absolutely wonderful for them, it seemed. She would leave them and let them stew in their uneasiness now.

"Oh, I hope you will excuse me." Sophia let her shawl trail elegantly behind her as she moved away from them. "I believe I should look to see how poor Bobs does. I would not want to impose on your hospitality for too long." She smiled at them and went out the library door.

Linnea looked at Sophia's retreating figure and

sighed. It was as she thought. The smile on Rothwick's face, his charming words, his elegant bow over Miss Amberley's hand: all these showed her that he was still in love with her. How could he not be? The girl was beautiful. She turned to look at her husband and gave him a stiff smile. She could not remember if he had ever said anything as charming to her. He had teased, he had confused her, he had made her laugh, but soft words . . . ? She thought not. She fingered the letter she had in her hand. It was from Miss Brinkley, her former schoolmistress, inviting her to visit should she pass through Bath at some time. Perhaps this would be a good thing to do. Perhaps she would be able to clear her mind if she were away from William for a short time. Certainly it seemed as if a fog came over her brain whenever he was near. And they had a marriage of convenience, did they not? Surely it would be permissible for her to see a friend on her own.

"I am truly better, Linnea," said Rothwick.

She looked up, startled out of her thoughts. "Oh, of course. I can see that." Her smile was constrained as she continued. "And I know I have been coddling you overmuch. I was only trying to be useful. I—we shall be glad to have you for supper at last. Good day, my lord." Rothwick took a step forward, but Linnea backed away toward the door, gave one last uncertain smile, and limped out of the library.

The earl sighed and dropped the hand he had raised to stay her. She was skittish again. And finding him with Sophia helped not one bit, he was sure. He looked around the library, at the book he had laid down on the table beside his chair, and then out the window. The sun had broken out through the clouds at last, and the sight gave him new vigour. Rothwick stretched his arms, feeling the muscles pull and some of his joints crackle. He had been in bed too long. Surely going out into the fresh air for some exercise would do him good. He would do that for a few hours each day to get his strength back.

"Must you play such dreary music?" Richard growled. He eyed his sister with discontent, a day later. Sophia made a lovely picture at the pianoforte, with the late afternoon sun streaming down upon her golden hair and reflecting the coral pink of her muslin round gown onto her cheeks. She merely looked at him, wide-eyed, and pounded upon the keyboard with more enthusiasm, making the room echo with dirgelike notes.

He gave it up. Indeed, he did not know why he tried to put any control over his sister. It was useless. He should have learned that by this time. Richard shrugged and slumped farther onto the chair. God, but staying at Staynes was tedious! Rothwick was civil enough—even cordial—but Richard could see that the man was not totally well and needed to rest more than he let on. So he generally tried to stay out of the earl's way and occupy himself with roaming the estate, looking in on Bobs, and hoping that the groom would hurry up and become better so that there would be no excuse to stay on.

There was not even the chance that he could find the bill for the sapphire set. Twice he had tried to go through his sister's chambers. The first time he had had to dive under the bed when a maid had come to change the bed linens and had a devil of a time trying not to sneeze when he had breathed in a noseful of dust. The second time he had been able to go through her wardrobe and chest of drawers, but there was nothing amongst her things except frippery little items she always carried with her when she traveled. He sighed. No doubt Sophia's abigail still had the bill in her safekeeping, but Murphy was not here this time.

Richard's gaze went toward the window, and he sat to attention.

"Hallo! It looks as if a caller has come." He saw a curricle breeze up the drive to Staynes, then recognized the figure within. "I do believe it's Sir James Marlowe, Sophie."

The mournful notes from the pianoforte ceased momentarily and then started up again. Richard slid a look at Sophia. She was obviously trying not to look eager, but he could see her flicking glances toward the window, as if she wished she could see out from where she was. They were in the parlour, and Richard fully expected the guest to appear at the door within a few moments.

So, apparently, did Sophia. Her glances soon left the window to settle on the door. But time went by, and no butler appeared to announce Sir James; neither did their host or hostess enter the room. Sophia bit her lip, and Richard noticed it with a certain glee. It seemed Sir James was not so easily led. Sophia left off playing the pianoforte and joined her brother at the window.

"I wonder what is delaying Sir James?" she murmured carelessly.

Her brother grinned. "Oh, I am sure he is talking with Lord or Lady Rothwick about estate matters or such."

"Well, surely that cannot take up all his time!" Sophia turned away from window. "No doubt he will weary of such talk soon, and will want to see me."

"Why in the world would he want to see you?" Richard wondered if there was something he had missed between the two. Had he not noticed an elusive similarity between his sister and Sir James? No. Surely there was nothing in it. Why, hadn't Sir James put Sophia neatly into her place not a few days ago?

Sophia looked at him with surprised eyes. "Why, of course he will want to see me!"

"Don't be so sure of that, dear sister! Not every man will come to heel at your whim."

A complacent smile touched her lips. Richard grimaced. Good God, but Sophia was disgustingly vain! He wished fervently that Sir James would send her to *point non plus* in the very near future. He sighed. Doubtful, that. No one besides himself had yet seen past her beauty. He turned and looked out the window again, and a slow grin grew on his face.

"My, my. It seems Sir James is walking with Lord and Lady Rothwick around the side of the house." He glanced at Sophia.

Sophia bit her lower lip again, then brightened. "And what an uneven number is three! I shall go down directly and make sure Lady Rothwick does not weary her foot overmuch and volunteer to entertain the two gentlemen." She jumped up from the window seat immediately and swiftly left the parlour.

Richard made a movement toward the door to follow her, then subsided. No. He was not going to let himself be drawn into any of Sophia's mischief-making any more than he had already. Besides, it would be an opportune time to search her room once again.

Rothwick did not know what it was about Sir James that made him uneasy. The man was cordial enough, even entertaining, with his repertoire of stories of far-off India. But as he watched him bending toward

Linnea to listen to her soft reply, he could not help feeling that the man was a little too . . . insinuating. Yes. That was the word. It seemed as if Marlowe walked a little too close to Linnea for comfort.

And how had he managed to get beside Linnea on this narrow path and leave him, Rothwick, behind? Damn it, she was Lady Rothwick, not Lady Marlowe! He gazed at the two ahead of him.

"Oh, I am not particularly interested in a Season in London, Sir James, truly," Linnea was saying. She glanced back at Rothwick, blushing a little.

"What, and deny yourself the pleasures of London?" Sir James turned to look at the earl. "Surely, Rothwick, you do not mean to hide this lovely lady away forever?"

"Of course not," Rothwick replied shortly. "She is my wife. She will, in time, be presented."

"Of course," returned Sir James, his voice smoothly cordial. He turned back to Linnea. "I hope you—and your husband—will allow me to call when you come to London, Lady Rothwick."

"It would be a pleasant thing, to be sure," Linnea said mildly. Rothwick thought he heard a note of uncertainty in it, however. What, did she think he meant to hide her away here forever? Surely she didn't think he would leave her to moulder away while he enjoyed the pleasures of London? He glanced at her again, and though he could not see her face, her shoulders hunched just a little, as if she were protecting herself from something. From him, perhaps?

Rothwick almost groaned. Did she not understand how he desired her? How he wanted to take off each layer of clothing, piece by piece, caressing her all the while? Just the thought of it made him want to take her away right now to his bedchamber. He took a deep breath, hoping the cool air in his lungs would cool the rest of him as well. He watched the two in front of him, farther up the path now, and noticed that Linnea hardly limped at all. Good! He would bring her to his bed tonight and be done with it.

With that thought, he felt almost cheerful. He glanced at Linnea and Sir James in front of him. Sir James was smiling and bent his head down close to hers again. A searing spark went through Rothwick's chest, which took him aback—only for a moment. It could almost have been jealousy . . . but of course he knew it was not. He had never made a fuss when he found his past mistresses with another. There were many willing women available. And he was not the jealous sort, after all. In fact, he would prove it to himself by unclenching his fists and leaving them to walk (in full view of the house, so it was quite proper) by themselves.

Linnea looked behind her to find that Rothwick had disappeared. Despondency clutched her heart, but she managed to smile at a witty remark of Sir James's. William did not even care if she walked with another man through the gardens. Well, so be it! Unconsciously she raised her chin in a defiant gesture.

"Is there anything the matter, my lady?" Sir James asked.

Her eyes flew to his, startled. "Oh, what— Oh, no, no, not at all."

Sir James's eyes grew assessing, though he continued to smile. "It is a pity Lord Rothwick apparently decided he had business elsewhere."

"Oh, I am sure it is something inconsequential and he will return. We need not bother ourselves with it."

"Inconsequential? Then I wonder that he left us by ourselves here."

Linnea glanced at him, flustered. "I, oh, I did not mean it was inconsequential, precisely. I suppose he felt wearied from walking so soon after his illness."

"Ah, yes. He has been ill, has he not?" They turned along a path toward some apple trees newly in bloom. "How inopportune for you. And lonely, I would imagine."

"No, really, I spent quite a bit of time caring for him, you see," Linnea replied. Her shoulders tensed, then she relaxed them. Heavens, there was no reason why she should feel so uneasy in Sir James's presence. He was all that was pleasant and amiable.

A corner of his mouth lifted disbelievingly. "That is quite different from having a man about who is hale and hearty, ma'am."

"I suppose that is true."

"What, do you not know? Well, then, perhaps I could show you." And Sir James quickly pulled her into a kiss.

Shocked into stillness, Linnea did not respond until his mouth was moving firmly upon hers. She felt no pleasure as she had with Rothwick; fury and insult burned in her instead. It gave her arms strength, and she pushed, then pummeled her fists against him. They had stopped under the apple trees, and though the branches were covered liberally with blossoms, Linnea knew that it was wholly possible they could be seen—at least most of them could be seen—if someone happened to look out one of the windows. She pushed harder, but he was quite strong and did not release her until out of sheer desperation she stamped on his foot. A gasp escaped him, and he drew back.

"How *dare* you, sirrah!" A sharp slap across his cheek made him gasp again and made Linnea wince with the pain that shot through her hand.

A wry grin crossed his lips, and he put his hand carefully to his cheek. "I dared because I was under the impression you needed some solace."

"Solace! I needed no solace! And I surely did not imply by either word or looks that I needed any from you—or anyone else, for that matter!" Her hand had curled into a fist, and Sir James grasped it quickly. "Let me go!"

"No. Not when you seem to be about to strike me again."

Linnea looked into his eyes and saw rueful and apologetic amusement there, instead of any rakish intent. She relaxed, Sir James released her, and she stepped back from him.

"So you love him, then," he said.

She blushed and said stiffly, "That is not your business!"

"I see you do. I was informed differently, you understand."

Slanting a suspicious glance at him, she said, "By whom, pray?"

"Oh, I will not tell you that. It is quite confidential."

"And far and above more important than my reputation, I daresay!"

He laughed. "No, it is not. But it would do me little good to reveal that information, and I am afraid I have besmirched my honor as a gentleman quite a bit in your eyes already in these past minutes."

"Pardon me if I did not think such a thing mattered to you." The angry sarcasm in Linnea's voice would have scorched him if it had been tangible.

Sir James grinned widely and put up a hand. "Touché! Believe me, I was grievously misinformed. I was told yours was a marriage of convenience, and a disaffected one, at that."

"It is not." Linnea bit her lower lip. Ever truthful, she said: "Well, it was, but it is not—not now. Not for me." She blushed. "Heavens, I have no cause to tell you this. Pray forget I have said it."

"Since I have not heard you say anything these past few minutes, I have nothing to forget."

Linnea could not help smiling a little. "I thank you, sir." She cast a glance at the house, but the windows were empty. She sighed in relief. He moved toward her again to walk beside her, but she moved quickly away.

"Ah. You are justifiably wary. I promise you, my lady, I will importune you no longer."

"I do not see why I should believe you."

He gave an impatient sigh. "I assure you, ma'am, I truly do not have an interest in assaulting you. Not now. Not in the future. I do not care to kiss unwilling women—nor can I particularly cozen to the idea of having my foot mauled by the heel of your shoe."

She gazed at him steadily but saw nothing except an amused impatience. "Very well, then, sir. You are forgiven."

"Thank you." He glanced at the sun overhead. "I will leave you, ma'am. I am sorry for any inconvenience I have caused. Will you excuse me if I pay my respects to Miss Amberley?"

"Of course."

Sir James bowed and left.

Linnea gave another look at the house. Was there a slight movement at one of the windows? Surely not. She shook her head. At any event, if anyone had looked just now, they would have had nothing to comment upon.

*   *   *

But she was quite wrong. Two figures had stood riveted at the sight of Linnea and Sir James walking under the apple trees.

Lord Rothwick stood at the window of the library, his hands clenched, feeling as if his breath had been struck from him. Then anger flared within him and burned its way to his brain. The library ceased to exist for him, the walls, the window: it was as if his whole mind were focused on the scene before him. The tree branches had obscured the upper half of the pair, but there was no doubt what was happening. No man or woman could come that close to each other and not be doing what he was sure they *were* doing—damned near consummating what should have been his marriage! He moved decisively from the window and flung open the library door, almost upsetting Potter.

"Damn you, man! Get out of my way!"

The valet stared at him, mouth agape, hands clutching some newly laundered neckcloths to his chest. "I, I am sorry, your lordship, I, I—"

"Shut up!"

Rothwick stormed past the man, oblivious of the servant's bewildered gaze. God, but he'd been a fool! Granted, his and Linnea's was a marriage of convenience, but it damned well didn't give her special license to do as she pleased. Their bloody marriage hadn't even been consummated yet, and by God he wasn't going to let anyone do it for him!

Rothwick thought over his reasons for leaving his wife and his guest to walk the gardens and realized what an idiot he had been. Granted, he hadn't heard anything disreputable about the man, but Linnea was a lovely woman, and who could resist that? He knew he could not. And she! Perhaps she was not completely up to snuff on the ways of the world, but certainly she knew what the bounds of propriety were!

Throwing open the door leading to the gardens, he glared about him, his muscles clenched in anticipation of giving Sir James a flush hit. But it was not Sir James who waited under the apple trees, stared at him guiltily, and blushed.

"Oh!" Linnea exclaimed.

"'Oh!' indeed!" snarled Rothwick. "And where is Sir James?"

"He . . . he has taken his leave—"

"After demonstrating the pleasures of London to you, I suppose!"

Linnea's cheeks burned brighter than before, and her eyes snapped with matching anger. "If you *must* know, he mistook me for a loose woman—*not* unlike *someone* with whom we are both acquainted!"

"And what, madam, did you do to provoke that mistake?" Rothwick asked, ignoring the second half of her sentence.

"I! *I* provoked! Why, my *dear* husband, I suppose he must have been inspired by your example!"

"*My* example! I saved your reputation!"

"Oh, is *that* the way of it? I thought you had ruined it, frankly."

"Oh, then our marriage is *my* fault, is it?"

Linnea's voice shook with anger. "Yes! Yes, it is your fault. *You* were the one who wanted a marriage of convenience, not I! I was against marrying you from the start! I had hoped we could come to lo—to like each other enough to be friends, but I see you had no intention of doing so, not with your stupid accusations! All you have done is lecture and tease me and—and kiss me to get *kippers* for breakfast!"

"Kippers? I do not recall wanting kippers. You are growing hysterical."

"I am *not* hysterical. You did so want kippers! . . . Ohh! This is a *stupid* argument! I hate kippers!"

"You may hate them all you like, but I want to know what you were doing with Sir James!"

Linnea glared at him and clenched her fists. She lifted her chin defiantly. "What do you think? You are so good at jumping to conclusions, after all!"

She looked at his angry and baffled face, and despondency seeped into her heart. Why was he so angry at her? If he saw Sir James kissing her, surely he must have seen her slap the man as well. But regardless, it must be *her* fault!

"The way you were pressed together, it looked as if you were well on your way to betraying our marriage!" Rothwick sneered.

"Ohhh! You vulgar, *stupid* man! I see I cannot talk to you!" Linnea barely restrained herself from slapping him also. She turned away and marched toward the house.

A hand grasped her forearm so tightly, she gasped. "You will stay right here, madam!" He pulled her to him, and she gazed up at his furious and suddenly confused eyes. "If you mean to betray our marriage, then you'll betray it with *me!*"

"What nonsense *are* you talking about—" But she was cut short by his kiss.

She could say nothing. His lips were fierce, possessive against hers. She could not move, for one of his hands cupped the back of her neck, and an arm crushed her to him. Her knees grew weak, and when he moved his mouth down her neck, she gasped and closed her eyes. Slowly, slowly, he pulled her down to the grass, and his hand slipped inside the bodice of her dress.

"Ah, God, Linnea, what you do to me . . . ," murmured Rothwick, his lips following the course of his hand.

Her eyes flew open again. What she did to him. What *she* did to him. Why was it that *she* did something to *him?* No, it was quite the other way around, and here he was again blaming it on *her.* No. Not this time. Not *this* time.

Linnea pushed against his chest and struggled out from under him. "No, my lord. Not again. You will not seduce me to get your way." She sat up, tugging the skirt of her dress from under his legs, and then stood.

Rothwick rose slowly to his feet. "Get my way?" he said, gazing at her with an odd expression in his eyes.

"Oh, yes. That is how you get what you desire, is it not? Teasing or kissing me until finally I agree to whatever you wish, however ill considered it is." She clenched her teeth against her rising tears. "But there is nothing behind those kisses, is there?"

She sighed. "You have made it abundantly clear that I am useless here. That I have little function in your life other than that of a figurehead of a wife. Something to display at court and in society when the time comes." Not even to breed children, she thought, but did not say it. The thought depressed her even further. She put her hands to her eyes, pressed them wearily, and then gazed steadfastly at him again. "I find I cannot live with that, my lord. I do not think I could live with you if that were all I am to do." He put up his hand and opened his mouth as if to speak, but Linnea forestalled him. "No, my lord. I do not wish to speak with you at this moment. I wish to go to my

chambers and rest for a while. I am quite weary of—
That is, I am quite weary." Linnea turned and walked
swiftly to the house.

Rothwick stared after her, his body frozen in anger,
frustration, confusion, and a curious sensation that
curled around his heart at the sight of her back so
proudly straight. He did not know why he had kissed
her, for he had been enraged at her apparent defiance.
He had wanted to possess her, to make her his at that
moment, so that no one could truly claim her afterward. No one, not even Sir James.

Sir James. Ah yes. He would have to find that gentleman. He went to the stables, in case the man should
still be there.

But he was not, for Sir James was taking leave of
Sophia. She was the other figure who stood riveted—
well hidden behind a rhododendron bush—at the
sight of Sir James kissing Lady Rothwick. Of course he
must have, for though she could not see all of them,
she could see enough to know that there was no other
reason for them to be so close together than kissing.

"I am glad," Sophia said fiercely to herself, despite a
tearing in her heart that made her want to cry. "He is
doing just as I instructed him." She turned away,
telling herself that it was not really necessary to see
her instructions carried out to the finish.

She walked slowly back to the house, intending to
go back to the parlour to play some more darkly ele-
giac music on the pianoforte. Suddenly she felt—more
than heard—a presence behind her and whirled
around.

"Miss Amberley."

It was Sir James. His color seemed heightened—it was hard to tell because of his darkened skin—and his expression was grave.

"Sir James." Sophia inclined her head in a dignified manner. She glanced at him and, seeing his intent, almost stern look, averted her eyes.

"I have come to take my leave of you." He came up and put her hand on his arm, escorting her away from the house. "I shall be going to London shortly after I return to my hunting box today. Perhaps I shall see you there someday."

Someday! Sophia's gaze flew to his face and saw a coolness there she hadn't seen before. What had gone wrong? Surely Lady Rothwick had not refused his advances—impossible! Why, if *I* were Lady Rothwick, she thought, I would have fallen into his arms and vowed my heart to him!

At once her heart soared—then sank to the bottom of her delicate little shoes. No. Oh, no. She was *not* in love with him. Not with Sir James. Why . . . why, didn't she urge him on to seduce Lady Rothwick? And, well, there was her revenge on Lord Rothwick still to be done! No, no. She could not afford to be in love with anyone now. Sophia looked away, swallowed the lump in her throat, and gathered her thoughts together.

"Oh . . . oh, I daresay I shall meet you there at some time. I am forever seeing everyone in London." She paused, then pushed on. "I see you have persuaded Lady Rothwick that you would be good company for her." She noticed that they had returned to her spot behind the rhododendron bushes, and she felt the surge of an unfamiliar emotion—guilt? But no. There was nothing to feel guilty about at all.

There was a slight pause, then Sir James said: "I fear

you flatter my arts of persuasion. However, I suppose I could say I would not be an unamusing companion."

Sophia felt near to tears. "No . . . no, of course not. I . . . I have found you most amiable." A caressing finger lifted her chin, and she gazed into Sir James's eyes. His stern look was gone, and there was an expression of warm amusement instead.

"My sweet one, you should not worry yourself." He drew closer to her. "You will get your revenge, I assure you."

"I . . . you, you should not address me in that manner."

"I know."

He pulled her into his arms and kissed her.

She did not struggle. She did not want to. This will be the last time I see Sir James—at least for a while, she thought. Surely it cannot be so terrible to kiss him just a little. Just a little. . . . Sophia put her hand to his cheek, and her other hand went up, too, around to the back of his neck. He drew her closer to him, and his hand left her back to flow down to her waist, caressing gently. His lips feathered across her cheek and behind her ear, and she sighed and sighed again. When he proceeded to kiss her neck, her legs trembled, and to steady herself she took half a step back—

Right into something sharp. She gasped with the pain and then realized where she was. The rhododendron bush! Why, she was as private with Sir James as if they were in a closed room! She pushed him away, breathing hard.

He gazed at her, a wry smile on his lips. "A little gesture of friendship, my dear, which I hope you do not mind. A farewell of a sorts, you see."

"A farewell. . . . Yes— No— That is, I, I understand.

Of course." Her mind was awhirl. It was different from any sort of farewell she had received in her life, but she supposed things were different in the places he had lived. An odd dizziness seeped slowly from her head, and she was able to gather a measure of composure. She took a deep breath.

"Do you think Lady Rothwick would ever be inclined to leave Staynes with you—for company, of course—someday in the future, perhaps?" she asked.

One corner of his mouth quirked up for a brief moment. "Oh, I imagine it might be possible. You will certainly know when it occurs."

Sophia felt her throat tighten. "Please do let me know," she managed to whisper. She looked up at him and held out her hand. "I wish you a safe journey, Sir James."

He took her hand and bowed over it. "Your wish is my command, sweet one," he said. He released her, and Sophia gave him half a smile, turned, and ran toward the house.

As a result, she did not see the odd smile on Sir James's lips or the half-raised hand he extended toward her retreating form. He dropped his hand again, seemed to shake himself, then turned toward the stables.

13

Linnea pulled her bandboxes onto her bed and flung her clothes at them. They missed their target, and as dresses, scarves, and sundry other items slipped to the floor, she sank onto a chair and burst into tears. Scrabbling for a handkerchief with one hand, she wiped her cheeks with the other.

Stop! Stop weeping, you silly woman! she told herself sternly. Linnea dabbed her eyes with the handkerchief she finally found, blew her nose, and gave a last resolute sniff. There now! She would call her maid to pack her clothes properly and take her along to Bath to visit Miss Brinkley. She was respectably married now, and Miss Brinkley would welcome her in her kindly way. She knew her former schoolmistress would make a temporary place for her until she was able to think more clearly and decide what she would do with herself.

"I am going on a short visit, Betty," she said after the maid had come into the room. "Please pack my clothes and other necessary items, and then quickly prepare yourself for travel. I shall need you to accompany me to an old friend's house."

Betty's eyes widened. "Yes, my lady, of course." The little maid had noticed her mistress's reddened eyes and wondered what had occurred to make Lady Rothwick so unhappy. And during her honeymoon, too! It must be his lordship again! Men! Why, didn't she herself find Thomas the footman cuddling the scullery maid? The scullery maid, of all people! The girl firmed her lips and set herself to work with a right good will.

Meanwhile Linnea sat down at her escritoire, took up pen, ink, and paper, and started to write. She paused, crumpled the paper, and took out another. Finally, after three balls of paper lay crumpled on the desk, she signed her name and sighed a sigh of completion.

"My lord, I am going on a visit to Bath. You need not fear I am committing any impropriety, for I shall be amply escorted."

That was all. Theirs was a marriage of convenience, in which each partner had independent concerns. She did not need to explain herself, she felt, for he certainly thought explaining *his* actions unnecessary. Her lips pressed together with a certain satisfaction as she scanned the note again. That was all he needed to know.

She sanded and folded the note. She looked at the ormolu clock on the mantelpiece and saw it was not long before dinner. She would have Bartle give the note to Lord Rothwick then.

Finally all was packed and she was dressed, with

Betty at her side. Bartle raised his brows momentarily but did not comment when she gave him the note and requested the traveling coach and footmen to accompany her.

As she sat in the coach, Linnea wondered briefly how long would it be before Rothwick noticed her absence. She pulled up her shoulders against the thought. He would know soon enough when he received the note.

Sir James wore a contemplative look on his face as he rode slowly back to his hunting box. The blond little witch had caught him by surprise. He had assumed from her insinuations that Lady Rothwick was not more than a courtesan at heart—and had been quite wrong. Miss Amberley—Sophia—had lied to him. Or, no, he thought, recalling her face when she'd told him of Lady Rothwick's supposed perfidy, it was what she believed. He grinned to himself. The vain little chit thought that was the only reason a man would choose another woman over her.

He should have suspected it by the jealous look in Rothwick's eye, but he had dismissed it as watchfulness lest Lady Rothwick commit an impropriety. And, he admitted to himself, he should have suspected it by Lady Rothwick's reserved demeanor. But Sophia had a way of turning a man's mind from pure reason—and that was a new experience for him.

The countryside passed by him unnoticed as he thought of Sophia. She was a clever little thing, oddly naive while she planned, plotted, and contrived—and vastly amusing. And she had actually upset the ordered workings of his mind. How had she done it?

Sir James grinned. She was certainly beautiful and entirely desirable. That, and the anger she had momentarily sparked in him by her resistance of him, had made him kiss her just to see her discomposed. Yet he had wanted to do more than kiss her; he had wanted to pull her down behind the bushes and make love to her, possess her, make her cry out with pleasure. She would be his own, and he would put a child in her to bear at his home in—

Sir James's hands tensed on the reins, making his horse come to a standstill as a wild possessiveness seized his vitals and left him almost breathless. He wanted her—more than that. He wanted Sophia to be *his* wife and no one else's. He had thought he'd seduce her, make her his mistress despite her rank and breeding. But then she could roam, as any mistress might. As his wife, she'd be his forever, by law. And he would kill anyone who dared touch her.

He would have her and most certainly make her his wife. Sir James kicked his horse to a gallop toward his hunting box. He had noted Lady Rothwick passing him in a traveling carriage not long ago and had almost dismissed it from his mind. A slow smile grew on his lips, widening fiercely. He would write a short note to Miss Amberley. He laughed aloud. The hunt was on.

Rothwick stared moodily at the wineglass next to him on the side table. It was half empty, but he pushed it away from him instead of draining it. Sir James had not been at the stables, and he hadn't been able to find him elsewhere. By the time he'd come back to the stables, the man's horse was gone. But the next time . . . ! The earl spent a few moments pleasurably contemplating what he'd do to him. Soon his savage visions faded, and he blinked.

The dinner bell rang, and he rose automatically. Linnea would be there, and it would be a devilishly awkward meal, but he would get through it. He grimaced. His temper had cooled, and he had to acknowledge that his words had been too hasty. In fact, he had been downright unjust to her. He would apologize once they left the dining room—

No, damn it. There were their guests, and they had to be accommodated. It would have to be later in the evening, when they retired for the night. He sighed and went down to dinner.

As he entered the room, he noted that Sophia and her brother were before him. She looked quite wan, although Richard seemed to be in fairly good spirits. They sat, and Rothwick waited impatiently for Linnea to arrive. The door opened and Bartle entered, bearing not dinner, but a tray with two notes upon it.

"Excuse me, my lord, but Lady Rothwick desired me to give you this," the butler said. He turned to Sophia. "And there is another letter directed to Miss Amberley." His face showed a faint disapproval at this irregularity, though he took the letter to her.

The earl opened his but looked up when he heard a gasp from Sophia. She had turned quite pale.

"Is something the matter, Miss Amberley?" She raised her gaze to him, and for a moment he thought anguish marred the polite expression on her face. He glanced an order to Bartle, and the butler dismissed the footmen and left the room.

"No, I— No, nothing. Nothing is the matter. I am quite well."

"Your family, then?"

"No. No this has nothing to do with my family. Please, let us go on with our dinner."

Rothwick nodded, looked down at the note in his hand, and felt the room take a quick turn.

She was gone. Linnea, his wife, was gone. He stared at his plate before him, as if he could somehow make her appear if he focused all his attention on it. But why? His mind was oddly blank, and then a mist of a thought coalesced there. He had raged at her, he had thrown unjust accusations at her, when she was most likely only a victim of a practiced seducer.

He raised his eyes and stared at the chair Linnea usually took during meals, not noticing Richard's curious glance or Sophia's anxious one. He hadn't even had a chance to apologize, to tell her he was wrong, to tell her he loved her.

He loved her. Rothwick's abrupt, sharp awareness of his surroundings enabled him to suppress the groan that filled his throat. He stood up suddenly.

"I am sorry to be so uncivil as to leave you to your dinner here alone, but I am afraid I must attend to matters of some import." He bowed briefly to Sophia and her brother and turned to leave.

"Lady Rothwick . . . "

The earl turned swiftly at Sophia's voice. The anguish he had fleetingly seen in her eyes was there in full force. A horrible suspicion rose in his mind.

"What do you know of Lady Rothwick, Miss Amberley?"

"I . . . she—" Sophia's voice broke, and she mutely extended her letter to him. He seized it, read it, and turned rage-hot eyes upon her.

"You conniving little—*chit!*"

Sophia flinched, and tears slid down her cheeks.

"I say!" protested Richard. "That's no way to talk to my—"

Rothwick strode to him and thrust the letter under Richard's nose so that he could not fail to read it.

"Good God!" Richard said faintly.

"Quite." Rothwick stalked to the door. "You will excuse me while I bring back my wife from the clutches of the bas—the *gentleman* whom your sister has thrown at her." The door slammed behind him.

Richard turned horrified eyes to Sophia. "Are you *mad?* What in God's name made you do this?"

His sister turned pain- and guilt-filled eyes upon him. "I . . . I thought—I was angry. . . ."

"It seems to me you hadn't thought at all!"

"But I did! I thought she was not good enough for Lord Rothwick."

Richard's glance was full of scorn. "You thought! *You* thought! After she kindly helped us when we had our accident—and I know you engineered it, my girl!—and invited us to stay at her home during her *honeymoon,* you couldn't find anything good about her *still?* And now, out of sheer vanity and spite, you connive with Sir James to abduct her!"

"No! I didn't mean it to be like that! I— Oh, God, Richard, we must stop him!" Sophia rose hastily from her chair, her eyes bright with alarm.

"I should say so! But Lord Rothwick will handle it quite well by himself, I am sure."

"No! I mean, we must stop Rothwick! You saw how angry he was. He will *kill* Sir James!" Sophia wrung her hands anxiously.

Richard's jaw dropped almost to his chest. "Are you completely insane? If Sir James has kidnapped Lady Rothwick, it is up to Rothwick to deal with him."

"No, no! I cannot let it happen!" She ran to her brother and clutched his coat. "Oh, Richard, please, please, you must follow them and take me with you!"

"No!"

Fresh tears ran down Sophia's cheeks, and she pounded a fist on his chest. "Oh, please, Richard! I will do anything you say, only take me to him quickly!"

Her brother opened his mouth to retort, then closed it, thinking hard. Pity for her obvious anguish and a sneaking glee at her discomfiture warred in his heart. And then self-preservation stepped in. Richard grinned slowly.

"Only if you give me the bill for the sapphire set."

Sophia frantically plunged her hand in a hidden pocket of her dress and shoved a folded piece of paper at him. "Here! Here it is! Take it, and let us go!"

He took and opened it. It was not blank this time, but most certainly the bill. He smiled and pocketed it. "Very well, then," he said.

Sophia seized his arm and pulled him toward the door. "Oh, hurry! Please hurry!"

"Perhaps we should stop for a moment and take some refreshment," Sir James said to Linnea.

He was riding his horse and bent to speak with her through the window of the coach. The coach had been going at a good clip, but his horse was faster and he had caught up with it before it had reached the road to Bath. The inn at the crossroads leading to Bath in one direction and London in another was but a mile ahead, but he had skipped his dinner in his haste and was now feeling devilish sharp-set. He smiled. How convenient it was that nature and his plans so easily dovetailed!

Linnea's stomach had finally unclenched since leaving Staynes, and her mind had calmed to a point where she could think clearly. She had left before dinner, and it was silly to continue on her journey when she knew it would be a long time to the next meal. Indeed, she should have left after dinner, but she had felt such anger and unhappiness, she would not have been able to eat one bite. But she glanced at Sir James skeptically.

"Are you suggesting I have dinner with you? Considering the trouble you have caused me, I am surprised you ask."

"My dear Lady Rothwick, I no longer have designs on you—in fact, I never did, so to speak. You might even think of me as a modern Cupid, rather."

Linnea laughed. "Oh, really? And how is that?"

"I have a whim to act the matchmaker."

"Then I think I will *not* have dinner with you."

"I assure you, my designs are focused completely on another lady."

"Honorable, of course."

Sir James smiled widely. "Of course. Miss Amberley will most certainly marry me."

Linnea's heart lifted, and she half thought of turning the carriage around but remembered Rothwick's accusations. She pressed her lips together briefly, then smiled politely.

"I give you my congratulations, then. When, may I ask, did she accept?"

"She has not—yet."

"Do you not think that is somewhat presumptuous, Sir James?"

"No. However, it will be less possible if you do not have dinner with me."

"And how can that be?"

Sir James smiled at her. "I will tell you when we have our dinner."

Linnea stared at him, twisting her lips in suspicion. She felt he was quite sincere somehow, and that despite his previous importunity, she could trust him this time. Her stomach rumbled gently and gave strength to her curiosity. How would he manage it, though?

"I will not suffer for it, or be taken advantage of, shall I?"

"No. And you may have your footman outside the door and your maid with you at all times for propriety's sake."

"Very well. I am quite hungry, I confess, and shall be glad of refreshment, and would not like to dine alone."

It was but a short distance to the inn at the crossroads. After escorting her to a private parlour, with Thomas the footman just outside the door and Betty the maid within, they sat down to a very fine table of roast capon and asparagus.

Linnea looked at her companion curiously. "So now will you tell me what part I am to have in your supposed future marriage?"

"Of course." Sir James took a sip of wine and gazed at her, smiling. "I have sent a letter to Miss Amberley, to be delivered at dinner. In it, I told her I have absconded with you—as she desired." The little maid at Linnea's side jumped up with a gasp, hastening to her mistress's side.

Linnea paled and rose from her chair. "You said—"

"Sit down—both of you—if you please!" His voice was soft, but there was a hint of steel in it. Betty stood stubbornly next to her mistress, but Linnea sat down again.

"Yes," he continued. "I did say you were quite safe, and despite my other . . . attributes, I keep my word. I expect your husband and Miss Amberley to arrive"—he took out his watch and looked at it—"oh, within the half hour." He slipped his watch back into his pocket and sipped his wine again. "Of course, there is always the chance that Miss Amberley will show your husband the letter and not come herself, in which case I shall have to think of another scheme. But that is life, is it not? Full of risk and challenges." He chuckled gently.

"You are mad," Linnea said.

"Oh, no. I know exactly what I am doing."

"And how do you know Lord Rothwick will come here?"

"It was in Miss Amberley's original plan to show him how unworthy you were—nonsense, of course. Regardless of what she may feel for me, she will show him the letter I sent her."

"He may very well not care."

Sir James smiled kindly. "But he does, of course. He is a proud man, your husband. And he loves you."

Linnea blushed and turned her head away. "Then you have seen something I have not." They were conversing on very private matters indeed, and she was uncomfortable, but she felt compelled to talk to Sir James. She did not want to believe it, lest her heart gain another tear in it, but if there was a chance at all . . .

"Oh, come now, my lady. I have seen the way he has looked at you—he is a man besotted!"

"He accused me of all manner of insulting things."

"He was jealous."

She raised her gaze to him. "Do you think so?" she asked hopefully.

Sir James grinned. "I barely escaped being thrashed to a pulp after he saw me kiss you. Lord Rothwick is a persistent man. I had a deuced difficult time eluding him this morning when he was storming about, wanting—I am sure—to kill me."

"Why are you telling me all this?" Linnea's eyes were suspicious again.

"Think of it as recompense for my, er, excess of civility to you this morning."

She raised her brows skeptically.

"Well, then, let us say I lack an audience for my, ahem, genius."

"Ah, *that* I can believe." Linnea relaxed and nodded to her maid to sit down again.

Sir James put a hand to his heart. "Lady Rothwick, you wound me. I—" A pounding on the door interrupted him, the door crashed open, and Lord Rothwick strode into the room. Sir James pulled out his watch and nodded gravely. "How gratifying. Precisely to the minute."

But he was not given much time to appreciate his prophetic powers, for Rothwick grabbed him by the neckcloth and pulled him out of his chair.

The earl had found them easily; Sir James's letter even said they would be at this inn. He had a temper, it was true, but never had he felt such rage as he did now. Linnea was *his,* and no one would take her from him. His thoughts had boiled over at the sight of Sir James, and his morning's frustrated anger converged upon his present wrath. Rational thought left him, and he became a primitive, seething mass of impending violence.

"Good. You are here. Now you will die."

"How crude," Sir James managed to croak through

the grip on his neck. "I would not have thought it. And you have such an impeccable reputation for elegant address in London. Gakk!"

With a jerk, Rothwick let him go, apparently recalled somewhat to a sense of civilized rules. "You will name your seconds, sir!"

"No!" cried Linnea. Both men ignored her, although Betty went to her side and put an arm around her shoulders.

Sir James smiled at him genially. "I think not."

"You admit your wrong, then."

"I only admit I might have been misleading in my letter to Miss Amberley." He looked past the earl to the doorway and sighed. "Alas, I see she is not with you. I shall have to think of another plan."

Rothwick stared at him, baffled, then contempt grew in his eyes. "You are a coward."

Sir James's smile faded, and his eyes narrowed. "Oh, no," he said softly. "You are quite wrong."

"Prove it, then."

A fist shot forward, and Rothwick jerked his head, feeling the rush of air past his jaw. He returned the punch, but Sir James was just as quick. Rothwick grinned fiercely. This was just as good. Better, in fact. Sir James avoided another hit and struck upward to the ribs. It landed, but only enough to make Rothwick stagger a little.

"Stop it! Stop it, I say!" cried Linnea. She looked around frantically and saw Thomas the footman watching the two men with fascinated attention. "You! Thomas! Stop them, please!"

Thomas scratched his head thoughtfully. "Pity to do it, your ladyship. Never seen such a good mill in all my life. Lots o' science, hardly any windmilling atall."

"You looby! Do what her ladyship says!" Betty shouted.

Thomas shrugged helplessly. "Can't. I might get hit."

"Silly coward!" hissed the maid.

"Yes, mum!" said Thomas, and settled down on a chair to watch the fight.

Rothwick was tiring fast. The rage that had pumped his blood full of energy was leaving him, and a touch of the fatigue he'd felt after the influenza seeped in. His mind was clearer now, and he knew he should have simply issued his challenge, taken Linnea home, and fought at a later date. As he dodged another blow, he noted that a small crowd had appeared at the door of the parlour. He almost groaned.

A feminine shriek pierced the air, and Sir James glanced away. Rothwick's fist drove toward his jaw in a flush hit, he felt a deluge of cold water across his face, and then he saw Sir James slump senseless to the floor.

Rothwick felt a hand shove him aside, and he pushed his wet hair from his eyes. Sophia had rushed to Sir James and was on her knees beside him.

"No! Oh, no!" she sobbed, cradling his head to her bosom. "I am so sorry! I didn't mean it to happen like this, truly I didn't." She turned fiercely to Rothwick. "You beast! You've killed him!"

"Good flush hit, yer lordship." Thomas peered at Sir James's purpling jaw. "Don't think he's going to stick his spoon in the wall, though. Still breathing."

Rothwick ignored him. He gazed at Linnea, who was still holding the water pitcher in her hands. She blushed and looked away. He moved toward her, then noticed the interested crowd at the parlour door.

He eyed them coldly. "This is not a raree show. I

would appreciate it if you all—including my servants—left us alone. Except the innkeeper." The
innkeeper, who had been torn between his admiration
for what appeared to be a bout between two superb
athletes and the ruination of his best private parlour,
shuffled toward him. Rothwick whispered something
in his ear, and the man's face brightened considerably.

"Of course, your lordship, anything you say, my
lord," he said, bowing profusely. He turned to the inn's
guests, still hovering about the threshold. "You heard
His Lordship! Out! Out!"

The guests moved away, reluctant, amidst much
grumbling that their entertainment was at an end. The
innkeeper shut the door firmly behind him.

Sir James's eyelids fluttered, then opened to stare
dazedly at Sophia. "Ah! Miss Amberley," he murmured.
He nestled his head more comfortably on her bosom.
"How delightful."

Sophia burst into fresh tears.

"Do stop drowning me, sweet one, and kiss me."

"I, I can't, I—"

"Silly chit. Kiss me now." He pulled her down to
him. They parted at last, and he said abruptly: "Where
is your brother?"

"He . . . he did not want to come here. He said it was
foolish of me to interfere."

"You were quite right to interfere, my sweet, but do
so in a less startling manner next time. I need to see
your brother, to inform him we are to be married."

"M-married?" Sophia stuttered, and blushed bright
red. "I have not said I would marry you!"

"But you will, of course. We have witnesses that
you have more than a slight affection for me." Sir
James grinned.

"Ohhh! No, no, I will not!"

"Your reputation is quite ruined now, my love. You must marry me." He looked at Linnea and Rothwick for confirmation.

"Well—"

"I think—"

"You see?" said Sir James, cutting them off. "They agree with me. You really have no choice."

Sophia gazed at him in consternation. "But, but—"

He cut her off with another kiss. "Say yes."

"Yes, oh, yes!"

He smiled at her tenderly. "That's a good girl. We shall be married as soon as I have talked with your parents."

A knock sounded at the door.

"Who the deuce is it?" shouted both Rothwick and Sir James at once.

"Er, it is I," came the muffled voice of Richard Amberley.

Sir James and Rothwick exchanged a look. "Come in," Rothwick said.

Richard peered cautiously around the door as he opened it. "Er, ah, I thought I would see if I might be of any help." His eyes widened at the sight of his sister kneeling next to the prone Sir James.

Lord Rothwick went to Linnea and grasped her wrist, pulling her toward the door. "I think, Amberley, you'll want to be alone with your sister and her betrothed."

"Betrothed!"

Rothwick shut the door behind him. He turned to Linnea. "Now, my dear, we will do what we should have done some time ago." He kissed her firmly, then pulled her along the hallway and up the stairs.

"Where are we going?" cried Linnea, struggling. They stopped by a chamber door.

"We are going to consummate our marriage, my dear," he said calmly. "I am going to make mad, passionate love to you until both of us collapse from exhaustion." He opened the door, picked her up, closed it behind them, and carried her to the bed.

"No!" Linnea said, attempting to sit up. He pulled her down again and gazed at her.

"Why not?"

"You have not said you love me at all."

"Oh, is that all?" replied Rothwick. He smiled at her tenderly, and her breath caught in her throat. "My foolish wife. Why do you think I want to kiss you? Why do you think I wanted to rip Sir James's flesh from his bones when I thought he had taken you away from me?"

She turned her face away but could not avoid the kisses that followed the unbuttoning of her cloak. "Knowing you, my lord, it could well be in a dog-in-the-mangerish frame of mind."

An impatient sigh burst above her head. She looked up at his amused and frustrated face. "I love you, my sweet simpleton. And if it takes me a hundred years to make you feel the same toward me, I will most certainly try. Now, kiss me."

Linnea put her hand to his lips and smiled. "You may try all you like, my love, but I already do." She pulled him down to her and kissed him.

They heard a tentative knock on the door.

"What in God's name is it *now?*" roared Rothwick, collapsing on top of Linnea in frustration. She stifled a giggle.

"'Tis me, Betty, your lordship. I was wondering what Thomas and I should do."

"Go to the dev—"

Linnea stopped his words with her hand. "Betty, I want both of you to take the coach and come back in an hour—"

"Five," growled Rothwick.

"Five hours, Betty," Linnea said, turning pink.

"Yes, my lady."

Rothwick sighed and kissed his wife once more. A fiery light grew in his eyes. "And now, my love . . ."

"Ohh, William . . ."

Linnea's little maid had not quite left when this last sighing moan drifted through the chamber door. She froze, blushed furiously, then ran swiftly down the stairs.

Say You Love Me by Patricia Hagan

Beautiful Iris Sammons always turned heads and was doted upon by her parents, whereas her fraternal twin sister Violet was the quiet one. An attack on their caravan by Comanche separated them irrevocably, but their legacies were forever entwined through their children, and through the love that ultimately bound them.

Promises to Keep by Liz Osborne

Cassie McMahon had always dreamed of a reunion with the father she hadn't seen since she was a child. When her hopes were dashed by his distant manner, she found consolation in the arms of a mysterious but seductive stranger. But Alec Stevens was a man with a secret mission. Could he trust his heart to this irresistible woman?

Cooking Up Trouble by Joanne Pence

In their third outrageous outing, professional cook Angelina Amalfi and San Francisco police inspector Paavo Smith team up at the soon-to-be-opened Hill Haven Inn. Soon they encounter mischief in the form of murders and strange, ghostly events, convincing Angie that the only recipe in this inn's kitchen is the one for disaster.

Sweet Deceiver by Angie Ray

Playing a risky game by spying for English and French intelligence at the same time, Hester Tredwell would do anything to keep her struggling family out of a debtor's prison. Her inventive duplicity was no match, however, for the boldly seductive maneuvers of handsome Nicholas, Marquess of Dartford.

Lucky by Sharon Sala

If Lucky Houston knows anything, it's dealing cards. So when she and her two sisters split up, the gambler's youngest daughter heads for Las Vegas. She is determined to make it on her own in that legendary city of tawdry glitter, but then she meets Nick Chenault, a handsome club owner with problems of his own.

Prairie Knight by Donna Valentino

A knight in shining armor suddenly appeared on the Kansas prairie in 1859! The last thing practical and hardworking Juliette needed was to fall in love with an armor-clad stranger claiming to be a thirteenth-century mercenary knight. Though his knight's honor and duty demanded that he return to his own era, Juliette and Geoffrey learned that true love transcends the bounds of time.

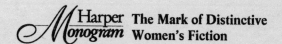